STEEL VENGEANCE
BLACKTHORN SECURITY
BOOK SIX

GEMMA FORD

Copyright © 2024 by Gemma Ford

All rights reserved.

No part of this book may be reproduced in any form or by any electronic or mechanical means, including information storage and retrieval systems, without written permission from the author, except for the use of brief quotations in a book review.

Mortlake Press

ISBN: 978-1-7385403-7-2

First Edition

Cover design by Deranged Doctor

Disclaimer: This is a work of fiction. Names, characters, places, and incidents are the products of the author's imagination or used in a fictitious manner. Any resemblance to actual persons, living or dead, or actual events is purely coincidental.

CHAPTER 1

ESHAWAR, PAKISTAN

STITCH TRAILED Abdul Omari as he and his entourage moved toward the local coffee shop. They moved as a unit, Omari dead center, surrounded by his four muscle-bound bodyguards. His security team wore the traditional robes, hiding who knows what kind of firepower underneath. From the bulges, it was clear they were packing.

Omari had shaved off the beard he'd sported back home in Afghanistan, trying to change his appearance. He'd also cut his curly hair short and ditched the turban. A high-value target on the U.S. radar, he kept a low profile, which was why he'd holed up in this part of Pakistan.

But not low enough.

Peshawar was near the Afghan-Pakistan border and chaotic enough for the warlord to disappear in. The streets were crowded, markets buzzing, traffic non-stop. Recent bombings and political unrest made it a prime spot for someone looking to vanish.

Stitch stepped back as a rickshaw rattled by.

He glanced around, making sure no one had clocked him. Everything seemed normal—locals doing their thing, vendors barking deals, taxis and rickshaws dodging potholes, and women carrying shopping bags, their heads wrapped in hijabs or scarves.

Then, his eyes locked onto a woman in a dusky blue headscarf over a shalwar kameez. She carried a canvas shoulder bag, her dark hair mostly hidden beneath the scarf. Unlike the other women who were either talking quietly amongst themselves, this one moved solo, eyes dead ahead—right on the target.

Omari.

There was no mistaking it. Her gaze was uncovered, sharp, and locked in. She moved fluidly, stopping now and then to glance at the produce, casually picking up an item here or there, dropping it into her bag, but her attention kept snapping back to Omari, tracking him.

At first, Stitch chalked it up to coincidence. Maybe she was just headed in the same direction—these streets were always packed. But three days straight? No way. She was tailing Omari, same as him.

The HVT disappeared into the café. He grimaced. Dirty glass windows covered with Arabic script blocked his view.

Shit, now he'd have to move. He crossed the street, heading for a tea house with outdoor seating, which would give him a better vantage point.

Like the locals, he was dressed to blend. His beard and deep tan made him fit right in. Back in the Afghan mountains, people thought he was one of them. The only thing that could give him away was his eyes—icy, intense blue. But today, with the sun blazing, his shades took care of that.

He ordered tea, paid the waiter, and settled outside. The two men beside him were engrossed in a game of backgammon. He watched them roll the dice then move their pieces across the beat-up board.

The woman had the same idea. She strolled into the shop next door, scanning an array of colorful scarves. She took her sweet time, trying a few on, admiring herself in the mirror by the entrance. Stitch could see her reflection. Behind her, the shopkeeper hovered, ready to make the sale. After some haggling, she decided on a cream-colored scarf, bought it, and replaced the blue one.

Smart. Changing her look under the guise of trying on a new purchase. Anyone who saw her go in might think it was someone else coming out.

But not him.

Now, he kept tabs on both the woman and Omari, who was tucked away inside the café. She moved on to the next shop, passing directly in front of him, not even sparing him a second glance. With his head bowed over his cup of tea, sunglasses on, she probably wrote him off as just another local.

Behind the shades, he studied her closer. Her skin was lighter than he'd thought. She wasn't from here, even if she'd nailed the look. Her clothes were perfect, obviously bought locally, and she wore the scarf like a pro. Her hair was a rich chocolate brown, he'd seen a flash of it when she'd swapped scarves.

Who the hell was she?

She could be one of Omari's mistresses. The drug lord apparently had more than a few. Maybe she suspected Omari was messing around with another woman. Not a stretch, knowing his type. Then again, maybe she was playing a different game.

What if she was a foreign operative? CIA, maybe? MI6?

Any number of intelligence services would be interested in Omari's whereabouts.

Stitch listened as she spoke to the shopkeeper, asking about something.

Urdu.

He was impressed. She had it down pretty well, but a few words were off. Still, it would fool most people. He frowned. Whoever she was, she'd prepped for this.

A black SUV rolled to a stop outside of the café. Three men stepped out—two with beards and skull caps, the third clean-shaven with a military haircut. The woman pulled out her phone, pretending to snap a selfie while holding up a necklace to her chest.

Stitch wasn't buying it. Her camera lens was pointed right at the men.

He took a sip of tea, his gaze pinned to the men who disappeared inside the café. A meeting, maybe?

The woman lingered for another few minutes, hopping between shops until it became obvious she was stalling. With one last look at the café, she headed off.

Making a split-second decision, Stitch got up and tailed her.

She moved with intent now, mission complete. No more playing the shopper. Twice, she checked over her shoulder, scanning for a tail. She'd had some training, no question. But she didn't see him. Stitch had spent a lifetime blending into shadows.

Rounding a corner, she made her way to an old, beat-up Honda scooter. Stitch watched as she hopped on, slinging the shopping bag across her chest.

Damn. He was on foot.

He threw himself in front of a rickshaw, forcing the driver to slam the brakes. Jumping in, he barked, "Follow that scooter!"

The driver shot him a weird look but hit the gas, swerving around a delivery van coming straight at them.

She didn't go far. Four streets later, she slowed, hopped the sidewalk, and parked in front of a butcher shop. Stitch looked around, then back at the shop. Dead carcasses hung from hooks inside.

A mile, if that. Barely worth the chase.

Stitch waited until she'd slipped into a plain door next to the butcher's shop, then he paid the driver and got out.

Was this where she lived? Or was it some kind of safe house?

He studied the crumbling structure with its sagging balconies that looked ready to collapse. If it was a front, it was a damn good one. The smell of raw meat mixed with the thick exhaust fumes, while flies buzzed overhead.

This part of town was more industrial—leatherworkers, jewelers, and other trades. But it was still packed. Wires crisscrossed the narrow streets, draped with laundry and flags.

No way to tell which apartment she went into. He could've followed her in, but without knowing where she was headed, it'd be a waste of time.

He scanned the exterior. The building was climbable. Plenty of footholds. But broad daylight wasn't the time for it.

Instead, he circled the block, taking in every angle.

Failing to plan is planning to fail, his special forces instructor used to say. Prep was key. That mentality had stuck with him long after he'd left the service. His wife used to tease him about it.

You need to be more spontaneous, she'd joke. But she had enough spontaneity for both of them.

Soraya.

He closed his eyes, letting the grief hit him, sharp and familiar. Then, he took a breath, shoving it back down.

Soon.

Omari was going to pay for what happened to her.

But first, he had to figure out who this mystery woman was and what she wanted with his target. He didn't need any more complications.

After finishing his rounds, Stitch found a bench up the street and sat down to wait.

CHAPTER 2

Sloane entered her apartment, a squalid one-bedroom flat above a busy street and locked the door behind her. God, she was tired.

Removing her scarf, she made a beeline for the bathroom and turned on the taps. A hot soak in the tub was what she needed to get rid of the dust and grime of the street. Even her eyes felt gritty.

While the bath ran, she plugged in her laptop and set her cell phone beside it. She'd use it to connect to an internet hotspot. It was the only way to get connectivity.

She thought about the three men Omari had met.

That was new. He usually met friends at the coffee shop, not out-of-towners. She could tell by the vehicle registration that they weren't from Peshawar. Maybe they'd hailed from across the border in Afghanistan. That was where Omari was from, although he couldn't risk going back in case the U.S. forces discovered where he was.

"We know already," she murmured, as she stripped off, tossing her clothes onto the bed. "We've got you in our sights."

Music emanated from the apartment next door. She didn't mind it, actually. The mismatched, jingly beat was strangely uplifting. Plus, it helped to know there were people close by. Sometimes, she felt so alone.

At first, she'd been delighted, if a little overwhelmed, at the prospect of being chosen for this assignment. She was a new recruit, after all. Matthew must have pushed to get her assigned. She didn't want to let him down. This was a test of her mettle, her first overseas mission.

She'd read ferociously in preparation, but coming here was nothing like what was in the books or online. As a westerner, she was conspicuous. As a woman travelling alone, even more so.

She'd quickly learned to dress like a local, to blend in. Her contact in Islamabad had helped her acquire the appropriate attire and headwear. One of the servants at his hotel had shown her how to fix her headscarf so that it looked natural, like an Arabic woman. With her dark hair and brown eyes, people assumed she was a local.

Then her contact had driven her to Peshawar. The trip had taken nearly three hours, and he hadn't spoken to her once. On arrival, he'd handed her the keys to the apartment, told her which number it was, and sped off leaving her standing in the middle of the dusty road with her suitcase.

The first thing that struck her was the smell of raw meat. It made her want to throw up. She'd never considered vegetarianism before, but in the three weeks she'd been here, she hadn't touched anything even remotely resembling meat. She could still smell it now, wafting up from the butchery below on the warm air, permeating the rickety windows.

Or maybe that was her imagination.

She walked naked into the bathroom. At least there was hot water. She hadn't been sure when she'd seen the state of the apartment. She poured in a few drops of scented oil she'd found at the market—lavender, she thought—and climbed into the steaming, fragrant water.

It was utter bliss.

She sunk down, feeling her body relax.

Her handler would be very interested in Omari's visitors. Perhaps this was the intel they'd been waiting for. Her orders were simple: observe and report back.

Nothing else.

It hadn't sounded that difficult at the plush CIA offices in D.C., however, here in Peshawar, things were more complicated. Logistically, following Omari had been a nightmare—until she'd got the scooter.

She'd bought it from Mohammed who owned the garage up the road. There'd been no argument when she'd offered to pay in U.S. dollars. The magic currency. He hadn't even asked if she had a license.

Another bribe ensured she could park it just inside the meat market. The store owner was happy to oblige. He even gave her a key to the back entrance so she could get it after hours when the front was closed, not that she'd ever had to use it.

Most of Peshawar shut down at night. Alcohol was prohibited, so there were no bars. It was only the odd teahouse and coffee shop, the tobacconist and the night market that stayed open. Despite this, the traffic only died down around midnight, but she'd gotten used to it. It no longer kept her awake like it used to.

After washing herself fully, she shampooed her hair and rinsed it using the jug she'd placed by the side of the tub. Much better!

Climbing out, she wrapped herself in a towel. Still dripping, she padded into the bedroom.

And screamed.

CHAPTER 3

Sloane dropped the towel and dived under the pillow for her gun.

It was missing.

Shit!

"Looking for this?" On the chair by the window, sat a man who looked like he could wrestle a grizzly bear—and win. He held her gun, twirling it between his fingers like it was a toy.

Her heart pounded as she realized two things at once: she was completely naked, and he was very much armed.

"Who are you?" She grabbed the towel and clutched it to her chest. Her hands trembled so badly she could barely hold on to the fabric. None of her training had prepared her for this—standing butt naked in a room with a mountain of a man, staring down the barrel of her own gun.

She could hit targets hundreds of meters away, track moving threats with precision. She could read a situation in seconds—friend or foe.

Foe. Foe. Foe. Her instincts screamed loud and clear.

But her weapon was across the room, and he had it.

The man just sat there, calm as anything, the gun now

pointing right at her, his eyes dark and unreadable beneath a layer of scruff on his tanned face.

"You're American?" She fumbled for clarity. Anything that would dampen the threat, steady her frantic heart.

He ignored her question. Instead, he asked one of his own. "Who are you and why are you following Abdul Omari?"

The hand holding the gun didn't waver. The eyes held steady, piercing in their directness. She could barely make out his features, thanks to the bushy beard that covered the lower half of his face. At first, until he'd spoken, she'd thought he was a local.

"I'm Sloane Carmichael," she said, falling back onto her legend. "I'm a charity worker with the Women's Empowerment League."

He scowled at her, his eyes narrowing. "Bullshit."

"W–What?"

"I recognize a cover story when I hear one. Who are you really? CIA? NSA?"

Something in her expression must have given her away, because his lips curled into a gratified grin. "Ah, the Agency. I should have known."

"I–I don't know what you mean," she stammered.

He smirked. "Please, spare me the pretense. I've been watching you follow Omari for days. Now, I want to know why."

"You're mistaken," she insisted, clutching onto the towel like it was a lifeline. "I work at the Peshawar Community Centre. I teach English language classes."

He got up. Holy crap, he was tall. He towered over her, his head nearly touching the ceiling. She took in the dark, wavy hair, wild and unkempt, the massive, boulder-like shoulders, and the menacing expression that sent chills down her spine.

As he approached, she stiffened. This man was raw

power. It emanated from every purpose-filled movement. His jaw was tense beneath the beard, his face a mask of barely controlled anger. Veins bulged in his neck.

Oh, hell.

Don't let him unleash that fury on me.

"Don't lie to me." His voice was a rough whisper. "Aid workers don't carry Glock 19s, change their appearance on a whim, and speak fluent Urdu."

Sloane grimaced internally.

Crap, she was made.

"That's for protection," she blurted out, knowing instantly how lame it sounded. "I'm a woman, traveling alone. This isn't exactly the safest part of the world."

He snorted. "How'd you get it past airport security?"

"I didn't. A friend in Islamabad lent it to me." That part was actually true. Except Jeremy wasn't exactly a friend. She'd met her handler for the first time three weeks ago when she'd arrived in the Middle East.

The grizzly stared at her for what felt like an eternity. She shivered under his gaze, and it wasn't because of the cold. His eyes were a striking blue, but icy—like the Arctic. Set against his deeply tanned face, they were both mesmerizing and unsettling.

She wondered what he'd look like if he cleaned up a bit, got rid of the scruff and that wild mop of hair. Then, she mentally slapped herself. Why the hell was she thinking about that? She should be worrying about whether or not he was going to crush her with his giant hands.

"What were you doing following Omari?"

"I told you, I wasn't—"

He tucked the gun into his waistband and took a step toward her. Her heart slammed into her ribs. Oh God… this was it. Was he going to strangle her in this dingy motel room?

But instead of lunging for her, he leaned over and casually picked her cell phone up off the bed.

She exhaled sharply, her knees almost giving out.

Thank God.

He glanced at the screen.

Ha! Good luck with that, buddy. It had a thumbprint lock.

Without a word, he reached for her hand and pressed her thumb against the button. To her overriding shame—or maybe it was fear—she let him, like a puppet on a string. His hand was warm, firm, and calloused. So different from Matthew's. A working man's hands.

The phone unlocked, and he dropped her hand like a hot potato.

She swallowed hard. The spot where he'd touched her still tingled.

Oh God, Matthew was going to kill her.

Who was this guy anyway? What right did he have to look through her phone?

She considered grabbing it, telling him to back off and get out of her apartment. But something told her he'd just ignore her. For starters, he was double her size. No way she'd win that battle. Hysterical laughter bubbled up in her throat, but she swallowed it down.

Not. Funny.

She was naked, unarmed, and completely defenseless. He was none of those things.

The phone lit up as he scrolled through her photos, stopping at the shots of the three men who'd met Omari at the coffee shop.

He held it up so she could see the screen. "Recognize these guys?"

Her stomach dropped.

Not waiting for an answer, he flipped through more of her pictures. Omari walking down the street, going into shops and teahouses, and standing outside what looked like his house—a two-story building with a secure garage and a gated entrance.

"Nice vacation photos," he said dryly.

Her legs finally gave out, and she collapsed onto the bed, still clutching the towel in front of her. "Mind if I put some clothes on?" she croaked.

He looked her over, his icy gaze lingering on the towel like he could see right through it. She wouldn't be surprised if he had x-ray vision. He seemed... otherworldly, like some kind of wild beast.

"Tell me what I want to know, and then you can get dressed." He pulled the gun from his waistband again but didn't point it at her. Instead, he held it casually like it was an extension of his arm.

She hesitated.

"Your name?" His voice was a low growl.

"Sloane Carmichael. I wasn't lying about that."

"Special Agent Carmichael, is it?"

Shit. Talk about breaking every rule in the CIA handbook. A lump formed in her throat, and she nodded.

Way to go, Sloane.

In under ten minutes, she'd let this guy ambush her, unlock her phone, get her real name, and find out she worked for the Agency.

Fantastic.

To be fair, he wasn't the type of man you said no to. Just looking at him, she knew he was dangerous. No—lethal. Probably a killer.

Those eyes... Cold, hard, unreadable.

"Why's the CIA so interested in Abdul Omari?" he asked.

She glanced at the door, and then up at him, a hulking shadow in the rapidly darkening room. By sitting down on the bed, she'd effectively cut off any possible escape route.

He'd be on top of her the moment she moved. Stupid, rookie mistake.

"Don't even think about it," he warned.

Her shoulders sagged. Was she that obvious?

"I don't know why," she said weakly. "My assignment is to watch and report back. That's it."

"They must have told you something," he pushed.

"Just that he's on a CIA watch list. I assumed it was terror related. He's got ties to the Taliban."

The intruder didn't react, he merely watched her, his dark expression giving nothing away. Self-conscious, she pulled the towel tighter around her.

"You can get dressed now," he said finally.

CHAPTER 4

Stitch watched as the CIA agent jumped off the bed and scooted toward the wardrobe, still clutching her towel. She may as well not have bothered. Her naked body was engraved behind his eyelids. Every time he closed them, he saw her.

Smooth skin, pink from her bath. Full breasts with dusky pink nipples. A dark patch of fuzzy pubic hair—

God help him.

Then she turned around, burying in the closet.

He sucked in a breath. That gently swelling bottom. What the fuck was she playing at?

"Hurry up," he growled.

Preventing her from getting dressed had been a tactic. He had her at her most vulnerable, ripe for interrogation. Yet, her nakedness was doing strange things to him. Things he hadn't felt in a long time.

His strategy may just have backfired.

"Close your eyes," she hissed, still fumbling. "You're making me nervous."

She wasn't the only one.

And he couldn't close his eyes. Not in enemy territory, even if he was the one holding the gun.

But he did look away. A neon sign from across the road came on and cast the floorboards and walls in a glowing red light.

It had been over a year since he'd seen a woman naked.

After Soraya... Well, he'd been in no fit state for any of that. Now, for the first time since his wife had passed, he felt the familiar stirrings of arousal. He wasn't sure who wanted her to get dressed faster, him or her.

Once the gold slip of material fell over her head, he breathed a sigh of relief. Then, he saw how it clung to her curves, skimming over her breasts and hips, and molding against her crotch. She wasn't wearing underwear. He groaned inwardly.

Goddamn. She was stunning.

Fucking awful agent, though, but an absolutely goddamned stunner.

"You call that clothing?" he rasped.

"It's a nightgown. It's all I could find at short notice." She shot him an accusatory look.

He shook his head. "Okay, sit down."

She perched at the end of the bed. Her dark hair hung in wet tendrils over her shoulders, dampening the flimsy material over her breasts. He could see her nipples jutting out, teasing him. His mouth went dry.

Averting his gaze, he resumed his seat by the window and placed the gun on his lap. It was loaded, he'd checked, not that he planned to use it. Interestingly, the barrel was threaded, which meant it was made for a silencer.

He needed to find out what she knew. Who her handler was? The 'friend' in Islamabad.

"Who are you?" she asked.

"Doesn't matter who I am."

"What are you going to do with me?" Fear flickered across her face.

"Nothing, as long as you tell me the truth."

"I have told you the truth. What more do you want?"

She was angry, but afraid to show it. The flush in her cheeks crept down her neck.

He leaned forward. "I want to know everything that you know about Abdul Omari. His daily routine, who he's met since you've been watching him, where he goes, and what he's been up to. And I want to know the name of your contact."

She gulped. "Is that all?"

He gave a little smirk.

"Let's start with his routine."

Reluctantly, Sloane picked up the phone. "He lives in the upmarket Hayatbad district, west of here." She bent forward to show him the photograph he'd already seen of the double-story house with the gated front entrance and garage.

He wished she hadn't. He kept his eyes glued to the screen.

"Every morning, he leaves home around eleven, is driven into town where he goes to his favorite coffee shop. He seems to prefer coffee to tea."

The cherry lips formed a pretty pout.

"Sometimes friends meet him there. Locals. I've seen the same men several times. Look, here they are…" She got up and stood beside him, leaning over to show him the shots.

Christ, was she fucking doing this on purpose? Did she have any idea of the effect she was having on him?

As she thumbed through the photographs, he caught a whiff of vanilla. Wet hair tickled his hand. He fought not to jolt away.

"Then he walks up and down the street, greeting people,

flanked by his bodyguards, before getting back into the car and going home. His routine hardly ever varies."

"Except for today," growled Stitch.

"Yeah," she said breathlessly. "I haven't seen those men before. They looked like they were from out of town."

He agreed with her there. The plates had been different, and the dust coating the base of the vehicle signified it had driven a fair distance before arriving at its destination in Peshawar.

"Afghanistan," he muttered.

She straightened up. "That's what I thought."

"Can I see the photographs?"

She handed him her phone. He flicked through until he got to the ones she'd taken of the three visitors. He zoomed in. None of them looked familiar.

"Do you think they're Taliban?" she asked.

"Maybe."

He didn't elaborate. She had her job to do, and he had his. No way was he about to tell her who Omari really was.

A monster. A destroyer of villages, a killer of women and children, a taker of lives. A psychopath consumed by power and wealth and all the trappings that came with it.

Being Taliban was the least of his crimes.

Nothing Omari did was terror related, but if that was the story she'd been fed, so be it. Nothing to do with him. He wasn't interested in Agency business, so long as it didn't interfere with his.

Omari was going down, regardless.

CHAPTER 5

When Sloane's heart finally slowed to a reasonable pace and she no longer felt like she might faint from fear, she took a closer look at the beast of a man who had invaded her space.

She might not be the best field agent, but she was brilliant at reading people. That was her "gift," as Matthew called it. And the first thing she picked up about this guy was that he was in pain.

Not physical pain, but the kind that tore at your soul. She could tell he'd been to hell and back and was haunted by it. It was all there, plain as day. The tension in his muscular frame, his clenched fists, the veins popping in his neck, the rigid jaw. His intimidating posture and angry glare barely concealed it. And his eyes—icy blue, filled with hurt.

Grief? Hatred?

Something.

Definitely something.

No doubt he was dangerous, but she didn't think that danger was aimed at her.

It was aimed at Omari.

He wanted something from Omari. But what?

A shiver crawled up her spine. Whatever it was, it wasn't good.

He knew his way around a gun. Military, maybe? A soldier? He moved like one—disciplined, efficient, totally focused, light on his feet. She'd trained with soldiers at the academy—she knew the type.

Plus, there was that sexy tattoo peeking out from under his right sleeve. She could just make out the tip of a trident, its sharp lines etched in bold black ink against his tanned skin.

Her knack for reading people was why she'd been recruited. Her instructors were impressed by how quickly she could sense someone's emotions. It came naturally, like breathing.

She was reading him now.

That's what happens when you grow up with an alcoholic father, she thought with a sniff. His unpredictable moods and frequent outbursts had kept her on edge. She learned when to disappear, when to calm him down, and how to talk him out of a drunken rage. Too bad she hadn't been able to talk him off that bridge. That was ten years ago. She'd been seventeen.

"Why do you want to know about Omari?" She turned back to the smoldering ball of tension standing in front of her, still scrolling through her phone.

He glared at her. No, not at her—through her.

His mind was on Omari, the Taliban official they were both tracking. Raw, unfiltered hatred poured off him. It was so strong she could practically feel it.

"None of your business," he snapped.

"Except you came here demanding to know mine?" she shot back.

His eyes narrowed—dangerous slits of rage and pain. "I believe I'm the one holding the gun."

She sighed and sat back down on the bed. "Looks to me like we both want the same thing."

He didn't respond, just stared.

"To know what Omari's up to, right?"

Nothing.

She took a deep breath. "So, why don't we come to a compromise?"

He growled, but it wasn't a no. "What did you have in mind?"

Encouraged, she pressed on. "It's my job to follow him and report what he's doing, who he meets, all of that... And you want to know what he's up to, too."

His cold gaze didn't budge. "Go on…"

"Maybe we can work together. It's pointless for both of us to tail him. It just increases the chance he'll notice he's being followed."

He gave a small nod, acknowledging her point. "What will you tell your handler?"

"Nothing," she said quickly. The red light flickered behind him, casting his giant frame in shadow. She stayed still—she was finally getting somewhere. "He doesn't need to know."

He scowled. "You expect me to believe you're not going to report what happened here?"

"Why would I?" she said evenly. "It'd just make me look bad. This is my first assignment, and I've already screwed it up. I don't want my boss knowing I got ambushed by an American soldier and spilled details about the operation. They'd fire me. My career would be over."

He frowned. "What makes you think I'm a soldier?"

She waved a hand in the air. "Everything about you—even though you're trying to hide it. And you're clearly American. Doesn't take a genius to figure it out."

He snorted. "Fair enough."

"I don't know what you want with Omari," she said quietly, "but we have the same objective. It'd be stupid not to work together."

There was a long pause as he studied her. She stayed still while he decided if he could trust her.

He couldn't. They both knew that.

The question was, did he want the intel badly enough to go along with her plan?

"If this is going to work," he said finally, "you report to me. Got it?"

She hesitated. What choice did she have? As long as he shared his information with her, did it matter who was in charge? Men and their egos. Besides, this would give her a chance to learn more about him, figure out what he really wanted with Omari. Once she had that, she'd have something valuable to feed back.

"What about my handler?" she asked. "He'll get suspicious if I don't report regularly."

"Keep to your schedule," he barked, his voice sharp, like he was used to giving orders. "Don't make him suspicious. He needs to think it's business as usual."

"I'll have to report the three men from today."

He nodded. "Go ahead."

She blinked, surprised. "Now?"

He nodded toward her laptop. "Why not? You're all set up."

She grimaced. "Not quite. Give me a minute."

The soldier watched as she plugged in her phone and connected it. Once she had a signal, she composed an email to Jeremy, attaching the photos. While she typed, he circled in, peering over her shoulder. His presence behind her was unsettling. The hairs on her arms stood up as if alerted by his magnetic force.

"Is Jeremy your handler?" he asked, leaning in closer to look at her screen.

"Yes." She could feel his breath on her cheek.

"Last name?"

"I don't know." She hesitated. "He never told me."

She hit SEND, and the email whooshed out of her inbox.

He stepped back while she closed the laptop and disconnected her phone. When she was done, she glanced up and found him staring at her. "Is your real name Sloane Carmichael?"

"Yes, I told you that already."

He shrugged. "I'm surprised. They usually give undercover operatives some kind of cover story. Maybe they figured you were better off telling the truth."

Or maybe they didn't think I was worth protecting, she thought suddenly. But no—Matthew would never put her at risk. He cared about her.

"I'm only supposed to observe and report back," she said defensively. "Not sure that warrants a fake identity."

"What if you get caught?" he asked. "Did they tell you what to do then?"

"I'm not going to get caught. And I've been through basic training." She hated the doubt in her voice. To be honest, her training wasn't that extensive. Ten months at the academy, then two months at the D.C. office before she was shipped off to Pakistan.

"You'd better hope you don't." For the first time, his icy blue eyes glittered with amusement. "You didn't put up much of a fight when I broke in."

"I'm still alive, aren't I?"

He tilted his head in acknowledgment. "I guess so."

"And now we're working together," she continued.

"We are."

"Some might say that's a win for me. Maybe this is my chance to gather intel on you. Ever think of that?"

This time, he smiled—just a little. The corners of his mouth lifted, and his gaze softened. "Of course."

Her breath caught.

Damn.

When he lost that steely edge, when he allowed himself to be human, it did something to her. She felt her pulse quicken.

"What's your name?"

There was a pause. "You can call me Stitch."

"Stitch?"

"Yeah."

Okay, fine. Stitch it was.

After a moment, he said, "It's sure going to be interesting working with you, Special Agent Carmichael. How about I take the morning shift, and you take the afternoon?"

Oh, no. That wasn't going to work. "Can we swap? I teach at the community center three afternoons a week."

"Fine. Makes no difference to me."

They stared at each other until he finally broke eye contact and backed toward the window.

"You can use the door, you know," she said, regaining her composure. He was, without a doubt, the most unnerving, intimidating man she'd ever met.

"I'd rather not be seen." He threw a leg over the windowsill and hopped down onto the rickety balcony. It groaned under his weight but held.

"See you tomorrow," she called.

But he was already gone.

It wasn't until then that she noticed he'd left her gun on the bed behind her.

CHAPTER 6

Stitch hovered in a narrow alleyway, the shadows providing just enough cover as he watched Sloane hurry past. She carried the same canvas bag slung casually over her shoulder, her pace quick and deliberate. He was practically invisible in the loose-fitting men's robes he wore, the folds of the fabric helping to obscure his bulk. A turban wrapped tightly around his head further masked his identity. To blend in better, he hunched his tall frame, pulling inward to disguise his height and broad shoulders.

The air was thick with dust and the distant hum of traffic, but he barely noticed, too focused on the sight of her. Even with the black scarf covering her head and wrapping around her neck, there was no mistaking the sensual sway of her hips.

Hips he'd seen naked, curving into a waist so small his hands could easily wrap around it, flaring into that soft, perfect bottom. His pulse quickened as the image flashed in his mind—her bending over to pull something out of the closet, her skin illuminated in the morning light.

Fuck.

He blinked hard, shaking the thought, forcing himself to focus on the task at hand.

Omari was a hundred meters ahead of Sloane, his usual entourage surrounding him like a wall. He chatted with a shopkeeper, laughing as he patted the man's shoulder, before disappearing into a restaurant. It was noon—maybe he was grabbing an early lunch.

Sloane lingered in the market, browsing stalls, trying on sunglasses, and pretending to admire jewelry. But when it became clear Omari was dining alone, she made her way back to the scooter she'd left parked a few blocks away.

This time, Stitch was ready. He had wheels of his own—a beat-up Vespa that was perfect for navigating the chaotic streets. He'd scouted a rental place earlier that morning, making sure he had a way to keep up with her without standing out.

Sloane started up her scooter, merging effortlessly into the thick stream of traffic. Taxis, rickshaws, and worn-out vehicles jostled for position on the pothole-riddled roads. He followed at a careful distance, not too close, but there were so many bikes and scooters she'd never notice him.

Two miles down, she turned off the busy main road, weaving through a series of side streets until she reached a broad, squat building.

Peshawar Community Center, read the sign in bold Arabic lettering. A security guard stood at the entrance, cradling a shiny black assault rifle. Next to him, a Western woman in jeans and a loose shirt puffed on a cigarette.

Stitch frowned. A guard like that for a community center? Something didn't add up.

The building itself was plain, nothing special. Tattered awnings covered the wide windows, and the corrugated iron roof looked as if it had been slapped on without much care. The concrete walls were rough and unfinished, like so many others in the border town. Everything here felt temporary, as if people didn't expect it to last.

The streets were quieter out here, fewer distractions, so he stayed back, out of sight. Sloane parked by the front door, exchanged a few words with the smoking woman, then tucked her helmet under her arm and went inside.

Stitch parked his Vespa a block away, near a school. Through the wrought-iron gates, children played in a dusty courtyard, their voices ringing out over the barren landscape. There wasn't much to absorb the sound around here—just dry roads, a few low concrete buildings, and, in the distance, parched fields that had long since been abandoned.

For a moment, he just listened. Schools sounded the same everywhere, from Pakistan to the States. Laughter, shouts of joy, innocence—before the world sank its claws into them, burdening them with the weight of culture, expectation, and survival.

He turned back to the community center. It was another blistering day, sweat trickling down his back, dampening the fabric of his robes. The woman had finished her cigarette and disappeared inside, but the guard remained, eyes alert, rifle in hand.

Stitch stayed put, watching. He could see shadows moving behind the wide windows. Class was about to begin. There was no need to risk getting closer. Now he knew where she worked, and at least that part of her cover story checked out.

He headed back toward town. It was his turn to tail Omari, who'd be finishing his lunch soon. As it turned out, the Taliban official wasn't in any rush. An hour later, Omari finally emerged from the restaurant, patting his stomach like a satisfied man.

Stitch followed at a distance as Omari was driven home in a bulletproof SUV, two bodyguards flanking him in the back seat. When the vehicle turned into a gated neighborhood, Stitch knew there'd be no new intel today.

He turned back, heading toward Mrs. Bhatti's. In this upscale neighborhood, a man rumbling past on a battered Vespa would raise too many questions.

Mrs. Bhatti smiled when he let himself in. "It's good to have you back, Stitch."

Hearing his old nickname tugged at something in his chest. It had been a while since anyone called him that. Back in his SEAL unit, it was all he ever heard. The guys had been like brothers. The life-or-death missions, the adrenaline, the camaraderie—it felt like another life now.

He'd been halfway through med school when he decided the Navy was where he belonged. The guys used to joke he'd swapped saving lives in the OR for saving them on the battlefield. Funny thing was, he'd stitched up more people in combat than he ever had in a hospital.

"It's good to see you too, Mrs. Bhatti. What's for dinner?"

The rich scent of spices floated in from the kitchen. He remembered how much she loved to cook—and how she always insisted on feeding him.

"You can't fight on an empty stomach," she'd say, wagging her finger.

Stitch retreated to his room, collapsing onto the bed. The afternoon light filtered through the blinds, casting stripes across the floor. The house was quiet, but his mind wasn't.

He'd come here to rest, to clear his head, but instead, Sloane kept creeping into his thoughts. The image of her in that slip—the one that clung to her like a second skin—kept flashing through his mind. He could still see the way it molded to her hips, the soft curve of her waist. It stirred something in him, something he hadn't felt in a long time.

And that's what bothered him most.

It had been over a year since Soraya's death, and not once

had he looked at another woman. Not like this. The guilt hit him hard, twisting his gut. His late wife's face flickered through his mind—the way she used to laugh, the warmth of her touch. She'd been everything to him, and he'd lost her. Now, he was thinking about someone else, feeling something for someone else.

He clenched his fists, closing his eyes to block it out, but Sloane's face lingered, that spark in her eyes pulling him in. How could he be attracted to another woman? Not now. Not yet. It felt wrong.

But no matter how hard he fought it, the pull toward her was undeniable. And that scared the fuck out of him.

CHAPTER 7

Sloane smiled at her class, a lively group of women eager to improve their language skills. Some arrived quietly, wrapped in full burqas, while others wore modern clothes paired with headscarves. Not everyone had permission from their husbands or families to attend.

The Women's Empowerment Group provided the classes for free, knowing many of the women couldn't afford to pay—or wouldn't be allowed to, even if they could. Aaliyah, the American-Pakistani woman who ran the center, had told her about a recent incident when an angry man stormed in and dragged his young wife out of class by her hair. "Right in front of everyone," she'd said, shaking her head.

Since then, they'd hired a security guard, with strict orders not to let anyone in who wasn't on the list or working at the center. His presence gave the women a sense of security they hadn't had before.

The lesson began, but as she taught, Sloane's mind drifted to the wild-looking American soldier who'd broken into her apartment the night before. He'd held her at gunpoint, but what should've been a terrifying experience had somehow turned into an unexpected partnership. She had nothing new to report to him yet, but the thought of seeing him later made her shiver in a way she couldn't explain.

It was crazy. He was pushy, demanding, arrogant—and dangerous. The simmering anger he carried around, the kind that could explode at any moment, should have made her wary. He wasn't in control of it, no matter how much he thought he was. She'd seen that flash of obsession in his eyes when he'd talked about Omari.

He was as much a prisoner of his hatred as she was of their arrangement. He might be controlling her now, but his own demons controlled him, making him unpredictable.

So why did the thought of seeing him again send goosebumps across her skin?

Matthew didn't have that effect on her, and she was crazy about him. Although, she had to admit, Matthew had started to feel more distant in her mind. Blurred around the edges. She hadn't even spoken to him in the three weeks she'd been here.

"We have to maintain absolute radio silence," he'd told her before she left. "All communication goes through Jeremy, and it has to be via email."

She still didn't understand why. No one was bugging her phone. No one even knew she was here. What harm would one phone call do? But orders were orders, so she hadn't argued.

The rough-edged soldier, however, kept creeping into her thoughts, uninvited.

"Oh, I'm sorry. Could you repeat that?" she asked, flashing an apologetic smile at a woman in the front row who had asked a question.

Focus, she told herself. She could think about him later.

It was midsummer, and by the time she got home around

six, there were still a couple of hours of daylight left. Two hours until he arrived.

On her way back, she'd stopped at a small grocery store to pick up bread, vegetables, and spices for a stew. Cooking always grounded her, reminding her of her grandmother, who had taught her the basics after her father had passed away.

Her grandmother had also been the one to teach her Urdu, a language that had been passed down through the generations. Her great-grandmother had been born here, and Sloane had always been told she looked like her—a resemblance she'd noticed in the grainy black-and-white photo that had sat on her grandmother's mantle. Now, three generations later, Sloane found herself in the country of her great-grandmother's birth.

She'd expected to feel some sort of connection when she arrived, but it hadn't happened. The land still felt foreign to her, despite the language. But that's why Matthew had recruited her—because she spoke it fluently.

Her thoughts wandered back to the day her life had changed. She'd been standing in the school playground, waiting with Freddy, one of her students, whose father had not arrived to collect him. Another teacher had been chatting with her in Urdu when Freddy's father had swept in, full of apologies.

Apologies. A business meeting had run long.

She remembered the way he'd smiled, charming and self-assured, his tailored suit and expensive cologne making it clear he wasn't just any businessman. She hadn't known it at the time but meeting him would set off a chain of events that would change everything.

Normally, it was his wife who dropped off their son—a coiffed blonde who drove a flashy red convertible, always perfectly put together. After school, it was a younger woman, dark hair pulled back in a bun, who picked Freddy up. The au pair, maybe? A nanny? Either way, both parents were obviously too busy, too important, to be deeply involved.

She had no idea that Friday afternoon how much her life was about to shift.

Sloane let herself into her apartment. Damn, it was stifling hot. She opened a window, but it didn't help much. It just let in the metallic meat smell from below.

A cool bath would help wash off the sweat of the day and cool her flushed cheeks. It had absolutely nothing to do with wanting to look nice for him.

After bathing and washing the dust out of her hair, she got dressed. Appropriately, this time. That gold nightgown… Ugh. She'd practically been falling out of it, but it had been preferrable to sitting naked in front of him.

Luckily, he'd been too caught up in his simmering rage to notice what she'd been wearing. Or not wearing, as it turned out.

Cringing, she selected a safe, black skirt and a strappy top. If it was this hot back home, she'd be flouncing around in a bikini, but that clearly wasn't an option here.

The one-bed apartment was a mess. She cleared up, putting her dirty clothes in a bag to wash, and moving the small table and two chairs from the kitchen to the bedroom. At least that way she'd have somewhere to sit, other than the bed.

She shook her head. Why was she bothering?

He wasn't a guest. He was an enemy. An American soldier using her to get information about Omari. So, why was she so nervous?

To take her mind off his imminent arrival, she unpacked the groceries and set about making a stew. Working over the stove made her hot again, so she splashed some water on her face and took a few deep breaths.

Where was he?

The sun had almost set, yet there was no sign of him.

She switched on the bedside lamp and the room was cast in a rosy glow, enhanced by the red electric signage on the building opposite. Too anxious to eat, she saved the stew for later and paced up and down the dimly lit room, waiting for his broad shadow to appear at the window.

An hour later.

It was pitch dark outside now, save for the flickering red light. Her handler would be expecting her surveillance update. She picked up her laptop and placed it on the table. It was fully charged, as was her phone. Connecting to the internet, she sent off a quick message. Nothing new to report.

He hadn't replied to last night's email, which had included the photographs of the three Afghan men. She wondered what her superiors would make of the three men from across the border.

Jeremy never responded. His job was to forward anything of interest on to his boss. Was that Matthew? She wasn't sure. The man who'd recruited her had been vague about his position at the agency.

Another excruciating hour passed, and Sloane's stomach growled. It was getting late, and she was tired and hungry. Well, she wasn't waiting any longer.

Perhaps he'd changed his mind and wasn't coming?

She ignored the pang of regret that flashed over her. That was a hunger pang. Nothing more. It was better for her if he didn't come. She could go back to doing her job without having to report to him anymore.

Sloane helped herself to some vegetable stew, eating quickly in case he arrived while she was busy, but she needn't have worried. He didn't show.

After supper, she washed up, made herself a cup of peppermint tea, and settled down to read. But the words floated in front of her. Still no soldier.

She frowned. Maybe something had happened to him. Perhaps he'd been called away. It struck her how little she actually knew about him. He'd been tight-lipped, while she'd sung like a canary. It was embarrassing!

Who did he work for? The U.S. government? Or did he have his own agenda? There was something rogue and untamed about him. He didn't strike her as a man adhering to the rules.

Sloane yawned. It was now nearly ten o'clock and she was battling to keep her eyes open. Should she even try? He wouldn't come now, would he? Not at this late hour.

At half past ten she turned out the light. If he couldn't stick to their arrangement, neither would she. It didn't matter to her. What did she care if she didn't see the broad-shouldered, wild-haired, grizzly bear of a man again?

Yet, it was with this image in her head that she drifted off to sleep.

A SOFT SCRAPING SOUND WOKE her, followed by a low creak and a cool breeze. Someone was in the room! Before she had time to react, a giant hand clamped down over her mouth.

She cried out in fright, but it came out as a muffled murmur. Panicking, she tossed her head from side to side, but the hand held firm. She lashed out, trying to push her attacker away, but it was like shoving against a brick wall. Solid and unyielding.

Her heart raced as all kinds of horrors rushed through her mind. Was she being attacked? Was it Omari's men? Had they found out who she was?

"Shh…" a deep voice hissed.

She recognized that low, growling baritone. It was *him*. Thank God.

She quieted down, and he slowly removed his hand.

"Didn't mean to startle you," he grunted. "But I had to be sure you didn't have anyone waiting for me."

"Who would I have waiting?" she asked, her confused mind still on Omari. Then she blinked. Duh. The CIA, of course.

"No," she said quickly. "Nobody's here but me."

"I know. I checked."

He stood back, giving her space, and she scrambled into a sitting position. The thin strap of her gold nightgown had slipped off her shoulder, the silky material barely covering her left breast. Hastily, she pulled it up. Thankfully, it was dark in the room, except for the annoying red flicker from the building across the street that the gauzy curtains did nothing to block.

"What time is it?" she muttered.

"Half past eleven."

"I didn't think you were coming."

No reply. Instead, he backtracked to the small wooden table and sat down. The outline of his hulking frame pulsed red, in time with her pounding heart.

Leaning over, she turned on the bedside lamp. The amber glow replaced the pulsing red light.

She ran a hand through her hair, fully aware she must look like a wreck, but he was staring at her with a heated intensity that took her breath away. She cleared her throat, and the heat vanished, replaced by the cool, distant look she was used to.

"Anything interesting to report?" he growled.

"No, nothing unusual today."

"Tell me where he went."

She sat up, the sheets tangled around her.

Great. Exposed, vulnerable, and unprepared. This was becoming a pattern.

Still, if she got up to get dressed, she'd have to walk around in front of him in her nightgown. Again. Why did he always catch her off-guard like this?

"Do you think we could arrange a time for these meetings in the future?" she asked, pulling the sheets around her waist. "So I can be prepared?"

"I like to keep things unpredictable," he said. "Less chance of an ambush."

She sighed.

"You were saying?"

She gathered her thoughts. "Omari left home around eleven, as usual, and was driven into town by his bodyguards. He walked around, spoke to a shopkeeper and a few locals, then went into a restaurant for lunch around noon. I waited for about half an hour, but no one else showed up, so I left. I had to be at the community center by one."

"Ah yes, your cover story."

"Actually, I *am* a teacher," she huffed. "Or I was before the CIA recruited me."

He raised an eyebrow. "A teacher who speaks fluent Urdu. I can see why that would be appealing. When were you recruited?"

"Ten months ago."

"For this assignment?"

She shrugged. "I don't know. Maybe. I did a crash course in D.C. and was assigned this mission."

He nodded.

There was a pause before he said, "I looked into your handler, Jeremy. Couldn't find anything on him. Do you know where he's staying?"

"The Marriott," she replied. "That's where we stayed the first night I arrived."

"Unlikely he's still there."

"Why would he leave?"

"Too easy to track him down, especially since you saw him there. And it's expensive. If he's the Agency's point man in Pakistan, he'll have cheaper, less conspicuous accommodation somewhere else. The hotel was for your benefit."

Okay, that made sense.

"Do you have a phone number for him?"

"No, just an email address."

"And if there was an emergency, if you didn't have WiFi or access to your laptop or phone, how would you contact him?"

She fell silent. She wouldn't be able to. If she didn't have access to email, she'd be screwed. He hadn't given her a backup plan.

"Nothing's going to happen to me," she grumbled, though she felt shaken. Just a few minutes ago, she thought Omari's men had broken in. "I'm just observing."

"Your cover could get blown. You could be kidnapped or held for ransom. It's not uncommon around here." He lowered his voice. "A woman traveling alone is especially vulnerable."

She suddenly felt like a lamb being led to slaughter.

Matthew.

She brightened. She could call him.

"I have my boss's personal number," she told him. "I could call him in D.C."

Strict radio silence.

Matthew's voice echoed in her mind. But surely, in an emergency...

"You have your boss's direct number?"

She flushed.

"Well, he's not just my boss. We're... friends. He was a father at the school where I taught."

Too much information. Stitch didn't need to know that. He had no right to know. But something about his solid, imposing presence made her want to trust him. Hell, she *needed* to trust him. She was alone out here.

"Did he recruit you?"

She nodded. "He overheard me speaking Urdu to another teacher and introduced himself. We became friends, and then he offered me a job."

There was another long pause. He sat silently, studying her in the dim light. She knew what he was thinking, and it was true.

"He's divorced, if you must know," she said defensively.

He shrugged. "None of my business."

That's right. It wasn't.

"How about you?" she asked, figuring it was time to turn the tables. She was tired of spilling her guts to him. This man had a way of getting information out of her without even trying. Either he was extremely good at his job, or she was terrible at hers. Probably the latter.

"What about me?"

"Omari?" She raised an eyebrow.

He grunted. "Nothing to report. Followed him home after the restaurant, but I had to turn back. Too conspicuous."

She nodded. Omari's neighborhood was a no-go zone for strangers. Anyone unfamiliar would stand out immediately.

"So that's it, then? Nothing to report on either side."

He got up. "I'm going to give you my number." He picked up her phone from the table and handed it to her. "Unlock it."

She held her thumb over the button until the screen lit up. He took it back. Since her bed was little more than a mattress on the floor, she was painfully aware that he could see right down her top, but his eyes stayed on the phone as he typed in his number.

He handed the phone back, and she saved the number under *Stitch*.

"Why do you call yourself Stitch?" she asked softly.

"I was a Navy medic, once upon a time."

"Navy?" She'd been wrong, he was a sailor, not a soldier. Not that it mattered.

He gave a nod.

"But not anymore?"

He shook his head. "No, not anymore."

He didn't look much like a medic. The unruly hair, the grizzly beard, the hard, rugged features. There wasn't an ounce of softness in him. And then there was his size. Medical professionals didn't look like that. This guy could pass for a professional wrestler, with his massive frame, rock-hard body and broad shoulders. Even the loose men's clothing couldn't hide how muscular he was, his thick thighs filling out the baggy trousers.

Sailor? Yes. Medic? No.

"So, what are you now?" she asked.

He ignored the question. "If you need help, or you get into trouble, call me."

"Okay." She set the phone on the bed beside her.

How ironic that this rough, mercenary-like sailor was the closest thing to an ally she had. He was the only one who'd given her a contact number in case of emergencies. Not even Matthew had done that.

She looked up at him—his hard, angular face, his shadowy, towering presence, and those massive arms. One thing was certain: if she ever got into a tight spot, there was no one else she'd rather have on her side.

CHAPTER 8

Stitch felt an almost magnetic pull as she stared up at him, her lips parted like she'd been about to say something but changed her mind. Her pale skin glowed in the dim light, dark hair messy and tangled around her face.

And that damn nightgown.

Jesus.

He'd have to come earlier next time. He couldn't handle seeing her in that slinky thing, barely covering her, her breasts practically spilling out, nipples hard under the gold fabric. It was screwing with his head.

A few inches forward, and he could kiss her. Feel her soft body melt into his.

Shocked by his own thoughts, he took a step back.

"Where are you staying?" she asked.

He hesitated. "Not far. I've got a contact here."

"Do you know Peshawar well?"

She wasn't looking at him with fear anymore—just curiosity. He'd lost his edge. That's what happened when you went soft. The damsel-in-distress thing had gotten to him.

"I've been here before," he said, not offering more. She didn't need to know the details.

But what if she gave his number to her handler? They could track him.

Shit. He hadn't thought that through. He blamed that gold nightgown and what was underneath it.

It was a burner phone, anyway. Easy to ditch if needed. No way it could be traced back to him.

On the plus side, if Omari or his goons figured her out, she'd let him know. Made sense to have a way to contact him.

But that wasn't the real reason he'd done it.

She was alone. Totally alone. Her handler didn't give a damn about her, that much was obvious. Her boss probably didn't either. Hell, maybe not even her *lover*, whoever the hell that was. How could they send her out here on her own with no backup? No support. Just a damn email address.

A naive teacher plucked straight out of a school—or maybe seduced—given a crash course in weapons and surveillance, then dropped into a volatile part of Pakistan to follow a potential terrorist on a CIA watchlist.

No way in hell.

Something else was going on here. Something they hadn't told her. And he was damn sure going to find out what it was.

THE NEXT DAY, Stitch watched as Sloane sat at a teahouse across the road from the restaurant Omari and his crew had disappeared into. Same place as yesterday. Same time. Noon.

He blended into a crowd of men by a fruit stall, but his eyes were locked on the restaurant. Something was about to go down.

The "Closed" sign was up on the restaurant door—he'd

seen it earlier. Two of Omari's men stood outside, hands behind their backs, probably gripping weapons. Their heads moved back and forth like radar, scanning for any incoming trouble.

He frowned when he spotted Sloane. She was right across the street, smack in the line of fire.

He didn't want her to know he was watching her, but if things got ugly, he couldn't let her get caught in the crossfire. So, he left the stall and headed to the teahouse.

Her eyes widened when she saw him.

"What are you doing here?"

"Mind if I join you?"

She shrugged. "Sure, but it's my watch."

"I know. Did you notice the 'Closed' sign and the guards?"

She nodded. "Yeah. I think they're expecting someone."

Almost certainly.

"Do you have your weapon with you?" he asked.

She shook her head. "No, I don't carry it on surveillance. It's just for protection at the apartment. Why?"

He glanced at the two men guarding the door.

"I think something's about to go down."

She stared at him. "What makes you say that?"

"I don't know. Call it a gut feeling."

Just then, three black SUVs rolled down the street, windows tinted, and dust covered.

"Here we go," he muttered. "Showtime."

Sloane stiffened beside him.

The convoy pulled up in front of the restaurant, blocking their view of the entrance. Four men jumped out of the first vehicle, guns in hand, making no effort to hide them. Any nearby shoppers scattered.

The armed men set up a perimeter around the convoy.

"Holy shit," Sloane whispered, reaching for her phone, but he clamped a hand on her arm.

"Not now."

The back doors of the second and third SUVs opened, and two men with turbans stepped out of each, flanked by bodyguards.

"I can't get a visual," Stitch murmured, trying not to make it obvious by craning his neck.

"Me neither," Sloane whispered back.

Moments later, the four VIPs were ushered into the restaurant, along with a few guards. The rest stayed outside, watching over the SUVs.

"Who are they?"

Stitch clenched his jaw. He had a good idea but wasn't about to tell her. "No clue. Maybe Afghans. I didn't get a look at their faces."

"I need a photo," Sloane whispered. "This is huge."

"It's too risky from here," he said. "We'll have to wait for them to come out."

"But I won't get a clear shot with the cars in the way," she complained.

He thought for a second. "Over there." He nodded toward a shop next to the restaurant. It sold all kinds of cheap stuff, with racks of scarves, hats, and sunglasses out on the sidewalk. "If you can get behind the scarves, you might be able to snap a few shots without drawing attention. I doubt they'll notice."

"That's risky," she breathed.

Stitch met her gaze. "Yeah, but if you want the shot…"

He needed that shot too. It was the only way he could confirm his hunch about who they were.

She hesitated, eyes darting between him and the shop.

"Okay," she finally said.

. . .

FORTY MINUTES HAD PASSED, and still no one had come out. Other than the guards, the street was deserted. No one was dumb enough to walk anywhere near that restaurant.

"We'd better move." Stitch stood up. "Time to get into position."

She slung her bag over her shoulder. "They could be in there for a while."

"Yeah, but we're too exposed sitting out here. Let's head toward the fruit stalls. More cover, and we can still see the restaurant."

She followed, and he was glad to see she didn't glance back at the guards watching them.

"Got another scarf or something in your bag to change your appearance?" he asked.

"You mean because they've already seen us?"

He nodded. "Yeah. Don't want them recognizing you if you walk back this way again."

"I can buy one from the store." She nodded toward a shop selling tunics, burqas, and headscarves.

He watched as she bought a midnight blue hijab and slipped it on in front of a mirror. It covered her dark hair and made her skin look even paler, more translucent.

"Good." He looked away before his thoughts could go further.

They crossed the street and sat down on a wooden bench near the fruit sellers. Her thigh brushed against his, and he jolted like he'd been shocked.

"Sorry," she murmured, giving him an odd look.

Shit, he had to get a grip. She had him on edge, through no fault of her own.

He shifted to give her more space. Physical contact wasn't something he was used to anymore. It had been too long, and he'd forgotten what it felt like to have a woman touch him—even accidentally.

He leaned back, keeping the restaurant in his peripheral vision. The minutes dragged by. He could feel the tension coming off her in waves as she shifted, crossing and uncrossing her legs.

"You don't have to be here," he said quietly.

She shook her head. "We need that photo, right?"

He couldn't argue with that. "It would help."

She took a deep breath. "I'll do it. I'm the only one who can. That's why I'm here—to watch and report." She was brave, holding it together despite her obvious fear.

"It'll be fine," he reassured her. "I've got your back."

She exhaled softly. "Let's hope it doesn't come to that."

Silence fell again. The waiting was always the worst part.

"What made you join the Army?" Her voice was soft, breaking the tension. He could tell she needed to talk, needed something to keep the nerves at bay. "I mean, if you were studying to be a doctor."

He hesitated. Normally, he wouldn't talk about personal stuff—especially not with a foreign operative. Anything he said could be twisted, used as leverage down the line. But Sloane didn't give off that vibe. She wasn't playing games.

"It was the Navy, not the Army," he corrected, but not unkindly. "I always wanted to be an operator, but I was interested in medicine too. Both my parents were doctors, so there was pressure to follow in their footsteps." He paused, then added, "I dropped out of med school and signed up. Figured I could have the best of both worlds."

"And did you?" Her eyes searched his face.

He shrugged. "Yeah. They gave me medical training, but not your typical stuff—trauma medicine, the kind you use when the bullets start flying and there's no hospital around. It was the best decision I ever made."

"Why are you here?" she whispered. "Are you keeping Omari under surveillance too?"

He grimaced. "Something like that."

Just then, the door to the restaurant opened.

"That's your cue," he muttered.

She stood and casually walked up the road toward the scarf stall. Stitch slid his hand into his pocket, fingers brushing his Glock. He hoped to hell he wouldn't have to use it.

CHAPTER 9

Sloane's heart pounded like one of the submachine guns the guards were carrying. Every step she took brought her closer to the restaurant. Two of the security team stepped out, scanning the street. Omari and his associates would be coming out any second now.

She hugged the wall, staying out of their line of sight. Finally, she reached the rack of scarves. Pulling out her phone, she huddled behind the soft fabric, keeping herself hidden.

Through a small gap, she could see the men exit the restaurant—four of them, dressed in long shalwar kameez with turbans and thick beards. They had to be important, judging by the eight heavily armed guards surrounding them. Each guard gripped a semi-automatic rifle, fingers twitching near the triggers.

Oh, hell. She tried not to think about what those guns could do if they caught her.

Her hands were shaking so badly she had to steady the phone with her other hand. She managed to position it through the scarves, so the lens was clear. It was set on video mode, which was better anyway—you could capture more that way.

Using the screen as a guide, she tracked the four men as they made their way to the waiting vehicles. She got a good look at their faces as they passed, barely two meters from her.

Their bodyguards opened the car doors, and the men slipped inside, disappearing from view. Turning the camera back toward the restaurant, she spotted Omari standing in the shadows. He didn't come out. Zooming in on his face, she could see the smug expression. The meeting must've gone well.

Who were these guys? They looked like they'd crossed the border from Afghanistan, just like the ones she'd seen the other day. Could they be Taliban officials, like Omari? Were they planning something?

A chill ran through her, and she quickly stashed the phone. Maybe Stitch could fill in the blanks.

The vehicles sped off in a cloud of dust, kicking up pebbles as they went. Sloane stayed pressed against the wall, hidden behind the scarves.

Thank God. They were gone, and she was still alive. She was about to head back to Stitch when she heard a shout behind her.

"You! Stop!" The guard yelled in Urdu.

She froze.

Crap. Crap. Crap.

Omari's men had spotted her.

One of the guards stomped over, his heavy boots clomping on the sidewalk. "What are you doing here?" he barked.

She stared at the ground, too scared to meet his eyes.

This was bad. Really bad. Time to play the helpless woman card.

He repeated the question.

"Shopping," she whispered, motioning toward the scarves.

The guard eyed her suspiciously, then grabbed her arm. She gasped, trying to pull away, but his grip tightened.

A deep voice behind her said, "There you are! Stupid woman."

Stitch!

And he was speaking in Urdu. That was a surprise—and damn, he'd nailed the dialect.

The guard whipped around.

"My wife," Stitch growled. "She's always wandering off." He grabbed her other arm, yanking her roughly toward him. The guard released her.

"Apologies," Stitch muttered, giving a respectful half-bow.

The guard hesitated, looking like he wasn't entirely sure if he should let her go. But after a moment, he gave a sharp nod and walked away.

Sloane exhaled shakily.

"Come on," Stitch muttered under his breath. "Let's get the hell out of here."

"Oh my God." Sloane leaned against the wall as soon as they rounded the corner, out of sight. "That was close."

"It was," Stitch agreed, scanning the street before looking at her. "You okay?"

She took a few shaky breaths, trying to slow her racing heart, then nodded. "Yeah, I think so. Thank you. I thought it was game over."

"Did you get the shots?"

"Yes."

"Let me see."

He didn't give her much time to recover—just like him. He was all business, all focus, while she was still trying to catch her breath.

"Yeah," she said, fumbling with her phone before handing it over.

He scrolled straight to the video, his expression unreadable as he watched. His eyes darkened, his jaw tightening with each passing frame. No sign of nerves or hesitation. Just that same quiet intensity he always had, like everything else in the world didn't exist for him.

Only the mission.

She couldn't shake the image of the guards with their AK-47s. She'd seen them before during training, but seeing them in the flesh? Different story. Her hands were still shaking from it.

His eyes darkened when the four men came into view. There was something in his expression—recognition, yes, but also something else. Anger. Pain.

"Who are they?" she whispered.

Stitch didn't answer right away. He watched the video through to the end before speaking, his voice rougher now. "I'm gonna send this to myself, okay?"

She nodded, but that wasn't good enough anymore. She had to know.

"You know them, don't you?" she pressed. "You know who they are."

His jaw clenched, the muscles ticking under his skin. He glanced at her, and for the first time, she saw something raw flicker in his eyes—something he'd been keeping buried deep. "Yeah. I know one of them."

She waited, sensing there was more.

"He's a local Taliban drug lord," he said, but his voice was tight, like the words were knives in his throat.

"Drug lord?" she gasped.

"Yeah," he ground out. "They control the poppy fields in Helmand Province. Each one's got a district, taxes the farmers, moves the drugs to labs on the Pakistani border. They've got stakes in the distribution network too. It's big business."

"In Afghanistan?"

He gave a sharp nod, his gaze flicking away like he didn't want to look her in the eyes. "Omari handles the distribution to the ports. Ships the heroin and opium out. Most of it heads to the West."

Sloane blinked, trying to piece it all together. "So... this is about drugs, not terrorism."

He was silent for a beat, then gave a bitter laugh. "It's always about both. The drugs fund their operations. It's all part of the same dirty web."

Sloane swallowed hard, feeling the weight of his words sink in. Before she could respond, two policemen walked by, heading for the restaurant.

"They're conveniently late," Stitch muttered.

He straightened, shaking off the moment, his walls going back up. "Come on, let's go," he said, his voice steady again. "We'll talk back at your place."

CHAPTER 10

His place was closer, but Stitch wasn't about to compromise the Peshawar safehouse—or Mrs. Bhatti—by bringing a CIA agent there.

He was on foot, having decided against renting a motorbike that morning. The plan had been simple: finish his surveillance detail, head home, then meet up with Sloane for their evening briefing.

"You want a ride?" she asked when they reached her scooter.

"Sure," he said. Beats walking in this heat—and they needed to talk anyway.

Sloane pulled off her hijab and slipped on her helmet, fastening it under her chin. Her dark hair spilled down her back. She stuffed the headscarf into her bag and straddled the scooter.

He caught himself staring at the way her ass filled the seat.

"You coming?"

He hesitated a moment, then climbed on behind her.

The little 50cc Honda sank under his weight but fired up

without a problem. He rested his hands on her waist, feeling the dip of her curves, the way her hips flared out beneath his fingers.

Lord help him.

They chugged the four blocks to her place, and every single meter was torture. Every bump sent her sliding back against him, her ass pressing into his thighs. He prayed to God he wouldn't pop a hard-on.

Her hair whipped in the wind, brushing softly across his face. He could have leaned back, given her some space, but he didn't.

It had been so damn long since he'd held a woman that he'd forgotten what it felt like. Just for a moment, the anger and grief he carried with him everywhere faded, replaced by the feel of her body against his.

Desire crept in, and by the time they reached her apartment, he was uncomfortably hard. He hadn't thought that part of him still worked.

"Thanks for the ride," he said quickly, hopping off the back of the scooter before she even killed the ignition. Hopefully, she hadn't noticed.

She took off her helmet and smiled, shaking her hair loose. Now that he knew how soft it was, he had this urge to bury his hands in it. What the hell was wrong with him? One ride on a moped, and this woman had him all twisted up. He shouldn't be feeling this way. It wasn't right.

But his body didn't seem to agree.

"I didn't think we were gonna make it at one point," she said, grinning. "You're not exactly a light passenger."

He snorted. "These machines are built to last."

She wheeled the scooter into an open-fronted butcher shop. "The owner lets me park it here," she explained.

Stitch did a quick scan of the street. The butcher was busy with a customer, slicing meat. Shoppers, mostly men, moved up and down the street with purpose. A truck was parked further up, outside what looked like a hardware store.

No one was watching them. Just two locals on a bike in a busy part of town. Satisfied, he followed her inside.

Her apartment was on the second floor. The wooden staircase groaned as they climbed, passing several closed doors. The only light came from the windows on each landing, the glass long gone.

"Come on in." She pushed the door open.

He stepped inside and went straight to the window, checking the street again. Still clear.

"Are you always this paranoid?" she asked, tossing her bag on the bed.

"Occupational hazard," he grunted.

She smiled, and for a split second, everything felt okay. Like the world wasn't a mess. But it was.

"I guess so. Maybe I'm not paranoid enough yet, but I'm still learning this whole undercover gig. Want some tea?"

He nodded. Tea would be perfect.

While she headed into the kitchen, he sat down at the table and looked around. This was the first time he'd seen the place in daylight. It was spacious, but empty. The bed was just a mattress on a low wooden frame. There was a small table, a couple of chairs, and a wardrobe. No pictures, no decorations. Just the essentials.

"Did Jeremy find this place?" he called. "Or did you?"

"Jeremy," she replied over the sound of boiling water.

Definitely needed to keep an eye on that.

She came back with two cups of tea and sat across from him. The feel of her body against his was fading, and as it did, the anger resurfaced. His muscles tensed as he thought about Omari and the others.

Rasul Ghani.

That was the guy he recognized. Ruthless Taliban leader and all-around piece of shit.

He'd have loved to take them both out today, but the timing wasn't right. He wouldn't have gotten away clean, and Sloane would've been caught in the crossfire.

"Where'd you learn to speak Urdu?" she asked, studying him from over her cup, her dark eyes watching him carefully.

"I've spent some time in the Middle East."

Ten years, but who's counting?

"You speak it well," she murmured. "Like a local."

He reached for his tea, hoping she'd drop it.

"Are you going to tell me about the drug smuggling?"

"It's how the Taliban fund their militia."

"I've heard that. I just didn't expect Omari to be involved."

He was more than involved.

"At first, they taxed the poppy farmers. Now they're a full-blown cartel, handling everything from production to distribution. Afghanistan supplies most of the world's heroin."

She was hanging on every word. "And Omari?"

"He's the logistics guy. Runs the distribution network, the labs on the border, and the trafficking of raw opium and heroin. The guys he met with today are regional leaders, in charge of production and taxing in their areas."

"How do you know so much about it?" she asked. "Is the military involved?"

He shook his head. "No. I'm not military anymore. Haven't been for a while."

She frowned. "So, how do you know all this?"

Sunlight streamed through the window. It was stifling hot and sweat gathered on his brow. He wiped it away with his sleeve.

"I've been researching the network... ever since..." He trailed off, unable to finish the sentence.

"Ever since?" she pressed gently.

"It's personal." He wasn't going to explain it to her. But one thing was for sure—he recognized one of those men. He'd been after him for months. Him and Omari.

The silence stretched. She watched him carefully. He took a sip of tea, not wanting to meet her eyes.

"Are you going to kill them?" she asked, her voice quiet but direct.

He choked on his tea, coughing. "What makes you say that?"

"I saw it in your eyes the first time we talked about Omari."

He frowned. "What did you see in my eyes?"

She set her cup down. "I'm good at reading people. When we met, I saw the way you reacted to his name. You hate him. He's done something to hurt you. I could see the anger in your eyes." She paused, searching his face. "And something else. Grief, maybe?"

His head snapped up. "I didn't realize it was that obvious."

He was usually good at hiding his emotions. But this woman, a novice, had seen through him from the start.

Not. Good.

"So, are you?" she whispered.

"Am I what?"

"Going to kill him?" She held his gaze. "I know you want to."

Damn. He couldn't hide it from her.

"Maybe," he admitted, his voice low.

Without a fucking doubt.

He stared down into his cup. "If I can get him alone. He's always surrounded by guards."

The silence stretched again.

"What did he do to you?" she asked softly.

He didn't answer.

Killed my wife. My wife's family. My village.

How could he explain that to her? He hadn't even told his brothers in arms. Fellow SEAL operators he'd trusted with his life didn't know the whole story.

The silence hung heavy between them. Finally, she changed the subject.

"What about the drugs?" she asked.

He shrugged. "Not my problem."

"Don't you care that they're shipping heroin to the West? Kids are gonna get hooked. Some of them will die."

"If I take out Omari and Ghani, it'll slow things down."

"Until they get replaced," she pointed out. "Guys like that always have deputies waiting to step up."

She was right. He knew it. And yeah, the drugs mattered. But not enough to stop him from pulling the trigger when the time came.

"They're gearing up to move a shipment, aren't they? That's why those men met with Omari today," she said.

He didn't respond. But she was right about that too.

She might be a rookie, but he could see why her boss had recruited her. The language skills coupled with her natural intuitiveness were valuable assets in any field agent.

"Yeah, those men were here to talk logistics. I'd say there's a deal going down. A new shipment."

"Maybe the Agency is trying to stop it?" Her eyes lit up. "Perhaps that's why they have me watching Omari."

"Could be."

Sure, why not? Let her feed them intel on Omari's agenda, find out when things are happening and swoop in and bust the shipment. That was more the DEA's remit, mind you, but what did he know? The internal workings of the CIA were a mystery to him.

"I just don't know why they couldn't have told me that in the first place?" Hurt flashed across her face.

She was thinking about her boss, the man who'd recruited her. Matthew.

"Perhaps they will now," he said. "Once you show them what you've got."

She nodded, but he could see she wasn't convinced.

"What now?" She cradled the teacup. "Are we still working together on this, or have you got what you wanted?"

Now he knew what Omari and the CIA were up to, there was no reason to keep working with Sloane. But for reasons he wasn't about to get into, he was reluctant to call it quits.

"It wouldn't hurt to find out a bit more about this shipment," he murmured, after a beat.

She exhaled, unable to hide her relief. "I was hoping you'd say that."

His stomach did a funny twisty thing, and he hoped he wasn't making the wrong decision. This wasn't his fight. Omari and Ghani were going down no matter what.

It was late when Stitch finally made it back to the safehouse. He'd walked the four blocks from Sloane's apartment to town, then all the way back to Mrs. Bhatti's. His landlady was already in bed, so he made himself a quick snack, showered, and collapsed onto his mattress.

Had sticking with Sloane been a mistake?

He had what he came for. He knew who she was, who she worked for, and exactly what Omari and his cartel buddies were up to.

Another shipment was on the way.

Scum. That's all they were. Drug dealers. The kind who'd burn entire villages to the ground just to keep their operation running smoothly. He clenched his fists, his entire body tensing with the rage that simmered just beneath the surface.

Breathe.

Let it go.

But he couldn't. He never could. That anger was the only

thing holding him together. Without it, he had nothing left. Soraya, his family, his home... all of it gone.

Revenge was his only companion now. The only thing driving him forward. Without it, who the hell was he?

But then, in the middle of the haze, Sloane's face flashed in his mind. Her laughing brown eyes. Those soft, cherry-red lips—sensual, kissable.

He squeezed his eyes shut.

No.

Hell no.

He couldn't be thinking about another woman. Not now.

It was too soon.

It's been over a year, a voice whispered in the back of his mind. But he shut it down. Time didn't matter. It was still too soon.

So why the hell was his body responding to her like that?

A year without sex will do that to you, he reasoned. It was biology, nothing more. When you're face-to-face with a woman like Sloane, your body reacted. Simple as that.

Even if his body was ready, his heart sure as hell wasn't. He needed to walk away. Let her handle her mission by herself.

Staying would only make things worse. It would complicate everything. She'd fail because of him. He already knew that much. In the end, he'd disappoint her like he disappointed everyone.

Omari would be dead.

Her mission would be over.

She'd get sent back to D.C.

Then what?

Not my problem.

He rolled over, pushing the sheets off. It was a hot, sticky night, and he was sweating again. All he seemed to do in this goddamn country was sweat.

Eventually, the exhaustion took over, and he sank into a restless sleep.

SORAYA, *laughing up at him. Her beautiful face framed by the sunlight, her kohled eyes sparkling with love and joy. Her hands cradled her swollen belly, glowing with life.*

"I'm pregnant," she whispered.

Then, without warning, flames erupted around them.

Blinding. Scorching.

The air turned to fire. Heat seared his skin. Smoke clawed its way into his lungs, choking him. He gasped for air, but the smoke filled him, suffocating him from the inside out. He spun around, desperate to find Soraya, but she was gone.

No. No! Where was she?

He yelled her name, but his voice was swallowed by the roar of the flames. The world burned around him. The walls of his home crumbled, turning to ash and embers. His heart pounded in his chest as panic gripped him.

Through the smoke, another face appeared. Sloane, untouched by the flames, smiling calmly as if the world wasn't burning around them.

"You coming?" she asked, her hand outstretched, as if they weren't surrounded by hell.

He hesitated, his body torn between running back into the fire to find Soraya or following Sloane into the unknown.

The heat blistered his skin, unbearable. The smoke seared his throat.

He reached for Sloane's hand.

HE WOKE UP WITH A START.

What the fuck?

He was drenched in perspiration. The room was stuffy,

oppressively so. He flung open the window and gasped in the warm, night air.

Please, no.

He couldn't let Soraya's memory fade. He had to hold onto it for all he was worth. She couldn't leave him. He wasn't ready.

As he whispered her name into the darkness, he knew he couldn't wait any longer.

Tomorrow he would kill Omari.

CHAPTER 11

*W*hy hadn't Matthew told her Omari was a drug lord?

Now that she knew, it all made sense. Her mission made sense.

Of course they'd want to keep tabs on him and see who he was working with. That way they could stop the shipment from getting into the United States.

Didn't he trust her?

She'd read about plausible deniability. Maybe that was it. He was trying to protect her. What she didn't know, she couldn't spill.

That's *if* she got caught.

And she almost had been. If it weren't for Stitch…

She'd emailed Jeremy the video clip, like she was supposed to. As of this morning, no reply. So she figured it was business as usual.

Omari seemed different today, almost like he had a spring in his step. He was laughing with his bodyguards, chatting more than usual with the local shopkeepers.

Yesterday's meeting had gone well. He was happy with the result.

If only she knew what was discussed. If she had details about the shipment, she'd finally have something solid to pass on to Jeremy. And to Matthew.

Matthew.

The man who'd been such a big part of her life six months ago was now just a shadow in her dreams. She missed him, missed his company. He used to show up at her door after work with a bottle of wine. They'd cook together and spend the night wrapped up in each other.

But it didn't feel as sharp as it used to. Time and distance had dulled the memory of his scent, the feel of him.

And it didn't help that she hadn't heard his voice. She'd been here for almost a month, and not a single phone call. Not one text asking if she was okay.

Yeah, he'd insisted on no contact.

But come on, really?

She was out here on her own. The only connection she had was an email address. What good would that do if she got into real trouble?

If Matthew didn't want to use his personal phone, he could've gotten a burner. Everybody else did. Even the sailor had one.

If you need help, call me.

Omari went into the coffee shop with a man she'd seen a few times before. Middle-aged, bearded, and sporting a belly that stuck out like he never missed a meal. Nothing about him seemed out of the ordinary.

The teahouse was across the street, and she took a seat outside, ordering a sweet green tea. She'd wait. Maybe Stitch would show up again like he had yesterday.

But honestly, it was probably better if he didn't. Omari's

guard had already spotted them together once. Twice would definitely raise suspicions.

She couldn't play the lost wife act again.

That had been quick thinking on his part, though. He'd sounded so natural, so convincing. The guard hadn't given her a second thought, just a clueless local woman who'd wandered off where she wasn't supposed to.

And then there was the ride home. His chest firm and solid against her back, his thighs pressing against hers as they rode. She'd never admit it out loud, but for that brief moment, she'd felt safe. Like nothing could touch her with him around. His body had been a shield, surrounding her.

And that feeling... it was addictive.

When the ride ended, she'd been oddly disappointed. More so when he jumped off the scooter like he couldn't get away from her fast enough.

For a man built like a tank, his hands had been unexpectedly gentle on her waist.

And now, she couldn't stop thinking about him in a totally different light.

Not as an enemy. Not even as a partner.

But as a man.

A hulking, rugged, broad-shouldered, hard-as-hell man.

THE RIDE to the community center took less than fifteen minutes.

Sloane parked outside, nodded to the security guard who recognized her, and headed inside. The moment she stepped in, something felt off. It was too quiet. The hallway was empty.

Then she heard a woman's cry echoing from down the corridor.

Her heart raced as she sprinted toward the sound. It was coming from the classroom where she taught English.

She burst through the open door to find a small group of women gathered around one of the desks.

"What's going on?"

Aaliyah, the woman who ran the center, looked up, her face tense.

"Fatima's not well."

Sloane recognized Fatima immediately. She was one of the regulars in her class. The young woman sat hunched over a desk, clutching her stomach, her face twisted in pain.

"Fatima, what's wrong?" Sloane asked in Pashto, crouching beside her. "Is there anything I can do to help?"

Fatima shook her head, her skin pale and slick with sweat.

Sloane shot a glance at Aaliyah. "Was it something she ate? Or something she took?"

Fatima let out another agonizing cry, her fingers gripping the desk like a lifeline.

Sloane pressed the back of her hand against Fatima's forehead—it was burning up. She stood, looking around at the other women. "We have to do something. Does anyone know what's wrong with her?"

One woman, dressed in a full burqa, stepped forward. "She made a terrible mistake."

Sloane frowned. "What kind of mistake? Did she take something?"

The woman shook her head, her voice barely a whisper. "No... she tried to get rid of something."

Fatima let out a pained moan, shaking her head, "No!"

"You need help," her friend said softly. She glanced up at Sloane. "She's bleeding. She needs a doctor. Please—"

Sloane's gaze dropped to the floor, where a thin line of

blood trickled down the leg of the chair. Everything clicked into place.

"You're pregnant?" Her voice was hushed. "You tried to terminate it?"

The woman in the burqa nodded, tears filling her eyes.

"He wasn't a real doctor," her friend said. "He hurt her. I made him stop, but... I didn't know what else to do. She can't go home. Her husband will kill her."

Sloane's stomach twisted. Surely her husband wasn't that cruel. "Why will he be upset?" Then she got it. "It's not his baby?"

Fatima shook her head, her face crumpling in pain.

Shit. In that case, he might really kill her.

The bleeding was getting worse. She needed medical help, and fast.

"We have to call an ambulance." Sloane stood up. "She needs a hospital."

Fatima grabbed her hand, her grip weak but desperate. "Please, no."

Her friend's voice cracked. "If we take her to the hospital, they'll notify her husband. So will any real doctor."

Sloane bit her lip. They couldn't leave her like this. She'd bleed out, and the baby—if it wasn't already gone—would be next.

The women looked at each other helplessly, the room filling with whispers. Fatima's cries grew louder, and more women gathered at the door. The lesson was supposed to start soon.

Sloane's heart raced. She jumped to her feet.

"I know a medic," She blurted the words without thinking.

Everyone turned to look at her.

"He's... a friend," she continued, even though that wasn't at all what they were. "An American. He won't tell anyone."

Aaliyah gave a quick nod. "Can you call him?"

"I think so."

Her fingers shook as she pulled out her phone and dialed Stitch's number.

Please, pick up, she prayed.

After a few rings, he did.

"Sloane? You okay?" How did he know it was her?

"Hi, Stitch." His name sounded strange on her lips. She'd never actually said it to his face, only in her head when she thought about him. "There's a medical emergency at the center. I need your expertise."

There was a pause. "What happened? Are you hurt?"

"I'm fine. It's not me." She took a deep breath, glancing at Fatima, who looked even paler now. "There's a woman here who really needs your help."

"What's wrong with her?" His voice had shifted into something sharp, focused.

Sloane exhaled, relieved he wasn't saying no. "She tried to terminate an unwanted pregnancy, but he wasn't qualified, and now she's bleeding out. I don't think she has much time."

There was no hesitation. "I'll be there as soon as I can. I need to pick up some supplies first. Give me twenty minutes."

The line went dead.

"He's coming," Sloane told the other women. She just hoped twenty minutes wouldn't be too late.

When Stitch arrived, Fatima was drenched in sweat, moaning and barely coherent.

It didn't look good.

"Thank God you're here," Sloane said as he strode into the room. "She's in a bad way."

They'd eased Fatima onto the floor, but it was clear she was in serious pain.

"Everyone back," Stitch barked, dropping to his knees. The women quickly scattered.

"Can you get them out of here?" he asked Sloane without looking up.

She nodded and ushered the women out of the room. As soon as they were gone, Stitch opened his rucksack, pulling out a military-grade medical kit, a bottle of disinfectant, and other supplies she didn't recognize.

With the room clear, he got to work.

"What's her name?"

"Fatima," Sloane replied, standing at the side, feeling helpless.

"Fatima, can you hear me?" he asked, his voice calm.

Fatima nodded weakly, her tear-filled eyes half-closed.

"I'm going to help you. I'll give you something for the pain, alright?"

Another nod.

Sloane held her breath as he pulled out a syringe and small vial of medication. With practiced precision, he drew up the liquid and injected it into Fatima's arm, all while murmuring reassurances in a calm, steady voice.

Sloane couldn't look away. It was like watching a completely different man. The aggression, the barely contained rage that seemed to define him, was gone. In its place was someone calm, focused, and gentle. His hands moved with precision, his tone soft and controlled.

Fatima's moans quieted, her body relaxing as the pain faded. Her eyes fluttered shut.

"Is she going to be okay?" Sloane whispered, afraid to hear the answer.

"Too soon to tell," he said, his tone grim.

He lifted Fatima's skirts, and Sloane quickly looked away, feeling the sudden awkwardness. "Should I wait outside?"

"Can you get me some warm water and a cloth for the blood?" he asked instead, his voice even.

Sloane nodded and hurried out. When she returned with the water and cloth, he was already working, bent over Fatima and stitching her up.

"Whoever did this was a butcher," he muttered, his eyes focused on the task at hand.

Sloane set the water and cloth beside him. "Will she be okay?"

"She will now," he said with a sharp nod, his focus never breaking.

"And the baby?" Sloane asked, almost afraid of the answer.

"The baby's fine. He didn't get that far, thank God. He just tore her up trying." He sighed, wiping the blood away with the cloth. "I've stopped the bleeding. She'll be sore, but she's going to make it."

Sloane let out a breath she didn't realize she was holding. "That's great."

She watched as he cleaned the area, applied antiseptic, and covered the wounds with gauze dressings. "I've given her antibiotics to ward off infection, but she should recover fully."

Sloane stared at him, feeling a wave of admiration. What he'd done was nothing short of amazing. He'd saved Fatima's life—and her unborn child's.

He pulled her skirt back down and packed up his medical supplies. "She needs rest. Someone should take her home."

"She can't go home," Sloane whispered. "It wasn't her husband's baby."

Stitch's brows shot up in surprise. They both knew what that meant here. Infidelity could get her killed. Honor killings were a grim reality, and going home like this could be a death sentence.

"She can stay here until she's well enough to move," Aaliyah said, stepping into the room. She shook Stitch's hand firmly. "Thank you so much, doctor."

He gave a curt nod and stood up. "Let's get her to a bed."

"Can I help?" Sloane asked as he bent down to lift Fatima.

"No, just lead the way."

Stitch scooped Fatima up effortlessly, as if she weighed nothing. He followed Sloane down the hallway to a small room at the end. Inside, there was a simple bed, a side table, and a thin wardrobe. A worn rug covered part of the floor.

He laid Fatima gently on the bed.

"Make sure she stays hydrated," he told Aaliyah. "She'll be sore for a few days, but as long as she stays off her feet, she'll be fine."

Aaliyah nodded, already moving to Fatima's side. "We'll take good care of her."

"Thank you," Fatima's friend whispered, her eyes filled with tears as she grabbed Stitch's hand. "Thank you for saving her."

"Koi baat nahi," he replied in Urdu. "You're welcome."

Sloane walked him to the door.

"That was an amazing thing you did," Sloane said, a little in awe.

He gave a small smile, the first she'd seen from him.

"Just happy I could help."

"Sorry I pulled you away from Omari."

The smile disappeared, and his eyes went cold. She instantly regretted bringing up the Afghan drug lord. She much preferred the calm, confident doctor with his steady hands over the grumpy, testosterone-fueled grizzly bear he usually was.

"No problem. He's holed up at home anyway."

"Will I see you tonight?" she asked softly.

He hesitated. "I don't think there's any need, do you?"

Reluctantly, she shook her head. "No, nothing out of the ordinary happened this morning."

"Okay, then. I'll catch you tomorrow."

He didn't say when.

"Okay."

With a sinking heart, she watched him stride back to his motorcycle, rucksack slung over his back.

CHAPTER 12

Stitch sat at the desk in his room, his Glock in hand. He double-checked that the chamber was clear, then popped out the magazine. Pulling back the slide, he released the lever and slid it off the front, disassembling the gun piece by piece. He laid the slide, barrel, recoil spring, and frame out in front of him.

Using a small brush and cleaning fluid, he worked methodically, cleaning each part before drying them with a rag. The motions were second nature—he'd done this so many times, he could probably do it in his sleep.

The weapon gleamed, clean and ready on the table.

He'd almost used it today. Before Sloane's call.

How ironic was that?

Instead of taking a life, he'd saved one.

Two, actually. He thought of Fatima's unborn child.

It felt good to help them. It had been a long time since he'd used his medical skills—since his village was destroyed. After that, there hadn't been a reason. Not until today.

From village doctor to vigilante. His life had flipped in an instant.

His medical knowledge had been the only reason they let him stay when he left the military. They'd needed him—badly—in that isolated village.

That's when he'd met Soraya.

He tensed, bracing for the wave of pain and grief that always followed thoughts of her. But this time, it didn't hit as hard. The ache was still there, but it wasn't as crushing.

Frowning, he reassembled the Glock. The familiar clunk of steel sliding into place steadied his mind.

Tomorrow, he wouldn't be distracted. Omari had been granted one day's grace, thanks to a woman who'd needed him.

One day.

Then it'd be Game Over for the drug lord.

Stitch met Sloane at the teahouse around midday.

She smiled when she saw him. He didn't smile back. He was here to do a job, and nothing was going to get in his way.

Didn't matter how good she looked in that copper scarf she'd picked up the other day, or how the color made her eyes flash with golden highlights.

"Omari inside?" he asked, his voice gruff.

"Yeah, they've been there since eleven."

"They?" He raised an eyebrow.

"He brought the whole family today," she said. "Wife and five kids."

For fuck's sake.

"Must be some kind of special occasion," Sloane added. "His wife showed up with a bunch of balloons. Probably one of the kids' birthdays."

Stitch clenched his jaw. That was a problem. Taking Omari out with his family around would be way harder. He wasn't about to traumatize the guy's kids by making them watch their dad get shot. That was a memory no kid should carry.

He wasn't that heartless.

Still, today was the day. No more waiting.

Somehow, he'd find a way.

He sat down, ordered some tea, and casually tapped the Glock in his pocket. The holster was slim, snug, hidden well under his long kameez. No one would spot it, not unless they were looking for it.

"Do you miss being a medic?" Her question caught him off guard.

"I guess I miss it sometimes," he said, his voice low. "It was mostly trauma care. Bullet wounds, shrapnel, burns—patching guys up fast, trying to keep them alive long enough to get to a field hospital. Not the easiest job in the world."

She hesitated, and he got the impression she wanted to say something but was holding back.

"What?" he asked.

"You're not just a sailor, are you?"

He tensed. "What makes you say that?"

She shrugged. "I met some navy guys during my training course. They don't teach you guys that level of expertise."

He sucked in a breath. Too damn observant for her own good. "No, I wasn't just a sailor."

"Marine? Special ops?"

"Something like that." He wasn't about to elaborate.

There was a brief pause.

"When's the last time you did any medical work?" He knew she was just making conversation, get him talking.

The waiter placed his tea in front of him, but he didn't touch it. Instead, he stared into the steam. "About a year ago."

The day his world had turned to hell. The village had been a massacre site—bodies strewn everywhere. He'd tried to save them, but it was impossible. The screams, the blood...

people he'd known, kids he'd treated for simple scrapes and fevers, now lying lifeless in the dirt. He could still hear their voices, still see the faces of those he couldn't get to in time.

He'd done what he could, but it hadn't been enough.

It was never enough.

She nodded thoughtfully, unaware of the nightmare he'd just relived. "Is that when you started digging into Omari and his drug network?"

His eyes stayed glued to the coffee shop across the road. "Yeah."

"Is that when it happened?"

His pulse quickened and he shot her a sharp glance. "When what happened?"

She couldn't possibly know.

"Whatever it was that Omari did to you."

He exhaled slowly. She didn't know. She was just reading him again, something she was annoyingly good at.

"I'm sorry," she said quietly. "I'm not trying to pry. It's just... you were incredible with Fatima yesterday. I can't figure out why you'd want to throw that away."

He frowned. "What makes you think I'm throwing anything away?"

She glanced toward the coffee shop. "Omari."

He ran a hand through his hair, irritation rising. The last thing he needed was her in his head. Not now, when he was this close.

"Look, my business with Omari is just that—my business. It's got nothing to do with you. I don't want you involved."

"Except I am involved," she said quietly. "Omari's my target. Whatever happens to him, I have to report it."

He shrugged. "Do what you gotta do."

It wouldn't matter then.

"I will," she said. "But I'd rather not have to report that Omari was assassinated by a U.S. Marine, or whoever you are, who got himself arrested—or more likely, gunned down by Omari's bodyguards."

He stayed quiet, his focus locked on the café across the street.

"I can feel it coming off you," she said, getting to her feet. "Tension. Anger. It's almost suffocating."

"You don't have to stick around. Your shift's over." His voice was hard.

She slung her bag over her shoulder. "You're right, I don't. I'm leaving. Just remember, whatever you do, there'll be consequences. Maybe you won't be around to face them, but others will. His kids. His wife. Me."

He kept his gaze forward, refusing to look at her.

She sighed softly. "Good luck, Stitch."

And she walked away.

BY THE TIME Omari and his family finally left the coffee shop, Stitch was in the tobacconist next door. His plan was simple: wait for the kids to get in the vehicle, then step out and take the shot. If everything went smoothly amidst the chaos, he'd slip out the back into the parallel street where his motorcycle was parked.

The escape route was clear. The back door was already open, providing an easy exit to the street behind. Plus, the store itself gave him cover. He could stay hidden while lining up the perfect shot.

He only needed one.

A blacked-out SUV pulled up outside the café. Stitch's hand slid into his pocket. No need to pull his weapon just yet —no sense in spooking the customers inside the shop. If they panicked, it could blow his whole chance.

The door opened, and two security guards stepped out,

scanning the street. Stitch pretended to be checking out a hookah on display out front.

The guards signaled for the family to come out.

The kids came first, running out, all hyper from cake and sugar. The driver opened the back door, but they didn't hop in. Instead, they ran up and down the sidewalk, pushing and shoving each other.

"Come on," he muttered under his breath. "Get in the damn car."

He didn't want to do this in front of the kids.

Omari's wife came out next, chatting with another woman. Sloane hadn't mentioned there'd be another family with them. Great. That meant there'd be another man to deal with too.

He waited, but no men appeared.

Where the hell were they?

Finally, the kids piled into the car, and the wife said her goodbyes, getting into the front seat next to the driver. No room for Omari.

The SUV drove off, and Stitch let out a quiet sigh of relief.

The woman stayed behind on the sidewalk, waiting for her husband. A few more security guards stepped out, and then finally, Omari and another man appeared.

"Get out of the way," Stitch grumbled, as the woman and her husband stood in his line of sight. With the wife and kids gone, this was his chance. He pulled his Glock out of his pocket and took aim, arm stretched just outside the shop door. No one inside had any clue what was happening.

"Move, dammit."

After what felt like forever, the couple said their goodbyes and started walking down the street. Omari was now alone, except for his four guards, but Stitch had a clear shot.

His heart beat slow and steady as adrenaline flooded his veins.

This was it. The calm before the storm.

His pulse stayed even—he'd been trained for moments like this his whole life.

Then, a woman screamed.

The guards all snapped their heads toward him, hands going for their guns. It was now or never. He was just about to squeeze the trigger when Sloane's voice hissed, "Not now. They'll kill you."

She yanked his arm and pulled him through the store toward the back exit. The guards were already moving toward the tobacco shop. They had seconds.

"Go!" she shouted. "I'll meet you at my place."

He didn't have time to argue. He jumped on her scooter and sped off down the street. In his rearview mirror, he saw Sloane disappear into the crowd just as the four guards burst out onto the street.

By the time they realized what had happened, he was already gone.

CHAPTER 13

Stitch was angrier than she'd ever seen him.

Sloane walked into her apartment to find him pacing, fists clenched, his face stormy.

"Why did you stop me?" he snapped. "I had him. I was about to take the fucker out."

Right now, he looked like Thor, god of thunder—bulging biceps and pure, pent-up rage. If she didn't know him better, she'd be scared to death.

"And get yourself killed in the process?" She tossed her bag onto the bed and unwrapped her headscarf.

"That was a risk I was willing to take."

"Well, I wasn't." She turned to face him.

He stormed toward her, blue eyes flashing fire. It took everything she had not to flinch.

"That's not your call!" he growled. "It was my decision. Now I might never get another shot. My wife's murderer is going to walk free."

She froze.

He must have realized what he'd said because he turned

away, running a hand through his wild hair, looking more agitated by the second.

Silence hung heavy in the air. Tension crackled between them. Her skin prickled, the hairs on her neck standing on end.

Did he just say his wife's murderer?

"Omari killed my wife," he rasped, his voice rough. She could see the veins in his neck. "He burned our village to the ground. He deserves to die."

Sloane stared at him, horrified.

"I–I didn't know. I'm sorry."

She'd guessed something bad had happened—maybe his unit was ambushed or his friends killed in some drug-related mess. But his wife?

That hadn't even crossed her mind.

"Now he's gonna tighten his security, be even more careful. Don't you get it? You've ruined my one chance at avenging her." He punched the wall, and she flinched. "You've blown it."

The plaster cracked under the force, leaving a fist-sized hole in the wall.

"It's not your only chance," she whispered.

Don't go there, Sloane, she told herself. But she couldn't help it.

"It's not your only chance to get him."

He spun around, ignoring the hole he'd made, ignoring the pain that must be throbbing in his hand. "What?"

"There's a better way."

He stared at her, eyes narrowed.

She sighed. "I probably shouldn't be telling you this, but every Thursday afternoon, Omari visits a graveyard on the western side of town. His driver drops him off at the entrance, and he goes in alone."

Stitch blinked. "He goes alone?"

She nodded, eyes downcast. Well, now she'd done it. By giving him the perfect opportunity, she might have just tanked her career with the CIA.

No Omari meant no target, which probably meant no job.

"Why didn't you tell me this before?"

She raised an eyebrow. "So you could kill him?"

His voice dropped. "Then why are you telling me now?"

She huffed, sitting down at the table near the window. "Good question. I've been asking myself the same thing."

"Seriously, Sloane."

She looked up. "Because I know you. You're stubborn. You'll try to take him out anyway, and in the graveyard, there's less chance of return fire."

Their eyes locked.

God, when he looked at her like that... with those icy blue eyes. She'd slay dragons for him—if she knew how. Omari was the closest thing.

"I don't want to watch you get shot to pieces in front of me," she added, breaking the intensity of the moment.

He snorted. "I had an escape route, you know."

"Still too risky. His guards had you in their sights. If you'd opened fire, they would've taken you out before you could get away. Plus, there were too many civilians around. You don't want collateral damage."

He gave a small nod, acknowledging her point.

"My way's better," she added.

He sank into the chair across from her. "Tell me about this graveyard."

"It's in the foothills, west of here. About a thirty-minute drive. I've followed him there for the past three Thursdays. Every week, same time."

"That's tomorrow," he said.

Their eyes met again. "Yeah."

"Thank you," he said softly, and then did something he'd

never done before. He reached out and touched her hand across the table. Her heart skipped a beat. He wasn't the touchy-feely type. "I mean it. You didn't have to…"

"No, I didn't." She pulled her hand away, feeling too much in that brief touch. If he left it there, she might like it a little too much. "But it's better than the alternative."

He tilted his head, studying her. She couldn't meet his gaze, so she stared at his hand. Big, rough, scarred. Not the hands of a doctor, but a fighter. A tattoo snaked out from under his sleeve, and she couldn't wondered how far up it went.

"What are you gonna tell your handler?"

She shrugged. "No clue. Maybe nothing. I never hear from him. He doesn't reply to my emails. Honestly, I'm not even sure if he reads them. I assume he does. Otherwise, why am I here?"

"He never replies?"

"Nope, not a word."

"What about your boss? Matthew?"

She frowned. "I haven't heard from him either."

Stitch raised an eyebrow. "Well, if you want my advice…"

She frowned. "Who says I do?"

He grinned. That rare, fleeting grin that almost made her forget what they were talking about. "Doesn't matter. I'm giving it to you anyway." His blue eyes sparkled for a second, and her stomach did a little flip. "Don't mention this. There's no benefit to you. Just act like you don't know anything."

"You mean don't tell them I handed Omari to you on a silver platter? That I'm complicit in a murder?"

He didn't respond. He didn't need to. That was exactly what she'd be doing.

Just to keep *him* from getting himself killed.

She sighed. No point getting worked up about it now. It

was done. She couldn't take it back. "I wasn't planning on mentioning it anyway."

He drummed his fingers on the table. "I know you're risking your whole assignment for me, and I get how hard that is."

"It's not just my assignment," she said. "It's the drug deal. Will it even go ahead without Omari?"

"Probably. There's too much money at stake to cancel it now. Omari's got people in his organization who can handle it. He's not a one-man show."

"So, the CIA can still intercept the shipment?"

"If that's their plan, yeah."

She felt a flicker of hope. "Then we need to figure out the details."

Silence hung between them as his fingers kept tapping. His face gave nothing away, but she saw warmth in his gaze. "Sloane, let's make a deal."

"Should I be worried?"

He laughed, deep and gravelly, and for a moment, she didn't even realize it was him. "When I get back from the graveyard tomorrow, I'll help you figure out the shipment details. I owe you that much."

"Really?" Her breath caught.

"Yeah. It's the least I can do."

"How?"

"We'll go to Islamabad, talk to the port officials. Someone's gotta know something."

"Isn't that dangerous?" she asked.

He shrugged. "Money talks. And we've got U.S. dollars."

She hesitated.

"If you want to get to the bottom of this, that's the way."

She thought for a moment. "You could ask Omari before you kill him. He'll know."

He hesitated. "That's not exactly the conversation I was planning to have with him."

"I know," she whispered. "It'd just save us time."

He was silent for a beat.

"I'll see what I can do," he said finally. "No promises, though."

Sloane gave a little nod. "That's all I ask."

CHAPTER 14

The graveyard was overgrown and forgotten, like it had been lost to time. Crumbling crypts with stone arches jutted up from the waist-high grass. Some were falling apart, rubble piled up around them. Tombstones leaned at odd angles, barely visible through the brush, and in the distance, purple hills rolled lazily, dotted with dried shrubs and bare trees.

It was a sad place. Isolated.

A perfect spot for a killing.

Stitch had gotten there early. According to Sloane, Omari left home at two for his weekly visit to the gravesite, and the drive took about half an hour.

It was already 2:15. He'd been waiting for 20 minutes, holed up in a hollowed-out crypt at the far end of the graveyard where the land blended into the hills. There wasn't much of a border—just a mess of weeds and crumbling stone swallowed by the wilderness years ago.

The crypt was big enough to keep him hidden but small enough to be overlooked. Other crypts were scattered around, some with arches still standing, some collapsed into ruins.

Sloane didn't know exactly where Omari went when he came here, only that he was dropped off at the entrance and walked in alone. Always alone.

Stitch wasn't surprised. The place was deserted except for the dead, and even they seemed forgotten.

Who was Omari visiting? His parents? Grandparents?

Stitch settled deeper into the shadows, letting the tall grass and the crypt keep him out of sight. Fitting that the drug lord would die near his ancestors.

He checked his watch. 2:20.

Footsteps. Someone walking through the grass. Stitch leaned forward, keeping to the shadows. Was it Omari? A little early, but maybe.

He crawled to get a better look—and his heart sank.

Shit.

It wasn't Omari.

Instead of the Afghan drug lord, a white guy with reddish hair walked casually along the path, dressed in chinos and a white shirt. Definitely a westerner, and definitely not trying to blend in.

Who the hell was this? What was he doing here?

The guy whistled softly to himself as he checked out the tombstones, pausing to read the inscriptions before moving on. Most of the writing was in Arabic, which told Stitch a lot.

Should he scare the guy off? Tell him to get lost before Omari showed up?

Then he heard tires crunch on gravel. Stitch ducked out of sight.

Too late.

This was happening, whether this guy was here or not.

Omari's voice cut through the stillness, telling his driver

to wait. Then he appeared, his white tunic stark against the dead grass.

The red-haired guy turned around at the sound of someone approaching.

Maybe Omari would tell him to get lost. Stitch could only hope.

He wanted Omari to himself.

He wanted that murdering bastard to know why he was going to die—and exactly who was pulling the trigger.

Voices. The two men were talking.

Stitch watched from his hiding spot.

What the hell? They shook hands.

He couldn't hear much, but it was clear—they knew each other.

It hit him then: This wasn't a gravesite visit. This was a meeting. A private meeting nobody knew about, not even Omari's closest people.

Keeping his Glock ready, Stitch crawled forward, belly to the ground, moving closer through the grass. They didn't notice him, completely unaware. Like a snake, he slithered up behind a pile of rubble, close enough to catch bits of their conversation.

They were speaking in Urdu.

"The arrangements are in place," Omari was saying.

"Good," the redhead replied. "When?"

"June 23. Container terminal D. The *Arabian Princess*."

"Excellent. The money will be in your account tonight."

Omari smiled.

The sight made Stitch's skin crawl. Who was this guy paying Omari? Was he in charge? Had he ordered the attack on his village?

Stitch pulled out his phone and silently snapped a couple of photos, then slipped it back into his pocket.

Omari had been paid. The deal was done.

If he shot Omari now, the shipment might not happen. The guy with him would want his money back—but would he get it?

Omari probably had offshore accounts. Cayman Islands, Panama, somewhere like that. Once he was dead, this guy's money would disappear into thin air.

Stitch doubted Omari's wife even knew about it. Not that it would stop them from going after her if things went sideways.

Whoever this redhead was, he wasn't Arabic. His accent was terrible. Stitch pegged him as American, but he wasn't totally sure.

That question was answered when the redhead shook Omari's hand and said, "Good work. We'll be in touch."

Definitely American.

Stitch frowned. Had he missed something in his search for Soraya's killer? Was there someone else pulling the strings? Maybe Omari was just the tip of the iceberg.

He studied the redhead as he walked off. Stocky build, hard face, straight posture. The guy carried himself like a soldier. Or maybe a merc. Come to think of it, this whole thing reeked of military precision.

If Stitch wanted to figure out who this guy was, he couldn't kill Omari. Not yet.

That left a bitter taste in his mouth, but he swallowed it. Before he pulled the trigger, he had to know if there was more to this than what he'd discovered.

He slithered back into his crypt and watched as the two men left. They headed in opposite directions. The graveyard walls were so broken down, you could get out almost anywhere.

Once they were gone, Stitch stood up and walked to his motorcycle, hidden behind a domed structure with crumbling turrets.

Once again, Omari had gotten a reprieve. He must be the luckiest bastard alive.

Stitch pushed his bike out onto the gravel road and kick-started it.

If someone else was running this show, he needed to find out who—and he knew exactly where to start. But he had one stop to make first.

"WHAT ARE YOU DOING HERE?" Sloane ran out of the community center after seeing him pull up through the window. "Is everything alright?"

She looked him over, half-expecting to see bullet holes, but he appeared to be in one piece.

"I'm fine."

She frowned, trying to figure him out.

The trauma of taking a life, the relief that it was over, the crash when he realized it wasn't going to bring his wife back —none of those emotions were there. Instead, he appeared normal. Almost upbeat.

"Is it over? Did you get him?"

He shook his shaggy head. "No, something came up."

She gaped at him. "You mean you didn't do it? Omari isn't dead?"

"No, he's alive and well, I'm sorry to say. Do you have a minute?"

It took her a moment to process. Omari was still alive. Stitch was unhurt, and he had something to show her.

She pulled herself together. "Yes, class is over for the day. I was just talking to Fatima."

"How is she?" he asked, momentarily distracted.

"Much better." She managed a small smile. "Thanks to you. You should come in and say hello."

"I will," he said. "But first, I want to show you something."

He pulled out his phone and scrolled to a photo of the red-haired man. "Do you know this guy?"

Sloane gasped, her hand flying to her mouth. "That's Jeremy! Where did you—? How—?" Her face twisted in confusion.

What was Jeremy doing here? And how did Stitch get a picture of him?

"I—I don't understand."

"He was at the graveyard," he said sourly. "Meeting Omari. It seems they have a secret weekly meet-up among the tombstones. That's why Omari goes in alone. He doesn't want anyone to know. Not even his bodyguards."

She stared at him, her head spinning. "What does it mean?"

He took a deep breath. "I'm not sure yet. I need to think about it. But it can't be good."

"You don't think—?" She stopped.

No, she couldn't say it. It was traitorous to even think it.

"I don't think anything yet," he said firmly.

She closed her eyes. The ground felt like it was shifting under her.

"I'm so confused," she whispered.

He took her arm and steered her toward the entrance to the center. "Let me check on Fatima, and then we'll meet back at your place later. I want to make a few calls and see what I can find out."

She nodded, unable to do anything else.

Jeremy here? Was he involved? What the hell was going on?

Holy crap.

What had she gotten herself into?

She exhaled shakily. This was way out of her league.

"It's an easy assignment," he'd told her. "Just observe and report back. No action required."

Yeah, right!

"I don't understand," she repeated, as he led her up the stairs. Her head felt foggy, like she was in a daze. Nothing made sense.

She tripped, but he steadied her. Thank goodness he was holding her up.

The security guard let them through.

"We'll make sense of it later," he told her. "I just needed to check that he was your handler. I've got some contacts who can help us figure this out."

"You have?"

What contacts? She thought he was working solo. A personal vendetta.

It was all so confusing.

"Leave it to me."

He flashed her a brief smile before stepping past her and heading into Fatima's room.

CHAPTER 15

Sloane groaned and went to stand by the window. It was way too hot to move and the heat made the stench from the meat market unbearable. She could feel her hair sticking to the back of her neck, and perspiration trickled between her breasts. As it was, she was wearing the lightest thing she had, a flowing maxi dress with thin straps and a plunging neckline, but even that didn't help much. She'd lost weight since she'd been in Peshawar, and it hung off her, exposing even more of her chest.

There was a faint knock on the door.

Stitch.

As usual, he'd arrived after ten o'clock at night. But this time, she was wide awake—sleeping in the heat was impossible. Besides, after what they'd discovered today, she needed answers.

"Hey there." She forced a smile, but he walked right past her into the room, always on alert. Did the guy ever relax? "Sorry about the smell, but I had to keep the windows open."

He grunted, unconcerned. She bet he'd had to handle a lot worse.

"You got a haircut," she said, surprised as he turned around. The wild-haired, mountain-man look was gone, replaced by a drop-dead gorgeous guy with a short, clean cut. He still had the beard for his Arabic cover, but it was neat now, not that wild, scruffy mess.

Suddenly, she could see his full lips and that sharp jawline. Without all the fuzz, his cheekbones looked way more defined.

She swallowed hard. Damn, he looked good. Really good.

And here she was, sweaty, frazzled, and red as a lobster.

Great going, Sloane.

"Yeah, it was time." He ran a hand through his new haircut. "Hope it hasn't compromised my cover."

He was still in the traditional shalwar kameez, but today's tunic was a pale blue, making his arctic eyes stand out even more. Instead of looking like some scruffy, middle-aged guy, now he looked like a hot, thirty-something straight out of a men's style magazine.

"I've got some cold iced tea." She gestured to a jug on the table.

"Thanks." He strode over and poured himself a glass.

She realized she was staring, but this new look was such a surprise, she couldn't tear her gaze away. The corners of his mouth quirked. "I don't look that different, do I?"

Hell, yeah.

"It's just a surprise, that's all." Heat stole into her cheeks, and if she hadn't already been flushed from the heat, she would have been embarrassed by it. As it was, she doubted she could get any redder. Still, she needed to put herself together. He was still the same, damaged, bitter fighter underneath, no matter how great he looked on the surface.

Turning to face the window, she said, "I can't believe Jeremy was meeting Omari. I'm still in shock. How do they know each other?"

"You weren't supposed to know," Stitch downed his lemonade in one long swallow.

"Did you talk to your contacts?"

He nodded. "Yeah. My best buddy, a guy I served with in—well, in Afghanistan—works for a private security company in D.C. They've got contacts everywhere. I asked them to check it out for us."

"Did you tell them about me?" She bit her lip. What would Matthew think of that? Strict radio silence meant not telling anyone else she was here.

"Not by name," he said.

She exhaled. "Good. I don't think the Agency would be too thrilled if your friend knew I was here."

"They're discreet," he assured her. "But my buddy Blade said they'd look into Omari's ties to the CIA, if there are any. Maybe the guy's a whistleblower, or maybe he's being paid for intel."

The thought had crossed her mind, too.

She tilted her head. "Omari might not be as bad as we think."

He let out a low hiss. "Oh, he's bad, alright—but that doesn't mean he's not playing both sides."

"The clandestine meetings—" she murmured. "If his men found out, he'd be in real trouble."

Stitch's lips pressed into a firm line. "He's walking a fine line. If he is dishing the dirt, he'll be considered a traitor. The Taliban won't stand for that."

"How soon will your friend get back to you?" she asked.

"As soon as he can."

Sloane ran a hand through her damp hair and stared down at her gown in dismay. It clung to her curves, the sheer fabric sticking to her damp skin. "I'm not sure what I'm supposed to do now," she admitted, throwing her hands in the air. "Should I confront Jeremy? Tell him I know he's meeting with Omari?"

"No." The word shot out like a bullet. "Do not say anything to anyone about the meetings. Not yet."

What about Matthew? He'd said not to call, but neither of them had expected something like this. Maybe she ought to tell him? He'd know what to do.

Unless...

"What if Jeremy's in on it?" She bit her lip. "Omari might be paying him off."

"It's possible," Stitch agreed. "But I heard Jeremy say the money would be in Omari's account by tonight, so it's more likely Jeremy's paying him for intel, not the other way around."

Okay, that made sense.

"Did you find out when the shipment's coming?" Sloane asked. "Did Omari say anything about that?"

"No, nothing." He refilled his glass. "We may still have to visit the docks and grease some palms."

Damn. "I guess that would've been too easy."

"Yep, guess so." There was an awkward pause, where his gaze lingered on her, curiosity mixed with something primitive, something that made her insides twist. She blew a strand of hair off her cheek. Phew, it wasn't just the temperature that was scorching.

"How about we sit on the balcony?" he suggested. "It's probably cooler out there."

She must really look bad for him to suggest that.

"It looks a little rickety," she said, doubtfully.

"It's sturdier than it looks. I've climbed up it, remember?"

She relented. If she carried on like this she was going to end up in a puddle on the floor. "Okay."

He carried two chairs outside, while she brought their glasses and the jug of lemonade. He was right—it was a lot cooler out here. The red neon sign across the street cast a surreal glow on the road below. The day's traffic had thinned out, with only a few scooters, and a couple of cars passing by. Most of the shops and workshops were shut. A few people hurried home, their heads down, bags slung over their shoulders, but no one was hanging around.

"Tell me about Matthew," Stitch said, once they'd sat down.

She arched her eyebrows, surprised. "Why do you want to know about him?"

"Call it a professional curiosity."

Sloane hesitated. Ever since he'd saved Fatima's life, she felt connected to him, like they shared some kind of bond. In a way, she'd saved his life too, preventing him from shooting Omari, after which he'd almost certainly have been killed. In a weird way, she felt like she could trust him.

Was that nuts? Trusting a guy with a vendetta?

Probably.

But right now, he was all she had.

"I fell hard for Matthew." She gulped, then fixed her gaze on the building across the street. "He was so suave, so confident and he moved in powerful circles. I'd never met anyone like him before."

Stitch gave a brief nod, but didn't interrupt.

"We had coffee a few times, then he invited me over for dinner. He cooked." She gave a half-smile. "He's not bad, actually. Anyway, one thing led to another and… Well, you know." She stared at her hands.

"He seduced you?" Stitch asked, his voice edged.

"It was mutual," she said quickly, looking up. "Michael's divorced, lives alone. I think he sees his son every other weekend. I was single." She shrugged. "Why shouldn't we get together?"

"No reason." He cleared his throat. "When did he offer you the job?"

"A few weeks after that. We'd been seeing each other pretty regularly, and one evening he said he had an opportunity for me. At first, I wasn't sure what he meant, but then he explained he worked for the U.S. government, and they were looking for someone with my skillset. He said he'd put in a good word if I was interested."

Stitch gave her an intense look, as if he were trying to read her. "Were you?"

"Not really. I enjoyed my teaching job. I loved the kids."

He frowned. "So why did you take it?"

She thought back to Matthew. How he'd told her how special she was, how unique. That her ability to read people was rare, and highly sought after. Speaking Urdu made her even more desirable. He'd flattered her—and she'd fallen for it.

"They offered me more than double what I was earning as a teacher," she admitted.

The money had been an added bonus. But really, if she was honest with herself, it was because she'd wanted to see more of Matthew.

He nodded, as if that explained it.

"I was enrolled in a training program for ten months, and after that, I got my first assignment—this one." She spread her hands. "And here I am."

"You said you hadn't spoken to Matthew?" There was something in his tone that irked her, put her on the defensive.

She bristled. "Not since I got here, but he told me not to contact him. The funny thing is, I didn't see him much during my training either, I was so busy with the program, and he was away a lot. Sometimes I find it hard to remember what he looks like. Do you know what I mean?"

There was a silence, then she remembered his wife.

Crap.

"Oh, I'm sorry. I didn't mean—"

Shit, now she'd put her foot in it.

"I still see her face," he said quietly. "Sometimes, I close my eyes and she's there, smiling at me. Then other times—" He faded out.

"How long ago did… did it happen?" she asked softly.

"Fourteen months ago. I wasn't there when they hit. I'd gone to the nearest town for medical supplies. I was heading back when I saw the smoke."

Sloane winced. "God, that's awful."

"I rolled into the village, and it was gone. Leveled. Bullet holes everywhere. A local Taliban militia had torn through and wiped it out, then torched it."

"Omari's men?" she asked quietly.

He gave a sharp nod.

His jaw clenched, hands balled into fists, his whole body tensing like a coiled spring. The hatred was practically radiating off him.

"Omari was the local Taliban leader. The village sat right in the middle of a new drug route through the mountains. They wanted to use it as a checkpoint, but the elders refused. Our village was poor, but we were honest. No one wanted to be part of their drug trade."

"And that's why they attacked?" she asked.

"Yeah. Sent a message. My father-in-law was an elder. They took him out first. Only a few survived. We buried the dead up in the mountains."

Sloane swallowed hard. "I'm so sorry."

He didn't respond for a moment, eyes staring off into the distance.

"I get why you want him dead," she said softly. "I think I would too." She was surprised by the antagonism she felt towards the Afghan, who up until now had been a nameless, faceless target. Now she hated him for what he'd done to the villagers, to Stitch's wife, to him. He'd completely destroyed their lives. Nobody had the right to do that.

"But you're still going to get him," she whispered.

Stitch's face flashed demonic red in the electric light. "Fuck, yeah. He's going down, I'm going to make sure of it."

CHAPTER 16

He'd lied to Sloane. He had to.

Until he figured out what the hell was going on, he couldn't give her the details about the shipment. If she reported back to Matthew, her boss would know Jeremy was involved. Hell, maybe he already knew. Maybe Matthew was in on it too.

A whole faction of the CIA could be dirty. Stitch had no idea how deep this thing went. The last thing he wanted was to put Sloane in the crosshairs. At the very least, she'd get pulled from the op and the whole thing would be shut down.

He couldn't let that happen. Not if he wanted to find out the truth.

He left her place around midnight. They'd talked for hours out on the balcony—her, about Matthew, and him about his life as a medic in that remote Afghan village.

That was a big deal for him. She had no idea just how huge.

After the attack, he'd completely fallen apart. Went off the grid, living in the mountains, hunting to survive. For a while, he wasn't sure he wanted to go on. The pain was... unbearable.

Living off the land was easy. SEAL training had more than prepared him for that. But as the weeks dragged into months, the grief morphed into anger, and the anger hardened into white-hot rage. That rage became his fuel—his focus. He swore he'd track down every person responsible for what happened.

That promise had brought him back. He'd crawled out of his hole, found a cheap, filthy flat in Kabul, and started working. He used every contact he had—local officials, poppy farmers, village elders to piece together the truth.

He had a list—and Omari's name was at the top.

Tracking the Afghani drug lord to Peshawar had taken months. He was hiding, all right, but not from the U.S. for terrorism. No, it was drugs—he was a kingpin in the growing Taliban-run heroin cartel.

He'd only told Sloane part of that story, sticking to the basics. He'd kept it light, sharing enough of his life without getting too deep.

The sharing part? That felt good.

Almost... normal.

For once, he wasn't the grieving widower fueled by grief and vengeance. He was just a man talking to a woman. A beautiful, interesting woman.

What was so wrong with that?

BY THE TIME Stitch pulled up across the street from the meat market, the sun was already blazing. The morning was barely underway, but the heat clung to the air, thick and relentless, promising another scorcher. The market was bustling— Saturday brought out the crowds. Carcasses hung from giant hooks, swaying gently as butchers moved between them, the smell of raw meat and blood hanging heavy in the air. He could already catch a whiff of it, and the busier the market got, the worse it would be. They needed to get on the road soon.

Sloane stepped out of her building, and for a moment, everything else faded. She was wearing a dark skirt, a silky blouse that caught the light just right, and a green-blue scarf wrapped loosely around her head. The color made her eyes pop, and as she waved at him, she gave him a smile that made him forget the smell of the market and the heat pressing down on him.

He found himself smiling back. He was doing that more lately—smiling, talking. Things he'd long forgotten how to do. Hell, he wasn't even sure he remembered how to be human anymore. But with her, it was coming back.

She stepped off the curb, moving toward him, but then the butcher from the meat market called out to her. She turned to respond, her body angled away from the road.

Something shifted in Stitch's peripheral vision—a dark figure, a motorbike weaving through the traffic. Full-face helmet, black gear, moving too fast. Warning bells went off in his head. The hair on the back of his neck stood up.

He saw it then—a weapon strapped across the rider's chest.

Fuck.

Instinct kicked in. He didn't think, didn't plan. He yanked his gun from the glove box and bolted out of the vehicle.

"Sloane, get down!" he roared as the biker skidded to a stop.

She swung around, but not fast enough. Everything seemed to move in slow motion, and he couldn't get to her in time. The motorcyclist raised the rifle and opened fire. The air exploded with the crack of gunshots, and the sidewalk shattered with concrete chips. Shoppers screamed and scattered, dropping bags and running for cover.

Stitch dropped to the ground, rolling and firing as he went.

Sloane twisted violently mid-turn, her body jerking as she hit the ground.

No. God, no.

"Sloane!"

He fired off more rounds, charging toward the shooter. The gunfire was deafening, each shot ringing in his ears. The biker turned the weapon on Stitch, but he rolled behind a car just as the butcher grabbed Sloane and dragged her to cover behind the counter.

She wasn't moving.

"You son of a bitch!" Stitch growled, breaking cover and emptying his magazine at the shooter. He knew it was reckless, but all he could think about was stopping this bastard before someone else got hit.

He saw the shooter flinch, grabbing at his shoulder.

Good. He'd hit him.

But Stitch's gun clicked. Empty.

Shit.

He sprinted toward the biker, ready to tackle him if that's what it took. But before he could reach him, the motorcyclist swerved hard, pulling a sharp U-turn and speeding off down the road. In seconds, he was gone, disappearing around the corner in a blur of black.

Stitch didn't stop. He ran straight for Sloane, who lay on the ground behind the butcher's cutting machine, her face pale, eyes closed. His heart pounded in his chest as he dropped to his knees beside her.

Not again. Please, not again.

"Sloane?" His voice was hoarse. He touched her face. "Sloane, can you hear me?"

Her arm was bleeding badly, but there were no other visible wounds. No bullets to the torso, no major damage.

Thank God.

Her eyelids fluttered, and she groaned. "Stitch…"

"I'm here," he said, his voice low but urgent.

She tried to sit up, wincing immediately. "My arm… what happened?"

"You've been shot. I'm going to need this." He unwrapped her scarf and tied it tightly around her arm, above the wound. "The bullet's still in there, but it's not too deep. You're gonna be fine." He glanced at her hand. "Can you move your fingers?"

She wiggled them, and he let out a breath of relief. No nerve damage.

She was still pale, the shock starting to take hold. He tightened the makeshift tourniquet. "This'll hold until I can get the bullet out."

The butcher was hovering nearby, his face etched with concern. Everybody in this border town had seen violence before, maybe too much of it. "The gun's empty," he said, nodding toward the pistol on the ground.

Stitch picked it up, tucked it into his pocket of his robe, then gave the man a firm shake of the hand. "Thank you." He'd pulled her out of the line of fire.

The butcher nodded once, then stepped back. Stitch gently lifted Sloane to her feet, wrapping an arm around her waist to steady her. "Come on, we need to get you out of here. I've got to treat that arm."

"We can go upstairs to my place," she said, but her voice was weak, shaky.

"Not a chance," he snapped. "You're coming with me."

"But… why? I'm just—"

"Isn't it obvious?" His tone was sharp, harder than he

intended, but the realization of what had just happened hit him full force. "That was an assassination attempt. Someone just tried to kill you."

CHAPTER 17

Sloane's arm was on fire. Every bump in the road felt like torture. She squeezed her eyes shut, trying to push through the pain. "How long?" she managed to grit out.

"Almost there."

A few moments later, they pulled up in front of a concrete block house with a faded orange awning. She glanced around, not recognizing anything.

"Where are we?"

"This is a safe house," he replied.

A safe house? Was this where he stayed? She had questions, but the pain in her arm was all-consuming.

"I feel sick," she mumbled.

"It's the shock."

He got out of the car and opened the back door, first scanning the sidewalk. Then he reached out his arms. "Come on, I'll carry you."

She shifted over, letting him scoop her up. He kicked the car door shut and carried her to the entrance. The door swung open just as they arrived.

"What happened?" asked a short, older Pakistani woman, maybe in her sixties. She seemed to know Stitch.

"She's been shot," he said, carrying her inside.

"Put her on the couch," the woman instructed. "I'll get some hot water and something to clean the wound."

She disappeared, concern etched on her face.

"Who is she?" Sloane croaked.

"A friend," he said, not offering more.

Sloane glanced down. The entire one side of her blouse was soaked in blood.

"It looks worse than it is," he reassured her.

"It hurts like hell," she muttered.

"Hang in there. You'll be okay." His voice was soft, almost gentle, with that rough, comforting edge she'd heard before. His "doctor voice," the one that had saved Fatima, that made her trust him completely.

She took a deep breath and exhaled slowly, trying to manage the pain.

"Good girl." He squeezed her hand, and she wished he'd leave it there. She needed someone to hold on to.

The woman returned with a bowl of steaming water and clean cloths draped over her arm.

"I'll be right back," Stitch said. "I need to grab my medical kit."

The woman set the bowl down on the coffee table. "I'm going to clean your wound," she said, her dark eyes meeting Sloane's, making sure she understood.

Sloane nodded.

The woman picked up a pair of scissors and carefully cut the sleeve off Sloane's blouse. Then, she soaked a cloth in the hot water and gently cleaned around the bullet hole.

Sloane lifted her head to look at the wound. It was a neat circle with burned edges and blood oozing out of it. It wasn't gushing, which she took as a good sign—no major arteries hit.

The woman didn't touch the wound itself, just cleaned around it and down her arm. The pain was so intense, her arm was turning numb. Sloane tried to wiggle her fingers, but the pain made her stop.

"Keep still," the woman urged. "Stitch will take care of you."

Oh, crap. She'd forgotten the bullet was still inside.

"Ready?" Stitch walked back into the room, carrying a tray full of medical tools. Sloane spotted a scalpel before squeezing her eyes shut.

No, she screamed internally, but she knew it had to come out. Better not to look.

"You're going to have to trust me." He knelt on the floor beside her. "I need to get that bullet out."

The woman stepped aside, letting Stitch work. It wasn't exactly an ideal setup for surgery.

He picked up the scalpel.

Tears welled up in her eyes, more from pain than fear. She'd never felt anything like this in her life. She tried to nod, to show she was ready, but the burning was spreading like a red-hot poker digging into her shoulder. She wasn't sure she could handle it.

"I'm going to give you something for the pain," he said, as if reading her mind. He must have known she was on the edge. "It'll knock you out. You won't feel a thing."

Thank God.

He filled a syringe with the same amber liquid he'd used on Fatima. She winced as he injected it just above the wound site.

The last thing she remembered before the darkness took over was the feel of his hand brushing her hair away from her face—rough calluses, gentle touch. Then everything went black.

CHAPTER 18

Where was she?

Sloane opened her eyes and looked around the room. It was plain and functional, with bare walls and tightly drawn curtains.

Why didn't she recognize anything?

The ache in her arm cut through her grogginess. She'd been shot! Stitch had brought her here and taken out the bullet.

She glanced at her bandaged arm. It still hurt, but not as much as before. She wiggled her fingers, sighing in relief when they moved. Thank goodness there was no lasting damage.

There was a soft knock on the door, and the woman came in.

"How are you feeling?" she asked.

"Okay, I think. I'm sorry for intruding like this."

The woman smiled. "Any friend of Stitch's is welcome here."

Sloane was even more intrigued.

"How do you know Stitch?" she asked, leaning back on the pillow.

"His team used to come here when there was trouble over the border. I called them my American heroes. So brave." She shook her head. "Fighting for their country. My daughter lives there, you know. She's in New York."

His team? Fighting across the border?

Sloane's mind swirled with questions.

"When was that?"

"Oh, a long time ago now. Many years." She patted Sloane's hand. "You've had quite a shock. Stitch said to keep an eye on you and not let you leave the house." She smiled. "He was very worried about you."

He was?

A warm glow spread through her, or maybe that was the anesthetic wearing off. Her head felt a little fuzzy.

"Thank you for helping me," she murmured.

The woman grinned. "Of course, dear. It's not the first time I've patched someone up. You should've seen the state of them when they used to come here." She shook her head. "Such dangerous work."

Sloane assumed "them" meant Stitch and his team. She realized she didn't know much about what he'd done in the military, before he left. They'd never really talked about it.

"You rest, dear. You've had a nasty shock. Someone tried to kill you."

Thanks for the reminder.

It still made no sense. Who'd want to kill her? A rookie agent, barely getting by undercover. A nobody.

Then she remembered the phone call.

Matthew!

She grabbed the woman's arm.

"Where's Stitch? I need to talk to him."

"Are you in pain?"

"No, I just need to talk to him."

"He's gone out, but he'll be back later." She made to leave. "I've made some stew, so let me know if you're hungry."

Sloane shook her head. She couldn't eat. Not now that she remembered.

Oh, God. Oh, God.

Please let it not be true.

But there was nothing she could do now. She had to wait for Stitch to get back—and he wasn't going to be happy with what she had to say.

"You did *what*?"

His icy blue eyes locked onto her, intense and unforgiving.

"I'm sorry. I thought it was best to keep him in the loop. I couldn't email Jeremy, since he's mixed up in this, so I figured I'd better report back to Matthew."

Needless to say, Matthew hadn't been thrilled to hear from her. But that changed when she told him what she'd found out.

"You should've talked to me first," Stitch said. He'd changed into a t-shirt and jeans, and she couldn't help but notice his tanned, muscular arms or how his jeans hugged his thick thighs just right.

His tattoo was on full display now—black ink twisting in a Celtic design down his forearm to his wrist. Another one covered his bicep, disappearing under his shirt sleeve.

"Why?" Her cheeks heated up. "You're not my boss. I don't report to you."

"I told you when we started this…"

"That was then. Things are different now. We know Omari's running drugs, and we know Jeremy's involved.

After you left last night, I thought it over and decided Matthew needed to know. If Jeremy's turning a blind eye or somehow involved in getting drugs into the States, the CIA has to be in on it."

Stitch stared at her for a long moment. "From your side, that makes sense."

Was he actually agreeing with her?

She frowned at him. "Thank you."

He moved closer and sat on the bed. The ancient springs creaked under his weight, tilting her toward him. He was all muscle and heat, freshly showered, his hair still damp. She had to fight the urge to touch those rock-hard thighs.

"But I need to know exactly what you told him."

She shifted as she struggled to stay put and not slide down the bed into him.

"Fine. I told him I saw Omari meet with four Afghan men, and they looked important. I sent him the video from the restaurant."

"What'd he say to that?" Stitch's blue eyes were more curious than cold, softening his usually sharp edge. She noticed an old scar along his jawline beneath his beard, and her fingers itched to trace it. She forced her eyes back to his.

"He already knew. Jeremy had reported that the Afghans were preparing to move a shipment."

"He knew it was drug-related all along?" Stitch's eyebrows shot up.

She nodded. "Apparently. I asked why he hadn't told me, and he said it was for my protection. In case I got captured, I couldn't spill what I didn't know."

Stitch shook his head.

The idea of being captured made her stomach drop. She'd be on her own. She knew that now.

Thank God for Stitch. If it weren't for him, she'd still be

clueless, still thinking Omari was some terrorist plotting an attack.

How naive had she been? Heat crept into her face. "Then, I told him about Jeremy."

Stitch's jaw tightened. "What'd he say?"

"He was concerned. He said he'd look into it and that I did the right thing by telling him."

Stitch's eyes stayed glued to her face.

Her next words came out hesitant, shaky. "Matthew's involved too, isn't he?"

She didn't want the answer. Didn't want to face the idea that her boss—her ex—was dirty.

Stitch sighed. "I'm sorry, Sloane. Looks like it. Hell of a coincidence that the day after you tell him about Jeremy and a potential CIA drug operation, someone tries to take you out."

She closed her eyes.

"I've been so stupid," she whispered, opening them again to stare into his. "I thought I was doing the right thing. He's my boss, after all."

And more than that, he had been her lover.

Her voice trembled. "I thought I could trust him."

"You can't trust anyone," Stitch said, his voice low, edged with a menace that made her shiver. "Not anymore. I don't know how deep this goes or who's involved. Could be an isolated case with Jeremy and Matthew getting paid to look the other way. But until we know for sure, you need to keep a low profile."

She nodded, feeling miserable. How could she have screwed up so badly?

"If the CIA's in on this, how am I supposed to get home?" Her voice hitched with sudden panic. "I can't stay hidden forever."

"You won't have to," he reassured her. "We'll figure it out."

That deep, rough voice could calm her when nothing else could. She only wished she could be as sure as he sounded.

"But how?" It felt impossible. How do you take on the CIA? It was just the two of them, in the middle of nowhere, with Matthew and the agency miles away.

"I told you, I've got friends who can help. Brothers I trust with my life."

"From your old unit?" She remembered what the woman had said.

His face darkened. "How'd you know that?"

"The woman told me your unit used this place as a safe house when you were operating across the border." She saw his face shut down, his eyes hardening, lips pressed into a tight line. A muscle twitched in his jaw.

"You get that look whenever you don't want to talk," she said. "It's like you shut off everything."

Frown lines appeared on his forehead. "You reading me again?"

She smiled a little. "It's not that hard."

There was a pause.

"It's not that I don't want to talk," he finally growled. "I just can't."

"Too painful?" she asked gently.

"Too classified," he corrected, his frosty eyes burning into her.

Ignoring his warning, she said, "She mentioned patching you up more than once."

"She shouldn't be telling you that," he muttered. "I'll talk to her."

"I asked," Sloane said quickly, not wanting to get the woman in trouble. "What do you expect? You never tell me anything."

He rubbed his temples, as if trying to smooth out the stress lines. "Okay. You deserve to know a little."

Her voice shook. "Especially since you're the only person I can trust."

It was true. Without him, she was as good as dead. Without his help, she'd never make it home.

Another, longer pause.

"We used this place as a safe house," he said, finally. "A place to lay low if we were injured or needed time to recover. It was safer here in Pakistan than over the border."

"Didn't that put her at risk?" She thought of the woman, probably playing host to a bunch of huge, intimidating operators.

"It was a managed risk. Besides, we made sure to take care of her." He grinned, a flash of mischief.

Her heart stumbled over itself as his eyes crinkled, playful for once. Where had this side of him been hiding?

As she caught her breath, he added, "Mrs. B's a big fan of anything American. Her daughter lives in New York."

"I know, she told me." She studied him. "She also told me your team often used to stay here after missions across the border."

He hesitated, not meeting her gaze.

"You're not a marine, are you? It's more than that." Her gaze dropped to his tattoo, the way he'd dashed across the road when the biker had appeared out of nowhere, his decisive actions, his ability to breach her room without her hearing him. "Navy SEAL?"

He sniffed. "You're good."

"I won't tell," she whispered, a shiver coursing through her. Navy SEAL operators were different. She'd read about them. They went into enemy territory, took on impossible missions, and hunted down terrorists. They blew stuff up, and yeah, they killed people with their bare hands.

He was one of them.

She should have seen it earlier. The controlled strength,

the way he read situations instantly, how he'd charged the gunman on the motorcycle like he had zero fear. She hadn't even noticed the guy coming down the road.

She'd never known anyone like Stitch. Matthew was the closest thing to a government agent she'd known, and he pushed paper behind a desk.

Stitch raked a hand through his hair. "Anyway, all that was a long time ago. I've been out for over a year."

She didn't miss the flash of despair on his face. "Why'd you leave?"

He looked down at his hands—scarred, marked by battle. "It's complicated. Maybe I should check your wound."

"It's okay if you don't want to talk about it," she said as he unwound the bandage. He'd already told her more than she expected.

She winced as he peeled off the gauze. It was still tender.

He focused on her arm, the neatly stitched wound. "We were ambushed in the Afghan mountains. Most of my team didn't make it back. Only two of us survived."

"I'm sorry," she whispered.

He exhaled, replacing the bandage. "I couldn't go back after that."

"What did you do?"

"I wandered around until I took refuge in a village in the mountains. I'd been there before, helping them out as a medic, so they knew me."

She nodded, listening intently.

"That's where I met my wife." Pain flashed across his face, raw and undeniable.

"The village Omari attacked?"

"Yeah." He closed his eyes, blocking out the memories.

Her heart ached for him. She wanted to help, but she didn't know how. Instead, she rested a hand on his arm, hoping to provide comfort. His muscles flexed beneath her fingers.

"I appreciate you telling me," she said. "Now I get it."

"I think you always did."

She held her breath. It was true, she'd sensed something had a hold on him from the start—she just hadn't known what. His skin felt warm and firm beneath her hand, the muscles hard and sinewy. She fought not to trace them with her fingers.

Oh, God.

Stop!

"I couldn't hide it from you. You saw right through me."

His face was so close now. Those blue eyes pulled her in like magnets. As he leaned closer, the mattress shifted, and she toppled toward him. Suddenly, she was clutching both his arms, his face just inches away. He reached for her, his hand resting on her hip.

She glanced down at his lips.

So close...

The pain in his eyes was gone, replaced by an intensity she hadn't seen before. Her heart pounded so loudly she thought it was about to somersault right out of her chest.

She didn't know what was happening, but right now, all she wanted was to kiss him.

And then it happened.

He closed the space between them, their lips meeting—soft, firm, deliciously hot.

Sloane closed her eyes and breathed him in.

Then she felt him freeze. His hand slipped from her hip, and he pulled away. "I'm sorry. I can't do this."

Her lips still tingled where he'd touched them. So brief, so sweet.

Almost a kiss.

"It's okay." She tried to hide her disappointment. "I understand."

The worst part was, she did. She really did. It was a miracle he'd even let his guard down this much after everything he'd been through.

Stitch stood up, avoiding her gaze. "Your arm's looking fine. I'll leave you to rest."

And then he left the room.

CHAPTER 19

Stitch turned off Bara Road and hit a dirt track running alongside a dry riverbed, opening up the throttle. The rented motorcycle kicked up dust and shot forward, bouncing over the uneven ground.

How had he almost kissed Sloane? What the hell was he thinking?

He wasn't, and that was the problem.

For once, he hadn't been thinking at all—he'd been feeling. The way she could read him, like she was inside his head, threw him off. She knew things about him no one else did.

Big mistake.

The wind slapped against his face, making his eyes water. He welcomed the sting and pushed the bike even harder.

Talking about his time as a SEAL operator, opening up about what had happened afterwards, made him vulnerable. He hated feeling vulnerable.

Then, out of nowhere, that overpowering urge to kiss her had hit him.

Where the hell had that come from?

He hadn't been attracted to anyone since Soraya. But

now, this American woman with deep chocolate-brown eyes and cherry-red lips had gotten under his skin.

Damn her for walking into the bedroom stark naked, fresh from her bath. Damn her for wearing that slinky gold thing she called a nightgown. Damn her curves, her softness, her inescapable sensuality.

He could still feel her hand on his arm, the warmth of it playing with his emotions. It wouldn't let him forget how, in that one moment, he'd wanted her. And how hard it had been to pull away.

Soraya.

He couldn't do it to her. It was too soon. Her memory was still too vivid.

"I'm sorry," he whispered, the wind snatching the words away before he could even finish.

The motorcycle was going as fast as it could now. The riverbed blurred beside him. If he wiped out, he'd be in serious trouble. He wasn't even wearing a helmet—nobody did around here. Common sense interjected and he slowed down, feeling drained. He was running out of road, anyway. The ground was turning gravelly, dipping dangerously towards the riverbed. Finally, he came to a stop.

Cutting the engine, he climbed off the bike, gulping down the hot, dry air. Everything was eerily quiet. No one was around. He spotted a grassy patch further up the bank. Leaving the bike where it was, he walked over and sat down, staring at the hills across the valley, the purple mountains stretching into the distance. Somewhere among those hills, he used to live. Back when he was happy.

But not anymore.

The grassy bank reminded him of a day about three months before the attack. Soraya had taken him down to the river for a picnic. Afterwards, she'd told him she was pregnant. He remembered the joy in her eyes, the way he'd hugged her, and how they'd talked about becoming parents. That dream had died in the fire, too.

Tears stung his eyes, and he fell back on the grass.

Soraya's voice echoed in his mind. "Are you happy here, my love?"

"What do you mean?" he'd asked. "Of course I'm happy."

"Because this isn't your world. This isn't your culture. I couldn't live with myself if I thought you were unhappy."

He'd taken her hand. "It is my world now," he'd said with a smile. "It is my culture. I'm happy here." And he'd kissed her, right there on the grassy bank.

His fists clenched the dry, brittle grass. The lack of rain had left it shriveled and gray. Everything died in this place.

I couldn't live with myself if I thought you were unhappy.

He stood up and brushed himself off. Enough with the self-pity. It was what it was, and he had to deal with it.

Soon, he'd get his revenge. The people responsible would pay. He'd make sure of it.

It wouldn't bring Soraya back, of course. He knew that. Or the life he should've had. Husband, father, village doctor.

But it would damn sure make him feel better.

He dropped the bike back at the rental place and paid extra for the condition it was in. He was walking back to Mrs. Bhatti's when his phone rang.

Only two people had this number. Make that three, including *her*.

"Blade?" he answered right away.

His buddy chuckled. "Glad to see you were expecting my call. How's life in our favorite border town?"

"Hotter than usual," Stitch replied.

"This is a secure line," his friend said, picking up on their code for 'trouble.'

"Someone on a motorbike tried to take Sloane out," he said. "I had to pull a bullet out and stitch her up."

"Shit. She okay?"

"Yeah, resting at Mrs. B's."

"You took her to the safe house? Was that wise?"

Blade knew Sloane was CIA. When they'd talked a few days ago, Stitch had laid it all out, no holding back.

"Yeah, she was pretty out of it on the way here. Besides, her own people put a hit out on her. She's got nowhere else to go."

"You know that for sure?" Blade asked.

"Has to be. Her boss was the only one she told about her handler, Jeremy, meeting Omari. No one else knew."

There was a pause.

"We did some digging," Blade said. "Well, Pat did. Quietly, if you get my drift. Didn't want to step on any toes."

"Find anything?" Stitch asked.

"Yeah. Matthew Sullivan runs a branch of the CIA focused on watching the Taliban's drug cartels. Officially, they track the big players and report back to Washington. Drug trafficking's blown up in the past few years, and it's a big deal for the U.S. government. They want to crack down, but the Afghan economy depends on poppy production. Shutting it down would tank the economy, and in its fragile state…"

He didn't need to finish.

After decades of war, people were already starving, and farmers turned to growing poppies because it was the only way to make a decent living. Stitch knew better than most how hard life was for rural communities.

"So, they might be getting paid to look the other way, or…" Blade hesitated. "And here's the kicker—they could be running the whole operation."

"Fuck."

"Exactly," Blade said. "Sullivan might seem like a desk jockey, but he was part of a specialist team sent to

Afghanistan in 2014 to help suppress drug production, get farmers to plant wheat, stuff like that. That year saw a huge opium crop, which tanked heroin prices, so wheat became more competitive. Heroin production dropped, but still enough to keep the Taliban going."

Stitch took it all in.

"So, these guys, this specialist team, would've made connections with local farmers, maybe even the Taliban warlords running things?"

"Yep. They were in a prime position to take advantage. Maybe not back then, but definitely later on."

Damn. It wasn't looking good for Sloane.

"How do we smoke out the bad guys?" he asked his friend.

"Pat's flying to the U.S. tomorrow to meet with a contact in the CIA. He's confident this guy's legit. They'll explain what we know and, hopefully, the CIA and the DEA can work together to intercept that shipment you mentioned and take down Sullivan and whoever else is involved."

Best-case scenario.

Stitch knew things didn't always go as planned.

"Alright, great. Tell Pat thanks from me."

Stitch knew Pat well. His son, Joe, had been part of their team. He was one of the men killed in the ambush that day in the Afghan mountains.

"Will do, buddy. And the good news is, you'll get to see me. Pat wants me to bring you something."

"Yeah? What's that?"

"I'll tell you when I get there. Meet me at Islamabad airport, 0800 hours tomorrow."

"Got it. Have a safe flight."

"Thanks."

They signed off.

Stitch felt better as he stepped into the house. Finally, things were happening. Sitting around with nothing to do was the worst. He'd always hated waiting for things to get moving. Unfortunately, in the SEALs, waiting was just part of the job.

Soon, Blade would be here, and they'd track down Jeremy.

Stitch had heard back from his contact—a short text earlier that morning with a location: The Best Western.

There was a bar there, one of the few still open for foreigners that hadn't been shut down or bombed yet. The memory of what happened to the Marriott a decade before made the owners of these sketchy drinking spots nervous. If you wanted a drink in Islamabad now, you relied on whispers from other expats. Personally, Stitch didn't think it worth the hassle.

His list, however, was getting longer.

Omari.

Rasul.

Jeremy.

Sullivan.

Once the ship carrying the drugs set sail, he'd finally do what he came to Peshawar to do.

And there'd be no reason not to.

CHAPTER 20

"I'm not staying here," Sloane snapped when Stitch told her he was heading to Islamabad to find Jeremy.

"You need to lay low," he said firmly. "This is the safest place for you."

"The safest place for me is with you," she shot back, her voice shaking despite her best efforts. "Besides, no one will expect me to go there."

He glanced at her wounded arm. "You've been shot. You need to rest."

"I'm sick of resting." She'd gotten so bored lying in bed that she'd spent most of the afternoon in the lounge talking with Mrs. Bhatti about him. Now she knew way more about Stitch than he'd ever want her to.

Like how he'd taken care of Mrs. B when she had food poisoning. How he'd go shopping for her, bring her little gifts from America, and even help her in the kitchen.

"He's not a bad cook," Mrs. B had giggled. "Though those big hands of his can get in the way."

Sloane had laughed.

"He needs a woman to look after him," Mrs. B had said knowingly. "He's been alone too long. Always taking care of everyone else. It's about time someone took care of him."

Mrs. B didn't know about the past year, and Sloane had kept it that way. It wasn't her story to tell, and Stitch wouldn't want people knowing. She tried not to even entertain the idea that she... that they...

No, that was ridiculous.

Despite the almost-kiss, he was still in love with his late wife. You could hear it in his voice when he talked about her. Sloane couldn't compete with that.

Mrs. B had also told her about the times Stitch or one of his team had come back injured, concussed, bleeding, and how they'd stayed hidden while they healed, waiting for things to cool down before heading back to the States.

The more Sloane learned, the more in awe she was of him, and the more she felt she could trust him. There was *no way* he was leaving her behind.

If anyone could keep her safe, it was Stitch.

"What's Mrs. B supposed to do if armed men show up?" she asked.

He smiled. "Probably more than you think. But you don't need to worry—no one knows you're here."

"They've probably searched my apartment by now. They know I'm not there. They'll think I'm hiding somewhere in Peshawar, not heading to Islamabad."

"You do realize Jeremy, your handler, is probably the one who put the hit out on you, right?"

She clenched her teeth. That sleazy bastard. "The last thing they'll expect is me going after him."

She stared him down, daring him to argue.

"I guess you've got a point," he said reluctantly.

"See? It's a no-brainer. Decision's made. I'm going with you."

He gave her a long, frustrated look, then threw his hands up. "Fine. You win. We leave in an hour."

THE DRIVE to the Pakistani capital took just under three hours.

They hit a police roadblock leaving Peshawar, and Sloane was so scared she nearly peed herself.

"Stay calm," Stitch muttered. "Don't look at them."

Two men in black uniforms with big guns peered into the car, then asked Stitch for his driver's license.

Sloane stared at her hands, silently praying they'd get through. The full burqa Mrs. B had given her made sure they couldn't see who she was, or her bandaged arm. The only thing visible through the narrow slits were her eyes, and she kept them down.

Stitch handed over his license. Her heart raced. Would they realize it was fake?

She tried not to think about the semi-automatic hidden under the carpet beneath the driver's seat. She'd done a double-take when he'd brought it out of the house.

"Just in case," he'd said, his face grim.

And then there was the Glock under her seat. The car was loaded with weapons. If anyone searched them, they were screwed.

By the time they reached the busy capital, her arm was aching from the bumpy roads, the painkillers had worn off, and she was starving.

"I know a place we can stay," Stitch said, glancing at her pale face. "You okay?"

"I'm fine," she lied. She didn't want him to regret bringing her along.

"After we eat something, take another painkiller," he said. "They're too strong to take on an empty stomach."

"Yes, Doc," she said obediently and watched the corners of his mouth lift.

They pulled up outside a cream-colored building with "Khyber Lodge" written on it. "It's reasonably priced and close to the airport," he told her.

They were picking up his friend tomorrow morning, one of the guys he'd served with.

"Are you ever going to tell me your real name?" she asked, once they'd checked in. To avoid suspicion, they were posing as husband and wife. She hadn't said a word—he handled everything.

The hotel receptionist hadn't even blinked.

"It's Vance," he said after a pause.

"Vance." She let the name roll off her tongue. "You know, you actually look like a Vance."

"Really?" He chuckled. "And what does a Vance look like?"

"Dark, broody, grumpy. Exactly like you."

That made him laugh—a deep, belly laugh that made his eyes crinkle. If she wasn't so mesmerized by the transformation, she'd have laughed with him.

God help me.

When he wasn't growling at her, he was totally gorgeous.

He shook his head and tossed his rucksack into the corner.

"Do you have a last name?" she asked.

"Now you're pushing it." He winked at her, completely unaware of her fluttering stomach, and pulled out his toothbrush. "I'm gonna take a shower, get rid of this road dust, and then we'll grab something to eat and pick up a few supplies."

She nodded, falling back on the double bed. It wasn't even a king, and it had a dip in the middle. They hadn't talked about sleeping arrangements.

"I won't be long," he said. "You should rest. You've been

overdoing it. Most people in your condition would still be recovering in a hospital."

"Except you," she muttered, her eyes half-closed. She couldn't picture him letting something like a gunshot wound slow him down.

His chuckle followed him into the bathroom.

ISLAMABAD WAS COMPLETELY different from Peshawar. It was sprawling and green, and unlike other capitals she'd visited, it had a strangely peaceful vibe. Maybe it was because it was so spread out. Every district seemed to have its own shops, restaurants, and a distinct look.

They caught a taxi to Centaurus Mall, one of the more modern shopping complexes in Islamabad.

"It's the best place to get something decent to eat and stock up on supplies," Stitch told her.

And he was right. The mall had tons of stores, selling everything from clothes and shoes to perfume and toiletries. There was also a big food court with a lot of international restaurants.

After Sloane picked up a change of clothes, a hairbrush, toothbrush, and a few other essentials, Stitch suggested they eat at an Italian restaurant on the third floor. It had a stunning view of the city.

"It's incredible," she said, gazing out over the white-topped buildings and domed mosques. In the distance were the faded hills they'd driven through to get here, hazy with low-lying clouds. For once, the weather wasn't sweltering.

Stitch—she was still getting used to calling him that—had cleaned up nicely.

Too nicely.

The casual black shirt he wore was open at the collar, showing off his tanned skin and just a hint of dark chest hair.

And those jeans… She couldn't stop staring at his butt when he walked ahead of her.

Neither could the other women. His dark good looks and muscular build meant he got plenty of attention. Trust him to be the hottest thing this side of the Khyber, while in her loose-fitting clothes, hijab, and face veil, she was practically invisible.

In a futile attempt to highlight her one visible feature, she'd bought eyeliner and rimmed her eyes with kohl. Not that he'd even noticed.

Eating with a face covering was an experience. How did local women manage it? She just kept dropping crumbs all over herself.

"This is gonna take some practice," she muttered, brushing herself off.

"You could take it off while you eat," Stitch suggested, glancing around the restaurant. "You're safe here."

"I'd rather not risk it." Jeremy was out there somewhere. "The CIA has eyes everywhere. What if I'm caught on a security camera or something?"

"I think you're being a little paranoid now," he said with a smile. "Like you said, no one expects you to be in Islamabad."

He was right. She was overreacting.

She took off the face veil but left her headscarf on.

The food was delicious, and after weeks of eating nothing but vegetables and fruit, she devoured a big bowl of creamy pasta.

Stitch did the same, twirling the spaghetti around his fork with surprising ease for such a big-handed guy.

"Mrs. B said you like to cook," she said with a smile, feeling her spirits lift.

"Mrs. B talks too much."

She laughed. "She's really fond of you. She told me so."

"Oh, did she now?"

"She said you used to bring her gifts from America."

He shrugged. "When we flew straight from the airport, yeah. Most of the time, though, we were dodging gunfire and limping across the border bruised and battered. I'm convinced if it weren't for Mrs. B, we'd have died in Peshawar more than once."

Sloane shook her head, but she had a feeling he wasn't exaggerating.

"Do you have family back in the U.S.?"

He shook his head. "Not really. My mother died when I was a teenager, and I never knew my father. I had an uncle, but we've lost touch."

She nodded. "Same as me. My mom passed away when I was young, and my dad when I was seventeen." That day was burned into her memory.

"Sorry to hear that."

She shrugged. "It is what it is. I moved in with my grandparents after my dad… passed away." She hated the word "suicide."

"Losing your parents forces you to grow up fast," he said.

"That's for sure."

Grief, guilt, remorse, trauma therapy, and long emotional talks with her grandmother. It had taken her a long time to deal with what her father had done.

"When do you think I'll be able to go home?" she asked, changing the subject. She didn't want to dwell on her painful past. The future was all that mattered now, even if it was looking a little uncertain.

He finished eating and set down his fork. "Not until Pat talks to his CIA contact and they've arrested Matthew, Jeremy, and whoever else is involved."

"How long do you think that'll take?" she asked quietly.

"I honestly don't know," he said. "Could be a while. These things take time."

"Yeah."

She couldn't expect him to know. He was just as in the dark as she was.

"It feels so weird being stuck here, you know? In limbo. I never thought I'd be in this position. I've always had a stable job, a nice home."

She'd made sure of that. After her dad's death, her home had become her safe haven. And when she'd moved out of her grandmother's house and got her own apartment, it had become her sanctuary.

"Right now, I feel like a fugitive."

"You get used to it," he said. "Living off the radar isn't as hard as you'd think, especially if you've got some cash and a good disguise." He nodded toward the veil on the table.

"I don't have much money," she admitted. "I brought a bit with me in case I couldn't use my credit card, but it's running out."

"I've got it covered," he said with a smile. "You're fine while you're with me. Don't use your card or they'll track you. You can bet they've already tried."

His words warmed her.

She'd be okay as long as she was with him.

But what about when she wasn't with him? And it wasn't just about protection. She'd gotten used to having him around—his strong, reassuring presence at her side. She didn't know what she'd do when he wasn't there anymore.

CHAPTER 21

"You take the bed. I'll be fine on the floor."

They stood there, staring at the bed. It was late, and Sloane was beyond exhausted. Stitch could see it in the dark circles under her eyes and the pale look of her skin. She needed rest, and the bed definitely wasn't big enough for the two of them—not without one of them ending up in the middle.

"Are you sure?" She glanced at him. "There's plenty of space."

"You must be delusional or seriously high on painkillers if you think we're both fitting in that bed."

She laughed. "Suit yourself."

She pulled back the covers and got in. It was true, she didn't take up much space, barely a third of the bed. "You really don't have to sleep on the floor. I'm so drugged up, I'll be out cold in five minutes."

With that, she rolled onto her side and closed her eyes.

He knew he shouldn't.

Ever since she came back from the bathroom in just her shirt, he'd been fighting his growing hard-on. He blamed those long, smooth legs that went on forever. And the way her nipples pressed against the fabric of her shirt.

Fuck.

It had been a relief when she finally slipped under the covers and pulled them up around herself.

Yeah, he was definitely sleeping on the floor. No way was he risking rolling into her during the night.

He adjusted the tightness in his pants, grabbed a pillow off the bed, then paused. Her breathing had already deepened. She was out. The painkillers, mixed with exhaustion, had knocked her right out. She lay on her good arm, her bandaged one folded next to her like a bird with a broken wing.

A wave of protectiveness surged through him. She looked so vulnerable, lying there with her eyes closed, her dark hair spilling over the pillow. He wanted to wrap her in his arms, hold her tight, and protect her from everything until this was all over.

Maybe even kiss the pain away.

He rubbed his forehead. Great, now *he* was fucking delirious.

There was no denying she was a beautiful woman, though. Any guy would struggle to pick the floor over her. Take Matthew, for example. The prick had probably taken one look at her and thought he'd score on that front too.

Recruiting a stunner like Sloane had probably been fun for him. She was single, available, maybe a little lonely. Easy pickings for a smooth-talker like Matthew. He'd wined and dined her—dinner at his place—then seduced her. He'd kissed those cherry-red lips, wrapped those long legs around him...

Stitch threw the pillow back on the bed with a sudden flash of anger.

Jesus.

Then, after he'd reeled her in, the bastard had sent her off on a dangerous mission to a foreign country where she didn't know anyone and was totally alone. Hell, there were a few things Stitch would love to say to Matthew Fuckhead Sullivan, if he ever got the chance.

Stitch pulled off his shirt and stripped down to his boxers. The carpet didn't look too clean. God knows when it had last been vacuumed. This definitely wasn't the Hilton. And Sloane still hadn't moved.

She was right, there was more than enough room. With that in mind, he checked the door, turned off the light, and climbed onto the bed.

STITCH ROUNDED a bend in the mountain road and saw the smoke. It rose in a thick, dark column into the sky, filling him with panic.

He floored the Land Cruiser, kicking up dirt and skidding around corners until he reached the village. The closer he got, the thicker the smoke became.

"Soraya!" He jumped out of the vehicle, the back of the military jeep loaded with supplies from town.

It was like running straight into hell.

The inferno tore through the village, consuming the thatched houses, burning the trees, destroying everything in its path. Gunfire cracked in the distance. He sprinted through the flames, dodging burning debris, heading straight for the house where he lived with his wife.

Thank God, it wasn't on fire. Not yet.

Smoldering embers on the roof told him he only had seconds before it, too, would go up in flames. He barreled through the door, nearly ripping it off its hinges.

"Soraya!"

No answer.

He ran upstairs to the bedroom—and froze.

She was lying on the floor next to the bed, shot multiple times.
No. No! Soraya!

He dropped to his knees, frantically checking her for any sign of life. Nothing. He was too late. There was too much blood.

He pulled her lifeless body into his arms and screamed to the sky, his voice raw with agony.

The heat around him grew unbearable. He couldn't breathe.

Still sobbing, he lifted her up and carried her outside, away from the burning house.

"Soraya," he choked, laying her on the ground. But she could no longer hear him.

"Stitch?" whispered a voice beside him.

She was alive!

"Soraya," he murmured, reaching for her.

"It's okay," she said. "You're having a bad dream."

Thank God. It had felt so real.

"I thought you were dead." He pulled her into his arms. She lay against his chest, her breasts pressed into him.

"Stitch, wake up."

"I am awake, babe. Finally, I'm awake."

The nightmare was over. Soraya was alive. Everything was going to be okay.

She felt so good in his arms. Soft, warm, familiar.

"I've missed you," he whispered.

His hands moved up her back, fingers sliding into her hair. It was as silky as he remembered. Somehow, she'd come back to him.

He held her head, gently guiding her face closer to his.

"Don't worry," he murmured when she hesitated. "It's okay. I'm not letting you go. I won't let anything happen to you."

He kissed her, soft and tender at first. God, he'd missed

this. The feel of her lips, full and sweet—fuller than he remembered.

She moaned softly and opened to him, and he deepened the kiss, claiming her mouth. The longing he'd buried for so long came rushing back.

His hands tangled in her hair, their breaths mingling, heat building between them until it was a swirl of need, want, and pure desire.

He tugged at her blouse, pulling it open. Her cool skin slid against his, and he cupped a breast, soft and round. He teased her nipple as he kissed her more intensely, the heat rising.

She moaned again, a sound that didn't quite fit.

"Oh God, Stitch."

Wait. That wasn't Soraya's voice.

Confused, he snapped out of the dream, his mind slowly making sense of what was real and what wasn't.

Sloane was on top of him, kissing him, her hands gripping his hair. He had a handful of her breast, the nipple firm between his fingers.

His tongue was in her mouth, and she was kissing him back, just as lost in it as he was.

It felt so good.

Too good.

With a groan, he froze. This wasn't right.

Realizing he'd stopped, she opened her eyes and pulled back.

"Stitch?"

He stared at her, horrified.

"Sloane... I... I thought—"

Her eyes were wide and heavy-lidded, her dark hair falling over her shoulders and brushing his bare chest. Her blouse was open, her breasts exposed, full and smooth. In the soft orange glow of the streetlight from the window, she looked sexy as hell. He could still taste her, still feel the heat of her mouth. His body ached with unfulfilled desire, wanting her even as she pulled away.

She rolled off him, looking unsure, cautious.

Fuck. What had he done?

"I'm sorry," he whispered. "I... I thought you were Soraya."

"Soraya?"

He nodded.

"You thought I was your wife?"

He sat up. "Bad dream."

Or maybe a good one, depending on how you looked at it.

She sucked in a breath. "Oh, God. So... you didn't mean to—?"

"No."

There was a painfully awkward pause before he added, "If I came on to you, I'm sorry. It was a mistake. I have these dreams sometimes... they feel so real."

"Oh." She was at a loss for words, and he didn't blame her. What an idiot! How could he have lost control like that?

Getting out of bed, he couldn't even look at her. There was only one thought on his mind, to get out of there. Now. Before he made it any worse.

Avoiding eye contact, he hurried into the bathroom and shut the door, leaving her staring after him.

CHAPTER 22

Oh. My. God.

Sloane stared after Stitch as he bolted into the bathroom. One minute she was trying to wake him up, and the next, she was in his arms, and he was kissing her like his life depended on it.

And, holy hell, it was good.

He was good.

No, he was fantastic. The best kiss ever!

And it was all a mistake?

She shook her head. Embarrassing? No, horrifying! He thought she was his wife!

Holy crap. That must've been one hell of a dream.

Lucky Soraya, getting to kiss him like that every night. Then she cringed.

Soraya was dead. She'd been killed in the attack on his village. It was tragic, and she shouldn't be thinking like that.

Clearly, Stitch still craved his wife. So much that she'd come to him in a dream.

But the way he'd kissed her...

Whoa. Her head was still spinning.

Who would've thought that tough, steel-nerved guy could kiss like that? Then she remembered how he'd taken care of Fatima, how gentle he'd been when he treated her gunshot wound.

Yeah, Stitch had a tender side. He just didn't show it much. Most of the time, he was all hard edges and badass attitude. The sailor, the tough guy.

But he was passionate, too. He'd totally claimed her, kissed her like he owned her as he tore open her blouse, exposing her breasts. His hands, rough and calloused, had sent shivers through her body, and her nipples still reacted just thinking about it.

Oh God.

How was she supposed to look him in the eye after this?

How was she supposed to deal with knowing how good it felt to be wanted by him, consumed by him?

She heard the shower running. He was washing off the taste and smell of her, trying to scrub away his mistake. A heavy ache settled in her chest. He belonged to someone else, but she was the one who wanted him, needed him.

Tonight had only confirmed what she'd been dreading for a while now. That she was hopelessly attracted to him.

The shower kept going, and she tried not to imagine his rock-hard body under the water, his muscles rippling, that chiseled back like a damn marble statue. She tried not to picture that perfect, firm ass just begging to be gripped, or those powerful thighs she couldn't stop thinking about. Was he leaning forward, head down, his strong arms braced against the wall? Was he thinking about her?

She lay down, squeezing her eyes shut, tears burning their way down her cheeks.

Tears of shame. Of want. Of pure, aching desire.

That kiss had only left her craving more. It was all she could think about as she curled up and tried to fall asleep.

The shower was still running.

She exhaled hard, trying to force herself to relax.

After a while, the deep sleep she'd been in before he'd woken her with his mumbling started to creep back. Her eyelids grew heavy.

Somewhere, in the back of her mind, she heard the shower finally stop.

But before he came back to bed, she was asleep.

CHAPTER 23

Stitch left the hotel early the next morning. Blade wasn't arriving until eight, but he needed some space to think. He grabbed a taxi to the airport and got a coffee from one of the pop-up stands outside. As the caffeine hit, he started to feel better. It's what he needed after a restless night.

How could he have done that to Sloane?

How had he confused her with Soraya?

The CIA agent was messing with his subconscious, playing tricks on his mind. And now his mind was playing tricks back.

But damned if she didn't feel good.

There was no denying the intensity of that kiss. The way her body had molded to his, her pelvis pressing into him in all the right places.

That soft moan—that's when he realized she wasn't Soraya.

Fucking hell.

He checked the digital clock above the Arrivals board: 07:57.

Almost time.

Sloane had still been asleep when he left, thank God. Not only couldn't he face her after what had happened, but the airport wasn't safe—too many cameras, too many prying eyes. They'd be monitoring every entry and exit point, watching for her.

He tossed the empty coffee cup in the trash and headed to Arrivals.

The more he tried not to think about last night, the more it gnawed at him. He'd come onto her in his sleep, kissed her in his dream…

And she'd kissed him back.

That's what really threw him. She hadn't pushed him away, hadn't slapped him, hadn't even told him to stop. She'd kissed him back, like she meant it. Soft, sensual kisses that had stirred his blood.

Up until now, she hadn't shown any sign she felt anything for him. Their relationship was strictly business—follow Omari, find out what's going on. At least, that's what he thought. But she'd kissed him with the same passion he'd had for Soraya. What a mess.

What was he going to say to her when he got back to the hotel?

He checked the time again. At least Blade would be there, offering a distraction. They had to focus on finding Jeremy, anyway. That's why they were here.

No need to bring up his stupid mistake.

He shook his head, cringing at the memory.

Idiot.

Passengers started trickling out into the Arrivals hall. The flight from Washington D.C. had landed. The crowd thickened, and then he saw Blade, grinning at him with his rucksack slung over one shoulder.

They bro-hugged, clapping each other on the back.

"Good to see you, man," Stitch said.

"You too," Blade replied.

"How was the flight?"

"Don't know. Slept through most of it."

Stitch laughed. Blade hadn't changed.

"Pat figured I could use some backup, huh?" Stitch asked. Joe's dad treated them all like sons after losing his own. He used to be a SEAL commander, but now he ran Blackthorn Security, a private outfit comprised of ex-special ops guys and SEALs. They handled everything from kidnapping and ransom to hostage rescue and black ops for the government and from what he'd heard, they were getting quite the reputation.

"Yeah, you know how he is. Sent me to help you track down this CIA handler, Jeremy Vale."

Stitch nodded. "Yeah, I've got a lead. We'll check it out tonight. How's Lilly?" Blade's wife, a military software designer, was smart and beautiful, and Stitch was pleased they'd finally gotten together.

"She's pissed I'm here. Too close to Afghanistan for her liking."

Blade had nearly died in Afghanistan last year, rescuing Lilly from the Taliban. He'd gotten her out, but not before being captured himself. Stitch had tracked him down and helped him escape.

"We won't be crossing the border," Stitch assured him. "Vale is here in Islamabad."

"Glad to hear it. So… how's Soraya?"

Stitch froze. He'd forgotten Blade didn't know. No one outside of Afghanistan did. After the attack, he'd gone dark for six months, totally off-grid. When he finally resurfaced, he was too focused on tracking Omari to tell anyone.

"What's wrong?" Blade picked up on his expression. "Something happen?"

Only Blade—and now Sloane—could read him like that.

"Yeah," Stitch muttered. "Something happened. Not long after you left."

Blade stopped walking and turned to face him. "Tell me."

So Stitch did. He told him about the attack, the fire, and how he'd carried Soraya's bullet-riddled body out of their burning house.

Blade didn't interrupt, just listened.

"They shot her," Stitch hissed. "The bastards broke in and mowed her down, just like they did her father and the other elders. Then they torched the village."

"Jesus, man. I'm so sorry." Blade stared at him, shocked. "Why didn't you say anything?"

Stitch shook his head.

He'd been lost in his grief, barely surviving. That wasn't something you just shared, not even with your brothers in the unit.

"Is this why you're after Omari? He's responsible?"

Blade was always quick to connect the dots.

"Yeah, he's one of them," Stitch said. "Omari's running the cartel. His men attacked the village because the elders wouldn't sanction their smuggling route. Through Omari, I found Rasul Ghani. He's a lower-level drug lord, keeps the poppy farmers on a tight leash. He met with Omari in Peshawar."

"And why are these assholes still breathing?" Blade's blue eyes locked on Stitch's. They didn't need to say anything more.

"That's where Sloane comes in."

"Ah," Blade nodded. "The rookie CIA agent."

"Yeah. I noticed her tailing Omari while I was tracking him. She was watching him, too—taking pictures." He paused. "So, we had a little chat."

He didn't mention that she'd been naked at the time. Blade didn't need to know that part.

"Turns out, Omari was her target, too. We teamed up on surveillance and figured out her handler, Jeremy, was involved. He and Omari meet every Thursday in an old graveyard outside Peshawar. Nobody knows about it, not even Omari's bodyguards."

Blade nodded. "Jeremy's not his real name, by the way. It's an alias."

Stitch wasn't surprised.

"His real name is Jonathan Hill. Pat asked his buddy at the Agency. Hill was part of that specialist unit I told you about. He's got connections in Helmand. Pat thinks he's either running the show or working with the Afghans."

"That's exactly what I was afraid of," Stitch admitted. "Until we take these guys down, Sloane can't go back home."

"Where is she now?"

"Holed up at our hotel. After the hit on her in Peshawar, she's better off with me."

"Damn straight. I still can't believe the Agency tried to take out their own agent."

"Yeah, it's gotta be her boss. He's the only one she told about it."

"Matthew Sullivan?"

"I think it was more than just business between them. He seduced her, recruited her, and then tossed her into the fire."

"Classy guy," Blade said sarcastically.

"Exactly."

"Pat said he'd call tonight with an update, but in the meantime, let's track down Hill, or rather Jeremy Vale, and see what he knows."

They stepped into a taxi headed for the hotel. Blade handed him a small packet.

Stitch opened it. "A USB device?"

"Sort of. It plugs into his phone and copies everything off his memory card."

"Nifty," Stitch said. "If we can get to his phone."

"We just need a good distraction," Blade grinned. "How hard can it be?"

Stitch thought about Sloane. Jeremy had to be wondering what happened to her after the failed hit. "I think I've got just the distraction."

He explained his plan.

"You think she'll go for it?" Blade asked, doubtfully.

"I'm sure she will. She wants this over as much as I do. If this is how we bring these guys down, she'll do it."

"Great. Can't wait to meet Agent Carmichael."

"She's not what you'd expect," Stitch said without thinking. "I think they recruited her just for this job. A one-off. She speaks the language and blends in, but they only gave her ten months of training. She's way out of her depth."

"Lucky she's got you, then."

Stitch didn't respond.

Blade changed the subject, filling him in on news from home. "Anna and Cole just had a baby boy," he said with a grin. "Cole's over the moon. Already bought him a tiny camo onesie."

Stitch chuckled. He'd worked with Cole before. He was a damn fine operator. Stitch had never met Anna, Cole's wife, but he'd heard they used to know each other a long time ago, but had parted ways after an op had gone south in Africa. Eventually, the conversation circled back to Afghanistan.

"Seriously, man, I'm really sorry to hear about Soraya."

"Thanks. It's been over a year now, so, you know—"

Blade wasn't buying it.

"You should've called. We would've been there for you."

"I know, but I had to handle it my way. I'm okay now—or I will be, once I tie up a few loose ends."

"You mean Omari and Rasul?"

Stitch didn't need to answer. Blade knew.

"Let me know if you need help with that," Blade offered.

"Thanks, but it's something I gotta do myself."

"I get it. But you might need someone watching your six."

Stitch looked at him. "It could mean going back to Afghanistan."

Blade shrugged. "So be it. Just don't tell Lilly."

Stitch smiled weakly. "Thanks. That means a lot."

And he meant it.

CHAPTER 24

Sloane jumped up as the door opened, and Stitch walked in, followed by one of the tallest guys she'd ever seen. Stitch was big, but this guy was a giant—easily six foot five or six, with a chiseled jaw and sharp, piercing eyes. He even had to duck to avoid hitting his head on the doorframe.

"Sloane, this is Blade. Blade, meet Agent Sloane Carmichael."

She shook his hand. It practically swallowed hers.

"Nice to meet you," she said. "Call me Sloane."

"Hey, Sloane. Sorry to hear about your arm." Stitch had given her a sling to keep the weight off, but the bandage was a different story.

"Thanks." She grimaced at Stitch. "I tried redoing it, but it's not tight enough."

"I'll fix it. Take a seat." He pulled out a chair and gestured for her to sit down.

Blade dropped his rucksack on the floor and pulled out his phone. "I'm gonna call Lilly real quick. She'll want to know I made it here in one piece."

Stitch nodded as Blade stepped out of the room, but not before giving them a curious glance.

Sloane sat down, and let Stitch take off the sling and ease her arm out. "You'll need to undo your shirt so I can get to it."

She hesitated, meeting his gaze in the mirror. Still no mention of last night.

He looked away.

So that's how it's gonna be, is it? Just pretend like it didn't happen.

Fine.

She unbuttoned her shirt and slid it off her injured arm. He helped, gently holding her elbow. She wanted to pull away, especially after last night's disaster, but she needed his help.

"Let me take a look," he said, in medic mode, calm and professional.

He stood right in front of her, his legs between hers, wearing jeans that hugged his thighs a little too perfectly and a black T-shirt stretched over his muscular chest.

Memories of last night hit her like a tidal wave.

His hand in her hair, holding her head still as he kissed her.

His rock-solid body under hers, their legs tangled together.

She sucked in a ragged breath and focused on his hands as he undid her bandage, trying not to notice how close he was or the clean, masculine scent that filled the air. His chest was inches away, and if she looked down—

Hell, no.

She wasn't going there.

Then the bandage was off.

Stitch frowned as he inspected the wound.

He leaned in closer to get a better look. His breath brushed against her chest, making her nipples react under her bra. She had to fight the urge to grip his hair and draw his head down to hers.

"What?" she asked, her mind barely able to focus.

"It's a little inflamed. I'm gonna give you another antibiotic shot." He straightened up.

"Is it bad?"

"Not too bad, but I don't want it to get infected."

He turned and dug through his medical kit, pulling out a syringe and a small vial. After drawing the liquid into the syringe, he tapped it to get rid of the air bubbles.

"This'll sting for a second," he said before jabbing it into her shoulder.

She gritted her teeth at the sting.

"Sorry."

He removed the needle, capped it, and tossed it into the wastepaper basket. She remembered seeing him do the same thing with Fatima.

"All done," he said. "Now let me rewrap it."

He placed a fresh strip of gauze over her stitches. The skin was puckered and warm to the touch. She shivered as he smoothed down the edges.

Then came the torturous part—winding the bandage around her arm.

With every turn, the back of his hand brushed against her breast. By the time he was finished, she was a hot mess of molten heat. Any longer, and she would have spontaneously combusted.

"Thanks," she croaked when he was done.

He gave a tight nod. "No problem."

She slipped her arm back into her sleeve, buttoning up her shirt as fast as she could. He studied her, without saying a word.

Was he thinking about last night, too? About how he'd ripped her shirt open? Maybe, because his gaze grew heated, and his eyes drifted back up to meet hers.

She refused to look at him. She couldn't.

"Sloane, I—"

He didn't get to finish because Blade walked back into the room.

"Lilly says hi." Blade nodded at Stitch. "She was really sorry to hear about Soraya."

Sloane slipped the sling back on.

"Thanks," he mumbled.

If Blade noticed the tension in the room, he didn't comment on it.

"So, you gonna fill me in on this lead?" Blade asked, sitting on the edge of the bed.

Stitch leaned against the dresser. "Yeah. My contact said a guy matching Jeremy's description was spotted at the basement bar in the Serena Hotel. It's a hidden expat bar. He drinks there several times a week."

"Are you sure it's him?" Sloane asked.

"Yeah, I showed him that photograph I took at the graveyard."

"He didn't tell me his last name." She frowned. "Not even his fake last name."

"Yeah, that's the name he's travelling on. He obviously has fake identity documents too, probably issued by the Agency."

Sloane shook her head. Obviously, she was important enough to know those kinds of details.

"I'm guessing he didn't want you to know his full name so you couldn't track him," Stitch explained. "Hotel bookings, flights, and so on."

The thought hadn't even crossed her mind.

So much deception. She really wasn't cut out for this spy stuff.

"When are we going to check out the bar?" she asked.

A look passed between Stitch and Blade—just a flicker of an eyelid, something subtle, but she picked up on it.

"What?" she asked.

Blade looked a little surprised, but Stitch grinned.

"She's good at reading people," Stitch said. "Knows what you're thinking before you do. Not much gets past her."

Blade raised his eyebrows. "Nice skill to have."

"I guess it is," Sloane replied. "But it kind of ruins the fun when you see everything coming."

Blade chuckled. "I can see that."

Except last night. She hadn't seen that coming—his gentle words, his protective tone.

I'll never let anything happen to you.

She'd wanted to believe he was talking to her. She'd wanted to believe it was real.

And that kiss…

Yeah, she definitely hadn't expected that.

"We've got an idea we want to run by you," Stitch said, his eyes on her.

Blade pursed his lips. "His idea, but it's a good one."

"Okay." She felt a nervous flutter in her stomach.

Stitch continued. "When we find Jeremy, we need to distract him long enough to download everything off his phone."

Blade held up a small USB-like device.

"This plugs into his phone and downloads the data," Stitch explained. "It only takes a few seconds, but we need him distracted."

"And that's where you come in," Blade added.

"Me?"

Wasn't she supposed to be laying low? And wasn't Jeremy the one who'd tried to have her killed?

"What better way to shock Jeremy than you showing up out of nowhere?"

"I don't get it." The nervous flutter turned into an all-round bad feeling.

"Well, what if you confronted him, like you were looking

for him?" Stitch said. "He is your handler, after all. You got shot, so naturally you'd want answers from him."

"If he wasn't a corrupt piece of crap, you mean?"

Stitch grinned. "Exactly."

She looked from Stitch to Blade. They both had that smug look, like they'd already made up their minds. This was happening whether she liked it or not. They were easier to read than a kid's book.

"You want me to confront him at the bar?" she asked, shaking her head. "Am I supposed to just walk up to him and be like, 'Hey Jeremy, remember me? You tried to have me killed?'"

"Something like that," Stitch mumbled.

Blade tried—and failed—to hide a smile.

She crossed her arms. "Well, you're right about one thing, it would shock the hell out of him."

"That's the point," Stitch said.

"We'd only need a minute, tops." Blade nodded toward the device. "It works fast."

"He'll know I'm here," she warned.

They both nodded.

"He might try to kill me again."

Another look passed between them, this one more obvious.

"Yeah, it's possible," Stitch admitted. "But if we want to bring these guys down, we need evidence. His phone is a burner, but it might have messages or numbers that can help us track the others."

"Or use it against him in court," Blade added.

She thought it over. They were right. Even if they stopped the drug shipment, they still wouldn't have anything solid on Jeremy or Matthew.

Heat rose in her chest as she thought about Matthew.

He'd seduced her, convinced her to join his shady CIA

unit, and then sent her off to die. Had he known all along she wasn't coming back? Was the whole no-contact rule just a way for him to remain unaccountable?

Asshole.

"If you don't want to, we'll figure something else out," Stitch said. "I get it if you're nervous. You did just get shot."

Anger coursed through her veins. No way. Jeremy and Matthew were going down, and if this was going to help it happen, she was in.

"I'll do it," she said firmly.

He narrowed his gaze. "You're sure?"

"Absolutely."

Blade slapped his thigh. "Great, we're on!"

Stitch grinned, and she saw something like pride in his eyes. "I knew you'd say yes."

Her heart did a teeny-tiny flip. Would she ever stop wanting him?

CHAPTER 25

Stitch stared at Sloane, his jaw practically hitting the floor.

When he'd told her to buy a dress for tonight, he hadn't expected her to come back with that.

The dusky pink dress hugged her like a silk scarf, showing off every damn curve. It highlighted the swell of her breasts, cinched at her waist, then flared gently over her hips and cute ass, draping around her knees in a soft swirl.

The color was perfect for her pale complexion and dark hair. She'd even found a pair of matching stilettos that made her legs look impossibly long. He couldn't stop staring at them.

The flowing, three-quarter sleeves hid the bandage on her arm, and her hair was blow-dried into soft waves that cascaded over her shoulders and down her back. On top of it all, she smelled incredible.

"Do I look the part?" She cringed at his stunned expression. "Is it too much?"

"No," he said, quickly. Fuck. Too obvious. "It's perfect," he added, and watched as her cheeks turned pink. If he'd thought she was sexy before, he'd been way off. She was off-the-scale exquisite.

As they walked through the lobby of the luxurious Serena Hotel, he wasn't the only one noticing. Men—young, old, didn't matter—sent her appreciative looks.

Feeling a surge of possessiveness, he took her arm. She shot him a surprised glance but didn't say anything.

There was something else, too. She'd lined her eyes, making them stand out even more. Mascara darkened her lashes, and when she blinked at him, his stomach did flips.

He wasn't used to that. Nerves weren't usually something he suffered with.

"Blade's waiting for us in the basement bar," he said, nodding toward an ornate staircase that curved down from the foyer.

Blade had gone ahead in a separate taxi to case the bar and make sure their target was there. Never walk into a situation unprepared. As they headed toward the stairs, a liveried bellhop stepped in front of them. "Sorry, this area is reserved for a private function."

Stitch pulled out his American passport.

Sloane, without any ID on her, leaned forward to give the bellhop an eyeful of her cleavage. The guy turned red and quickly lifted the gold rope, letting them through without another word. No local woman would ever pull a move like that.

"Nice one," Stitch whispered as they descended the marble stairs into the stylishly lit basement lobby. Pot plants flanked the corners, and recessed lighting gave the place a romantic vibe.

"It's all I could think of," she whispered back.

Once again, she'd read the situation perfectly.

They reached a marble lobby, with a single door. Stitch opened it, and they stepped into another world.

A long mahogany bar stretched along one side, with three stylish bartenders mixing cocktails behind it. In the corner, a pianist on a grand piano played smooth jazz that barely rose above the hum of conversation and bursts of laughter. The floors were covered with rich Persian rugs, leather sofas, and ornate cocktail tables. Soft lighting cast a warm, intimate glow over the room.

"Wow," Sloane whispered, glancing around.

The bar was full, but no one paid any attention to them. The crowd was well-dressed and elegant. The air was thick with the smell of expensive cologne and perfume.

Blade had texted earlier to confirm their target was here —already on his second gin and tonic.

"There's Vale." Stitch nodded toward a red-haired man sitting alone at the far end of the bar, nursing his drink and reading a newspaper. A few seats down, Blade lounged with a beer in hand, casually texting on his phone.

Stitch glanced at Sloane. She looked beautiful and determined, putting on a brave face. His chest tightened.

"Ready?" he asked softly.

She gave a nervous nod. "As I'll ever be."

The plan was simple—she'd walk over and distract Vale. His phone was either in his jacket pocket or on the bar next to him. Blade would swipe the phone, download the data using the device, and put it back before Vale noticed.

Stitch was on standby in case anything went sideways. The weight of his Glock at his ankle was a welcome reminder. It wasn't a foolproof plan, and a lot could go wrong. But it was worth a shot.

"Go ahead. Remember, I've got your back," Stitch said.

She gave him a grateful smile before heading toward her handler.

CHAPTER 26

Sloane walked toward Jeremy, her heart pounding so hard she thought it might leap right out of her chest.

Breathe. You can do this.

She must be insane—confronting the very man who'd put a hit out on her. Her handler, of all people. But what other choice did she have? Blade and Stitch were counting on her, and if she didn't do this, they'd never get the evidence they needed to bring these guys down. No matter how terrified she was inside, the plan was a good one.

If it worked.

As she got closer to Jeremy, she realized with a jolt of panic that his phone wasn't on the bar counter like they'd expected. Her heart leapt into her throat. No phone meant no data, and without that, this entire operation could blow up in their faces. She shot a glance toward Blade, her pulse quickening. He remained calm, his eyes zeroing in on Jeremy's jacket pocket.

It was in there.

She exhaled slowly, forcing her shoulders to relax. She had to keep it together. The last thing she needed was to let Jeremy see her sweat. If he even suspected something was off, he'd bolt, and everything they'd planned would fall apart. She had to be calm, confident, and completely in control.

Her breath caught for a second as she reached Jeremy. Every instinct screamed for her to turn around and walk away, but she couldn't. She planted herself next to him and flashed a smile that she hoped looked more poised than she felt.

"Hello, Jeremy."

He glanced up, eyes widening as he nearly knocked over his drink.

"Sloane! Jesus. What are you doing here?"

The look on his face was priceless. He'd gone pale, like he'd seen a ghost. Jeremy Vale, the smooth, unflappable CIA handler, was completely blindsided. Good.

"Surprised to see me?" she asked sweetly, raising an eyebrow. Her voice was laced with mock innocence, though she could barely hear herself over the pounding in her ears. She leaned casually on the bar, giving Blade the perfect opportunity to do his job.

Confusion, worry, doubt—all of it crossed his face in an instant. He fumbled for words, still trying to collect himself. "I—I thought you were in Peshawar. What are you doing here?"

"Looking for you." She shook her head. "Boy, you're a hard man to track down."

Behind him, Blade slipped his hand into Jeremy's jacket pocket. He pulled out the phone and got to work. Sloane was amazed at how smooth he was. Like a professional pickpocket. No one had noticed a thing.

Jeremy managed to regain some composure. "Your orders

were to stay in Peshawar and keep an eye on Omari. You shouldn't be here."

"You didn't answer my email," she said. "Those men looked important—Afghans, I think. Did you see my video? I was expecting some sort of response."

Jeremy opened his mouth, then closed it again.

It was worth it, just to see him floundering like a fish.

She leaned in closer. "I knew I was onto something when someone took a shot at me."

He blinked, stunned.

"Can you believe that?" she went on. "At first, I thought it was a mistake. Then I remembered—one of Omari's guards saw me right after I took the video. My cover's been compromised. I think you should pull me out."

Blade slid the phone back into Jeremy's jacket pocket and moved away. He gave Sloane the slightest nod. It was done.

"I—I'll speak to Matthew," Jeremy stammered. "Maybe you're right. Maybe it's time to pull you out."

She beamed at him. "Thank you. That's a relief. I wasn't sure what to do, and Matthew told me not to contact him."

"Where are you staying?" Jeremy got to his feet. "Let me give you a lift. I've got a car here."

"Oh, no. I don't want to put you out." She patted his arm. "I'll just get a taxi."

With that, she turned and walked back across the room.

Jeremy grabbed his jacket and started to go after her, but he didn't get far. Stitch bumped into him spilling his beer all over Jeremy's expensive shirt. "Shit! I am so sorry."

Jeremy stopped, momentarily stunned.

Stitch stepped in front of him. "I really am sorry. Let me buy you a drink to make it up to you."

Jeremy hesitated, swiping at his shirt. "That's okay. I've got to go."

He tried to push past, but Stitch caught his arm. "Listen, I feel really bad. You sure I can't buy you a drink? It's the least I can do."

Jeremy glanced over Stitch's shoulder, watching as Sloane disappeared out the door.

CHAPTER 27

"We got it," Stitch said as soon as he and Blade stepped into the hotel room. Sloane had gone ahead in a waiting taxi. It had been crucial to get her out of there as quickly as possible.

She sat on the bed, face flushed, eyes gleaming. He had the sudden urge to pull her into his arms and kiss her.

"Everything went according to plan," Blade added with a grin.

"When I didn't see his phone on the bar, I freaked out," she admitted, crossing her legs.

That dress.

Jesus, it was messing with his head.

The soft material shifted as she moved, briefly revealing perfect, creamy, kissable skin before she smoothed it down again.

"I saw him tuck it into his jacket pocket," Blade said, pulling out the device. "It's all here." He handed it to Sloane, who held it like it was a sacred treasure.

"Let's see what we've got," Stitch suggested.

Blade pulled a laptop out of his rucksack, placed it on the

dresser, and powered it up. Sloane passed the device back to him, and he slid it into the USB port. They gathered around the computer and Stitch caught a whiff of her perfume—the new one she must've been wearing tonight. It was heady, intoxicating… just like her.

Damn that dream.

If he hadn't kissed her, he wouldn't know how sweet she tasted or how good it felt to hold her in his arms. It would have been easier not to know. Now, he couldn't stop thinking about it.

He tensed as her hair tumbled over her shoulder, brushing against his hand. Soft and silky. Was there no end to the torture? Breathing in, he asked, "What's on it?"

"Almost there," Blade replied, tapping a few keys. A folder popped open, displaying a list of phone numbers. "Here's his call log."

"Oh, God." Sloane's face went pale as she scanned the numbers.

"What?" Blade glanced over his shoulder.

"That's Matthew's number." She pointed at the screen, her finger had a slight tremor. "Or at least, it's the number he gave me. I've dialed it enough times to recognize it."

"Makes sense Jeremy would be calling him," Stitch reasoned. "He was his boss too."

"It doesn't prove he was involved in the drug trafficking," Blade added. "But it does establish a connection."

"Most of these are going to be burner phones." Stitch nodded to the rest of the numbers. There were no contacts associated with them. No contacts in the phone at all.

Blade nodded. "Yeah, but that doesn't mean we can't trace them. I'll send this to Anna at HQ. She might be able to track where they were used."

"Too bad we can't hear the conversations," Sloane mused.

"We'd have to plant a bug for that," Blade said. "Wasn't enough time."

"On the bright side, we'll still get his close contacts." Stitch stepped away from Sloane, her perfume was making him lose focus. "Even if we don't know who they are." He was way too close to burying his face in her neck, letting his lips wander along her soft skin. Christ, he really needed to pull himself together. This was getting out of hand.

Soraya's face flashed through his mind, but he pushed the memory aside. For once, he didn't want to dwell on her or feel the weight of that sadness. Right now, he was with one of his team brothers and a beautiful woman. Couldn't he just enjoy the moment? He wasn't going to act on anything, but there was no harm in appreciating her presence and feeling a little thrill. Just being a regular guy for a change.

Blade sent the file off to Anna, then shut the laptop. "Alright, you two. I'm going to head to my room, call Lilly, and then crash. How about we meet for breakfast? Say 0800?"

"Sounds good," Stitch agreed, thumping him on the shoulder.

Sloane smiled and said goodnight.

Stitch knew his buddy was giving them breathing space. The chemistry between him and Sloane was too tense to ignore, and Blade was no fool. Stitch had caught his quick glance at the double bed before leaving, but he hadn't commented on it. It was too soon for jokes about him and Sloane.

Now that Blade had left, an awkward silence fell over the room.

"Um, I guess I'll go take a shower," Sloane said, straightening up.

Stitch sighed. They needed to clear the air before it self-combusted around them.

"Listen, about last night." He blurted out the words before he could stop himself. "It was a mistake. It won't happen again."

She gave him a cautious look.

He decided to lighten the mood. In the Navy, humor was often the best way to cope with tough situations. "But if it does, you have my permission to slap me."

He got a weak smile in response.

"I'm serious," he added with a grin. "If I cross a line, wake me up. Kick me in the shins if you have to."

"Okay." Her shoulders eased and some of the pressure dissipated. "Just remember you said that. I don't want to get wrestled to the ground because you think you're under attack."

Wrestling her to the ground—now *there* was an image.

"I promise I'll never hurt you."

Her beautiful eyes accentuated by makeup fixed on him. They were filled with something he hadn't noticed before.

Desire.

His pulse quickened. It wouldn't take much. All he'd have to do was close the distance between them—a few feet at the most—take her in his arms and kiss the living daylights out of her. He'd peel off that dress inch by inch and kiss his way down her beautiful body. He'd make her moan again, like she had last night.

God help him.

Fixing his gaze on the wall behind her—anything not to look at her—he said, "Go ahead."

She brushed past him, the fabric of her dress grazing his leg as she moved. Once she was safely in the bathroom, he took off his shirt and tossed it onto the bed. Then he kicked off his shoes. At least they'd cleared the air. He could always sleep on the floor if things got weird, but after last night, he doubted she'd budge from her side of the bed.

Stitch lay back, trying to shove the enticing thoughts about Sloane out of his mind.

Nope. It wasn't damn well working.

Frustrated, he got up, grabbed a bottle of water from the mini-bar, and chugged it down in one go. With a superhuman effort, he turned his thoughts to the problem at hand. He was now responsible for a rookie agent with a price on her head. Both her handler and her boss wanted her dead, and the only thing standing in their way were him and Blade.

Still, she couldn't have better protection. Nobody was getting to her through them.

Faced with the seriousness of her situation, his body cooled, and he felt more in control.

Then Sloane emerged, all flushed and pink, from the bathroom, and wrapped in a fluffy, white towel. Water glistened on her shoulders, and damp tendrils stuck to her neck. Her hair was twisted up in a messy bun.

Oh, *fuck.*

As she slid past him, he caught a whiff of fragrant soap and imagined what her skin must taste like. He wanted to lick those droplets right off her glistening body.

"My turn."

He leaped off the bed like someone had stuck a hot poker up his ass and disappeared into the bathroom before she noticed the rock-hard erection straining against his pants.

Much to his dismay, the room was steamy and still smelled like her—soap mixed with her perfume. Her cocktail dress hung on a hook behind the door.

Haunting him.

Grimacing, he stripped off his jeans and boxers and glared at his hard-on.

This was *her* fault.

All he had to do was think about her, and he was standing at attention. On the bright side, at least he knew everything still worked. It had been over a year since he'd sprung to life with this kind of enthusiasm, so in some respects, it was a relief. In others, it was uncomfortable, humiliating, and downright disturbing.

He turned on the water and stepped under the hot jets. The steam wrapped around his body, but all he could think about was her. How she'd stood here naked only moments before.

Had she been thinking about him?

He tilted his head into the spray, letting it beat gently against his closed eyelids. Heat crept through his body, easing some of the tension. Almost unconsciously, his hand slid to his cock, and he began stroking himself. What would it feel like to be inside her? To sink into her warmth, hear her moan in pleasure?

He groaned as his cock throbbed in his hand. He shouldn't be doing this to himself. It would only leave him frustrated, unfulfilled, even more confused. Yet he couldn't seem to help it.

He'd built walls around himself for so long, consumed by grief, not allowing anything in but the need for revenge. But somehow, she'd broken through. She'd gotten under his skin.

Now here he was, fantasizing about her. About all the things he wanted to do to her.

He pictured her wet, gleaming body, as if she were right there in the shower with him. He'd hold her tight, claiming her mouth with his, kissing her until she couldn't breathe.

"Jesus, Sloane," he muttered, as his hand moved faster, gripping harder. Heat crept into his face, but it wasn't just from the steamy water. All his focus was on the rhythm, on finding some release.

If he could just come, maybe he'd finally get her out of his system. The rush of endorphins might leave him relaxed enough to get some sleep.

Next to her.

Fuck. Who was he kidding?

The fantasy took hold. He'd kiss her breasts, feel her nipples harden against his tongue. Her neck would arch back, sighing in ecstasy. Her fingers would tangle in his hair, holding him close.

His cock jerked in his hand—he was close.

Then, he'd work his way down, nuzzling the soft curls between her legs. She'd groan and clutch at him, holding him to her. Slowly, he'd part her with his tongue and taste her.

His cock swelled painfully as the tension built. A growl escaped the back of his throat, and he braced himself against the wall with one hand as the first wave of pleasure hit him.

He'd taste her sweetness, feel her thighs tremble as she struggled to stay standing. He'd hold her up, gripping her soft, round ass, while he buried his face into her again and again.

She'd cry out his name as she came, her body quivering in his arms.

He moaned into the steaming water, his hand moving like a piston. The heat built in his groin, pooling low until it exploded out of him. Stars danced behind his eyes as he released, emptying himself.

She'd climax in soft spasms, clutching his hair and holding on for dear life.

"Sloane—" The last wave of pleasure ripped through him, leaving him drained and trembling.

Holy fuck.

He leaned against the wall, trying to catch his breath as he calmed down.

Goddamnit. He was still too fucking hot, so he blasted himself with cold water, neutralizing the desire still pounding through his body.

Better.

Now he could think straight again.

Stitch finished washing, ignoring the flicker of guilt tugging at the back of his mind. Better this than losing control and jumping her in the middle of the night. He didn't want Sloane to have to fend him off, despite the permission he'd jokingly given. He didn't want her thinking he couldn't keep it together, because nothing could be further from the truth.

Wrapping a towel around his waist, he opened the bathroom door. The room was so fogged up, he couldn't see his hand in front of his face. Sloane had switched off the light but left his bedstand lamp on.

To show him the way. To say: *It's okay. Let's try this again.*

But with an unspoken reminder.

Keep your hands to yourself.

She was wrapped up in nothing but the shirt she'd worn the night before, her long legs tangled in the sheets. His cock, at least for now, was blissfully calm as he gazed at her sleeping form.

Good.

Problem solved.

He slipped into bed beside her and switched off the lamp.

CHAPTER 28

Sloane stretched out and touched a leg. A hairy, male leg.

It felt nice, and for a second, she thought she was back in D.C., in Matthew's bed. Then she opened her eyes, and everything rushed back.

Budget motel.
Islamabad.
Him.

She jerked her leg away and stared at the window on her side of the room. The blinds were drawn, but light streamed in from underneath and around the sides. It was morning.

Matthew had tried to kill her. He was one of the bad guys.

Fully awake now, she replayed the events from last night —the hotel bar, Jeremy, the look on his face when he saw her standing there. Even though she'd enjoyed the moment, she couldn't muster a smile. It was still such a shock, they wanted her dead. She knew too much about their heroine importing scheme.

Still, it had felt good to confront him like that. It was now a game of cat and mouse, but they were winning. The fuck-you message she'd delivered last night had said: *You're going down, buster. You're not going to get me.*

And it was all thanks to Stitch.

How crazy was it that a month ago, she'd arrived in this city with nothing but a case of clothes and an assignment? Now here she was, teamed up with two Navy SEAL operators, about to take down a drug trafficking ring. It was surreal.

This had been the weirdest, most insane month of her life. She was now a CIA agent on her first mission. She'd been shot, met a man who made her pulse race, and now she was helping to dismantle a drug cartel. Real life would seem boring after this.

Then again, boring would be a relief.

Boring was safe. It meant she could go home, and not worry that a lone gunman on a motorcycle was going to take her out as soon as she let her guard down.

One thing she knew for sure—she wasn't going back to the CIA.

No freakin' way.

She was done with the Agency. It was pretty clear that the life of an agent wasn't for her. She'd take the chaos and mayhem of a school day over this any time.

Except for Stitch.

She could never regret meeting him—her scarred, rough, and damaged sailor.

Sitting up in bed, she looked over at him, still sleeping soundly. He was on his back, his broad chest rising and falling steadily. She admired his naked torso, the powerful muscles now relaxed in sleep, the tattoo winding down his arm.

She imagined what it would be like to caress the patch of hair on his chest, trace it down to his belly button, and over his chiseled abs.

"Sleep well?" asked a deep, growly voice beside her.

She gasped, her eyes darting to his face. Had he caught her staring?

"Uh, yeah, thanks," she replied, coloring. "You?"

"Fine." He tossed the sheet back and strode to the bathroom wearing nothing but his boxers. She knew she shouldn't, but her gaze dropped to his firm, muscular butt. The kind that demanded attention.

Once the door was shut, she sprung out of bed and reached for her clothes, wincing as she did so. Her arm still ached, even though the shot he'd given her had helped. She hadn't asked him to redress the bandage last night, since she'd dozed off before he'd gotten out of the shower, but she had managed to apply the gauze and a strip of band-aid she'd found rummaging through his medical kit.

He emerged, pulling on jeans and a T-shirt.

"Let me see your arm," he said, gesturing to the stool beside the dresser. "The band-aid's fine for nighttime, but you need to keep it covered during the day."

She sat and tried not to move as he wrapped the dressing around her arm. Those massive, scarred hands—so gentle. She still felt them holding her hips, moving over her back, in her hair.

I'll never let you go.

Words she longed to hear, but they were for someone else.

Not her. Never her.

A melancholy slapped her in the face, and she sighed.

"You okay?" He was looking down at her, his gaze narrowed.

"Oh, yeah. I'm fine."

"Don't forget the sling."

She nodded and got up. She slid her arm in and looped it over her head, wincing at the movement.

"Here, let me." He straightened it for her, lifting her hair out from beneath the band.

Now he was just messing with her. She took a step back. "I'm okay, thanks."

He moved away with a little nod. "Sloane, there's something you should know."

She bit her lip. "What?"

Her heart skipped a beat. Was he going to tell her she was on her own? That he and Blade could no longer protect her? That they were going after Omari themselves?

"The day I went to the graveyard to take out Omari—"

"Yeah?"

"I overheard the date the shipment is leaving Karachi."

She gasped. "Why didn't you tell me?"

He sighed. "I couldn't trust you. I knew you'd tell Matthew."

She fell silent, but his words gnawed at her.

"You were right not to," she admitted, eventually. "I called Matthew that night and told him everything. If I'd known about the shipment, I would've told him that too."

Stitch just nodded.

"I can't believe how naive I was." She shook her head. "I trusted him. I thought he… I thought he cared about me," she corrected. "But he was using me this whole time."

"You weren't to know."

"I should've figured it out." She looked up at him. "You did."

"I've had years of practice. You're new to this."

"I'm quitting the Agency," she said quietly.

He didn't seem surprised.

"This isn't who I am. I'm not the girl who chases bad guys, gets shot at, and takes down drug dealers. I'm a teacher. I like being a teacher and I don't care if that makes me boring."

"You could never be boring," he murmured, softly.

She barely heard him. "Besides, I'm a terrible field agent."

He smiled softly, his blue eyes crinkling at the corners. The look stopped her in her tracks, turning her brain to mush.

Oh, hell.

Don't look at me like that.

"I bet you're a great schoolteacher," he said, unaware of the effect he had on her.

It was too much. Her heart twisted painfully, and she looked away. "Thanks. I'm looking forward to getting back to it, once this is over."

An edge crept into her voice. "If this is ever over."

"We're going to end it, Sloane," he said, firmly. "You will be able to go home. Get back to your life."

God, that sounded so good.

And yet, terrible at the same time, for it would mean leaving him.

"Thanks for your help," she said, awkwardly. "I mean it. You could have deserted me and continued with your mission, but you didn't."

He gave a nod. "I'd never leave a team member behind."

Team member. The thought made her warm inside and she smiled. "Well, I just wanted you to know it means a lot."

He grinned and made for the door. "You're welcome. I'm going down to meet Blade. See you downstairs?"

She nodded, still reeling from that grin. "I won't be long."

CHAPTER 29

"The *Arabian Princess* leaves Karachi tomorrow," Stitch said as they walked to the restaurant. Blade was beside him, while Sloane, dressed in a flowing gold tunic and a scarf that covered her rich, chocolate hair, walked a pace or two behind.

"How do you want to handle it?" Blade asked.

"I'm guessing Omari will be there in person. He'll want to make sure the shipment goes off without a hitch. This means a lot to him."

"Agreed," said Blade, shooting him a knowing look. This was it. Once that shipment left the port, there was no reason for Omari to keep breathing. Finally, Stitch would have his revenge.

"What about Jeremy?" Sloane asked, as they reached the restaurant. "Do you think he'll show up?"

"I doubt it," Stitch replied, holding the door for her. "Jeremy's the muscle. He's here to keep you in check and make sure Omari holds up his end of the deal. With the shipment taken care of, Jeremy's job is done. The next one won't be for months."

"You're the only loose end," Blade said somberly, once they'd sat down at a table. "You're the reason Jeremy's still hanging around."

Sloane didn't reply, but Stitch saw the flash of fear in her eyes.

"It's a long drive to Karachi," Blade said. "We should leave tonight."

"What about me?" Sloane asked. "Am I coming with you?"

"No," Stitch said. He couldn't have her there, not when he was going to take out Omari.

"Why not?"

"It's too dangerous," he explained. "It's safer for you to stay at the hotel."

"You can't just leave me here," she protested. "Jeremy knows I'm in Islamabad. He's probably looking for me right now. How long until he starts checking all the hotels?"

"We paid cash. No names. He won't find you."

"But you don't know for sure."

Stitch felt torn. He wanted to keep her close, to protect her, but he couldn't risk having her interfere again. Whenever she was around, something always stopped him from finishing the job with Omari. This time, there couldn't be any distractions.

"Karachi's over a day away. What am I supposed to do if something happens, and I can't reach you?" Damnit to hell. He hated seeing her like this. Scared. Vulnerable.

Blade glanced at Stitch. "There's a way we can neutralize the threat."

Stitch didn't reply.

"You can't kill him," Sloane gasped, reading between the lines.

Blade shrugged. "You'd be safe. He's a bad guy, Sloane. He's working with the enemy."

She shook her head. "I couldn't live with myself."

And that was why she couldn't come to Karachi.

"Okay then, what if we get him arrested? That would take him out of the picture, at least for a while."

Stitch smirked. "It's not easy for a foreigner in a Pakistani jail."

"Exactly."

Sloane hesitated. "How are you going to do that? Give the police his cell phone data?"

Stitch had a feeling he knew where Blade was going with this.

"By now, Jeremy's probably told Matthew you came to see him," Blade explained.

Sloane watched him warily. "Yeah, but he already wants me dead, so what?"

"Exactly, he's going to be desperate to shut you up."

She shook her head. "I don't understand."

"In fact, I'll bet Matthew's already tried to reach you," Blade continued.

"He can't. I destroyed my sim card and left my phone in Peshawar."

"Yeah, but you know his number," Stitch said. By heart.

She paled. "You want me to call Matthew?"

Both men nodded.

"But why?" Her eyes were wide with trepidation. Stitch couldn't blame her for being scared. Matthew had betrayed her. He'd seduced her, recruited her, and then sent her out here to die.

"Because if you don't, it'll look suspicious," Stitch replied.

"But he tried to kill me?"

"Someone tried to kill you, yeah. You don't know it's him. You trust him, remember?"

"I think I'm going to throw up."

"It's a good plan," Blade said. "Tell him you lost your phone. Beg him to fly you home as soon as possible."

"Do you think he'll believe me?"

"Why wouldn't he? Under the circumstances, it would be odd if you didn't try to contact him."

"Then what? As soon as I get to the airport, he'll try to have me killed again. He'll probably have Jeremy waiting for me there."

"That's not going to happen," Stitch said quickly. "Jeremy won't get anywhere near the airport."

"He won't?"

Blade grinned. "No, we'll make sure of that. All you need to do is make the call."

CHAPTER 30

Sloane took the phone from Stitch, her hands trembling despite her best efforts to steady them.

"Keep calm," Stitch said, watching her closely. "You can do this."

She bit her lip, the weight of the moment crushing her. This was a man she had once slept with, a man she had trusted. And he'd betrayed her. Used her as a pawn in his twisted game and sent her out here to die.

How was she supposed to pretend she didn't know?

Sloane dialed Matthew's number, then sank into the chair in front of the dresser, her heart pounding. Stitch and Blade sat silently on the bed behind her, their gazes burning into her back like twin lasers.

"It's ringing," she whispered, gripping the phone.

A moment later, Matthew's voice cut through the tension. "Hello?"

Sloane swallowed hard, forcing the words out. "Matthew, it's me."

"Jesus Christ, Sloane," he bellowed, his voice full of exasperation. "I've been trying to get hold of you. Jeremy said you'd been to see him in Islamabad. What the hell's going on over there?"

She forced herself to stay calm, kept her tone deliberately even. "Someone tried to shoot me," she said. "But I got away."

Matthew's response was immediate. "I know, Jeremy told me. Are you alright?"

Sloane rolled her eyes. As if he really cared. "Yes, I'm fine."

"What happened? How did you get away?"

As if he didn't know.

"Some men came to help me. They pulled me to safety."

"Were you injured?"

The shooter must have fed back that he'd clipped her, but they wouldn't know how badly.

"It was just a graze," she said, hoping he believed her. "A local woman patched me up." That was true, at least. Stitch and a local woman.

"Thank God."

She gritted her teeth. "I didn't have access to my laptop, so I came here to find Jeremy," she explained, glancing at Stitch, who nodded his silent approval.

"How did you know where to find him?" More questions. He was trying to connect the dots, find out how much she knew.

She sniffed, to make him think she was crying. "Matthew, I want to come home. Please, can you fly me back?"

He didn't miss a beat. "Yes, yes, of course. I'm sorry you've had such an awful time. Do you know who shot you?"

You ordered it, you scumbag.

She clenched her jaw, but kept her voice controlled, her anger bleeding through. "No, but I think it's got something to do with the Afghans."

"Afghans? You mean the men Omari met in Peshawar?" He'd seen the video.

Sloane nodded. "Yes. I think they saw me. I can't think of any other reason why they'd want me dead."

"That could be," Matthew said, after a brief pause. "Listen, where are you staying? I'll send someone to get you."

She glanced at Stitch who nodded. They'd expected this.

"I'm at the Marriott," she lied, her pulse quickening. "Matthew... I'm scared."

Blade, sitting behind her, masked a grin, clearly enjoying the show.

Matthew's voice softened, playing the role of the concerned superior. "Okay, don't panic. I'm sending Jeremy around now. Can he reach you on this number?"

"Yes," she said flatly.

"Okay, you stay put. Jeremy will be there as soon as he can, and he'll get you on a flight out tonight. How does that sound?" So smooth, as always. God, how she hated him.

"That would be good."

Like hell.

She knew full well Jeremy would show up with a gun and a silencer.

"Hang in there, honey," Matthew added, his tone dripping with fake concern. "You'll be home soon."

The moment she hung up, Sloane sprang to her feet and paced the room in angry strides. "Honey? I can't believe he had the cheek to call me honey after he tried to kill me."

Stitch looked pleased. "You did great. He totally bought it."

"Hook, line, and sinker," Blade chimed in, a hint of amusement in his voice.

Sloane couldn't remember when last she'd been so furious. "What a lying bastard. I hope he rots in jail."

"That's the plan," Stitch said, a rare smile tugging at the corner of his mouth.

Sloane stopped pacing and turned to face them. "Let's

catch these bastards. I don't care what it takes. They cannot be allowed to get away with this."

"They won't," Blade reassured her.

Stitch took the prepaid burner phone out of her hand and gave her a bottle of water. "Here. Take a minute."

She unscrewed the lid and took a long drink, her pulse still racing.

Once she'd calmed down, she dabbed her mouth with the back of her hand and looked at them. "What's next?"

Blade leaned back, grinning. "Next, we have a little chat with Jeremy."

CHAPTER 31

Stitch waited in the car while the well-paid taxi driver went inside to book a room at the Marriott under his own name. Cash, of course. That'd confuse the cops when they came sniffing around later.

Once the room was sorted, Stitch pulled up his hoodie and headed upstairs to wait, while Blade kept watch in the lobby. It wouldn't take long. The shipment was set to leave Karachi tomorrow, and Matthew wasn't about to let Sloane screw things up.

They'd left Sloane back at the hotel. She'd promised to stay put. The brand-new prepaid phone they'd given her meant she could reach them anytime, if needs be.

Stitch glanced at his Glock on the table. He wasn't sure exactly how this was going to go down, but he was more than ready to give Jeremy a piece of his mind. Nobody tried to take out his woman, especially not on his watch.

Whoa!

Sloane wasn't *his* woman.

Even if he had reached for her. Held her. Tasted her.

Fuck.

His phone buzzed twice in rapid succession. The first message was the expected text from an unknown number.

It's Jeremy. Which room are you in?

Stitch typed a reply.

143.

Right after, another text came through, this time from Blade.

On the way up.

Game time.

Stitch set his phone to record and left it face down on the dresser, then he grabbed his gun and positioned himself at the door. Blade would follow Jeremy up—standard procedure when dealing with informants. Blade's boss, Pat—a former SEAL and all-round tough guy—was in the loop about the meeting. If things went sideways, he'd get the local authorities involved and make sure Jeremy was detained until they could ship him back to the U.S. They just needed something solid to pin on him.

A soft knock broke the silence.

"Here we go," Stitch muttered to himself.

"Sloane? It's Jeremy," called the voice outside.

Bastard even sounded friendly, Stitch thought, but he remained calm. His training kicked in, keeping him focused. He cleared his head and zeroed in on the task. With his Glock hidden behind his back, he opened the door.

"Who the hell are you?" Jeremy took a step back, clearly not expecting a muscle-bound stranger to greet him. Then his gaze narrowed. "Wait? We've met. You were at the bar the other night. You spilled your drink on me."

"That's right, Jeremy. I've been expecting you," Stitch said, icily.

"What are you doing here? Where's Sloane?" Jeremy peered behind Stitch into the room.

"Sloane couldn't make it."

"What is this? Some kind of set-up? I don't have time for this nonsense." He turned to leave, but bumped straight into Blade, who had silently positioned himself behind him.

"Going somewhere?" Blade rumbled, blocking his way.

Jeremy took a step back, gaze flickering between the two of them. His hand started moving toward his jacket pocket.

"I wouldn't," Stitch warned, levelling his gun. "Hands where I can see them."

Slowly, Jeremy raised his hands.

Blade reached a gloved hand into the CIA agent's jacket and pulled out a Beretta fitted with a suppressor, then quickly patted him down in case he was concealing a second weapon. "He's clear."

"Come inside. Let's talk." Stitch motioned for him to step inside the hotel room.

Jeremy did as he was ordered but remained tense. Blade followed, right on his heels, still holding Jeremy's gun.

"Take a seat," Stitch said.

"I'd prefer to stand." Jeremy glared at them. "What's this about? Who are you?"

"Friends of Sloane's," Stitch said, flatly. "We heard you wanted to talk to her?"

He forced a chuckle. "I think there's been some kind of misunderstanding. I'm here to help her. I'm taking her back to the U.S."

"With this?" Blade held up the Baretta.

The smirk left his lips. "That's for protection. I've got a license for it."

Stitch ignored him. "You and Sloane traveling together?"

"Yes." Jeremy wasn't a very good liar. Stitch expected more from a seasoned CIA special agent.

"Mm-hm. That's strange. The airport didn't have any flights booked in either of your names."

Uncertainty flickered across Jeremy's face. "Who the fuck are you?"

"We also work for the U.S. government," Stitch said, keeping his gun on Jeremy. "I've got a license for this too."

The agent's eyes hardened. "What do you want with me?"

Stitch didn't miss a beat. "Abdula Omari."

The name hung in the air for a second too long. Jeremy's mouth tightened. "What about him?" he hissed.

"You know him pretty well, don't you?" Stitch circled him while Blade stood between the agent and the door, cutting off any chance of escape.

"I know of him." Jeremy tried to sound casual. "But if you've talked to Sloane, you know about her assignment."

"Yeah, we do. We also know about yours," Stitch shot back.

Jeremy's brow furrowed. "I don't know what you're implying."

"I think you do," Stitch said. "You paid a hitman to take out Sloane because she found out about your relationship with Omari."

"I don't know what you mean?"

"Let me jog your memory." With his free hand, Stitch retrieved his phone off the dresser. He held up a picture of Jeremy shaking hands with Omari in a graveyard. "Ring any bells?"

Jeremy paled. He stared at the photo, trying to figure out how Stitch had gotten it.

"Was Sloane there?" Jeremy finally asked.

"No," Stitch set the phone back on the dresser, face down. "I was."

Jeremy stared at him. "Why?"

"Never mind. What were you and Omari discussing?"

Jeremy shifted his weight. "I think you already know."

"You tell me," Stitch replied. "It will save any misunderstandings down the line."

Jeremy sighed. "Fine. We were discussing the shipment. But if you were there, you already know that."

"Oh, I know." Stitch shot him a hard look. "The *Arabian Princess*, right? Loading dock D?"

Jeremy's body stiffened.

Stitch wasn't about to let up. "I'm more interested in the money you paid Omari. What was that for?"

Jeremy clamped his mouth shut, saying nothing.

"Was it the final payment for your little CIA-backed drug-running operation?"

Jeremy's eyes shifted.

Bingo.

"How long has Matthew Sullivan been running this show?" Stitch asked.

Jeremy stiffened as he went into defensive mode.

"That's not gonna work, Jeremy." Stitch looked him in the eye. "Either you talk, or we hand you over to the Pakistani police."

Fear crept into his eyes, but he tried to brazen it out. "For what?"

"Attempted murder, for starters. You did walk in here with a gun," Stitch said, calm but deadly.

Jeremy scoffed. "That won't hold."

"Wanna bet?" Stitch nodded at Blade. Blade aimed the Beretta and fired two quick shots into the mattress. The sound was barely louder than a cough, but the impact made Jeremy jump.

"Jesus! What the fuck are you doing?"

"Staging a crime scene," Stitch said.

Jeremy glared at him, but he was trapped. There was no way out of this.

"What were you saying about the money?" Stitch probed, as if Blade hadn't just fired a weapon.

Jeremy hesitated, then let out a deep breath. "I want a deal."

"Maybe," Stitch said coolly. "Depends on what you've got."

Jeremy shook his head. "No, I want a deal first. Then I'll talk."

Stitch raised an eyebrow, almost impressed. "Alright, here's the deal—you talk, you walk. You don't, and I call hotel security."

"How do I know you'll stick to your end of the deal?"

Stitch gestured to the gun in his hand. "Guess you'll just have to trust me."

Another sigh. Jeremy's shoulders slumped.

They had him.

Jeremy took a deep breath and began to talk.

"During the Afghan war, the CIA sent in a security team to crack down on poppy production. Our job was supposed to be replacing it with wheat and other crops, try to get the economy back on track." Jeremy glanced up. "But it was all bullshit. A joke. Nobody wanted to grow wheat—the margins were too small. So, we just ended up monitoring the poppy fields instead."

Stitch gave a nod. "Go on."

"Our unit was called Ghost Company. It was made up of soldiers, mercs, and private contractors. We were based in Helmand Province. Over time, we built up contacts—production, distribution, you name it. We helped streamline their network."

"In exchange for a cut," Stitch finished for him.

Jeremy nodded. "Yeah. We started making real money—better than any army paycheck. When the war ended, the official team got pulled out, but we kept things going on our own."

"And Matthew Sullivan heads up Ghost Company?" Stitch asked, his tone sharp, making sure it was clear for the recording.

"Yeah," Jeremy confirmed. "He led the original team. When it was over, he went back to D.C. to run it from there. The rest of us stayed in Helmand."

Stitch's voice dropped, more intense. "Whose call was it to hit the village in the Anjuman Pass?"

Jeremy frowned. "I don't know what you're talking about."

"Don't lie to me," Stitch growled, stepping forward until the gun was pressed to Jeremy's temple. "I *know* it was your guys who wiped that place out. I want to know who gave the order." His voice was barely a whisper, but every word carried a deadly weight.

"I told you—"

Stitch cut him off, the barrel digging into his skull. "Don't fucking lie to me, or I'll blow your brains out. You hear me?"

Jeremy's eyes locked on Stitch's, and he caved. "Okay, okay, relax! It was Sullivan. The provincial government blocked our usual supply route, so we had to find a new way through the mountains. The villagers resisted, and Sullivan told us to send a message."

"A message?" Stitch hissed. "That was a massacre."

Jeremy rolled his eyes, a hint of annoyance showing through. "What do you care about some tiny Afghan village?"

Stitch's voice dropped even lower, cold and venomous. "That was *my* village. My family. My friends. My wife, you piece of shit."

Jeremy just stared at him, wide-eyed.

Blade didn't move, though the arm holding his gun twitched, ready to back Stitch up.

Stitch's chest heaved, rage bubbling up, his finger itching to pull the trigger. It would've been so damn easy. Just a squeeze, and this scumbag's head would explode. But he held himself back. He needed confirmation first.

"I didn't know," Jeremy mumbled.

"Were you there?" Stitch snarled, pushing the gun harder against Jeremy's head. "Did you help kill all those innocent people?"

Jeremy paled, shaking his head. "No, I wasn't there. I swear. I was with Omari in Peshawar."

Stitch didn't buy it. "Omari wasn't in Peshawar then."

"He was close by, setting up labs near the border. I was helping oversee it."

Stitch knew about the labs in the foothills where they processed the raw opium. It was possible Jeremy had been there.

His blood pounded in his ears. He wanted to end this bastard right here. Maybe Jeremy hadn't pulled the trigger on Soraya and her family, but he was neck-deep in this filthy operation. Plus, he was the one who'd ordered the hit on Sloane.

I couldn't live with myself.

Sloane's words echoed in his head. He wasn't a cold-blooded killer. He couldn't just shoot the bastard without reason.

Then Jeremy gave him one.

The CIA agent twisted suddenly, going for Stitch's gun in a desperate attempt to surprise him. It was gutsy, but it didn't work. Before Jeremy could get his hands around the weapon, Stitch pulled the trigger.

At the same time, a loud pop sounded from Blade's direction.

Jeremy flew backward, his body hitting the floor with a dull thud. Blood pooled from the hole in his forehead, compliments of Blade, as well as the wound in his gut.

He was dead before he hit the ground.

. . .

"Let's get out of here," Stitch said, picking up his phone. It was still recording. They'd let the authorities sort through the bullet holes, casings, and trajectories when they processed the scene. Good luck with that.

Blade tossed Jeremy's gun onto the floor beside him. He'd been wearing gloves, so he didn't worry about prints. "Right behind you."

Stitch took a moment to wipe down both sides of the door hand, before slipping out of the room. Blade followed, closing the door behind him.

They took the emergency stairs, avoiding the guests who had come out of their rooms after hearing the gunshots. Hotel security wouldn't be far behind.

"This way," Blade hissed, slipping into the stairwell. They hurried down one flight and stepped into a plush, carpeted hallway, moving casually as they headed for the elevators. Blade pressed the button for down.

Stitch tucked his gun back into the holster under his shirt. "We've gotta get out before they lock down the hotel."

"I'd say we've got less than a minute," Blade muttered.

The elevator door finally pinged open, and they shot inside. Thirty seconds later, they were walking out of the lobby.

Blade and Stitch strode to the taxi rank and got into a waiting cab. As they closed the doors, they saw armed police storm up the steps to the hotel.

Blade gave the taxi driver the name of their street and the zone it was in, purposely not mentioning the hotel. Not that it mattered. In less than an hour, they'd be on the road.

"That didn't go according to plan," Stitch said, glancing at Blade.

His buddy grimaced. "Couldn't be helped. Did you get the recording?"

"Yep." He patted his pocket.

The cab merged into traffic.

They both knew Blade's shot had been the kill shot. Stitch's gut wound might've done the job eventually, but it wouldn't have been as clean or painless. "He was lying about being at the village attack."

Blade nodded. "I know."

One name crossed off his list, Stitch thought grimly, as they headed back to the hotel.

Taking a life was never something he did lightly, even if the guy was a scumbag like Jeremy. The man had blood on his hands, though, and that made him feel better about what had happened. He'd ordered the hit on Sloane, probably even had a hand in the slaughter that took out Soraya and the elders. Not to mention his role in Ghost Company.

Stitch wasn't going to lose any sleep over it.

"You know," Blade said, "there's no reason why Sloane can't come with us to Karachi."

Stitch shot him a glance. "There's no reason she can't stay here. We've neutralized the threat."

"Yeah, but if the Feds take down Matthew Sullivan, Sloane can go home. We can fly out of Karachi instead of coming all the way back. Hell of a drive, buddy, and honestly, I'm not sure I want to do it twice."

Stitch thought about it. Blade wasn't wrong. Sixteen hours of driving was a massive waste of time.

"I don't know. She's not going to like what we're going to do."

"So don't tell her."

"It's not that simple."

"Because she reads people?" Blade shot a look at him.

"Yeah. It's almost impossible to keep anything from her. She's too intuitive."

"And you're afraid she'll talk you out of it?"

"I'm not afraid of anything," he growled, making Blade grin. "It just complicates matters, that's all."

There was a brief pause.

"Sullivan is going to know she had help," Blade pointed out. "There's no way he's going to believe she walked in there and shot Jeremy. Twice. With two different caliber bullets."

Stitch sighed. "Okay, I get your point. She's still not safe. We'll take her with us."

"The shipment leaves in less than twenty-four hours," Blade said.

Stitch tensed his jaw. "We'd better move out then."

CHAPTER 32

"He's dead?" Sloane stared at them in disbelief. "But how? I thought you were going to get him arrested." They were in a rented SUV, heading out of the city on the Lahore-Islamabad freeway. Sloane sat next to Stitch, who was driving, while Blade lounged in the back.

"That was the plan," Stitch said, eyes fixed on the road.

"What happened?" she asked.

"He went for my gun." Stitch replied. "Stupid move. Gave us no choice."

"So you shot him?" Neither of them looked particularly torn up about it.

"We both did," Blade said from the back.

She glanced over her shoulder. "You *both* shot him?"

"Yeah." Stitch pursed his lips.

"Couldn't let him grab the weapon," Blade added.

A long silence followed.

"I can't believe Jeremy is dead." She stared out of the window at the rolling hills dotted with sparse vegetation. Not that she'd liked the man. He'd hired the shooter to kill her, and he'd done all those other terrible things. It's just killing him seemed so drastic. So... final.

"If he'd grabbed my gun, we wouldn't be here," Stitch said, misreading her reaction. "He would've killed us without a moment's hesitation."

"It's not that," she murmured, head spinning. "It's just a lot to get my head around."

"At least he can't hurt you now," Blade said.

"But Matthew still can."

"Sullivan doesn't know Jeremy's dead," Stitch reassured her. "Won't know for a few days, at least, until the cops ID the body."

"And that's not going to be easy," Blade added. "He probably has several aliases."

She exhaled, relieved. "What happens when they do?"

"By then this will all be over," Stitch said, an edge to his voice.

Sloane hoped he was right.

"I'm gonna get some shuteye," Blade said, stretching out across the backseat. "Wake me when it's my turn."

Stitch nodded.

Sloane turned to the window, watching the landscape change to wide, open plains that stretched for miles in all directions. It was obvious Stitch and Blade were used to working together. They had an unspoken bond forged from years operating in the same team, and an ease of communication that only came with knowing someone well. They were tight, like brothers, and would always have each other's back.

Had they really both shot Jeremy? She'd never know, but she believed them when they said he'd gone for Stitch's gun. It had been self-defense.

Turning away from the window, she stole a glance at Stitch. His blue eyes were locked on the road, cool and steady, like nothing fazed him. His hands gripped the wheel with this effortless confidence, the kind that made you feel safe and a little on edge at the same time. His tanned forearms flexed with every slight turn, showing off those cut muscles and that tattoo—dark and winding, tied to a career that he was proud of but never talked about.

With that chiseled jaw and slightly tousled hair he was both lethal and breathtakingly gorgeous—a dangerous mix she found impossible to ignore.

Too bad they'd never get to finish what they started. At least she had some memories. *That* night would be forever burned into her mind.

A soft snoring came from the back. She looked over her shoulder and saw that Blade was already out cold.

"That didn't take long," she remarked.

"He's always like that," Stitch said without looking away from the road. "Motion knocks him out. Cars, buses, helicopters—you name it, he's out."

She smiled. "You two are close, huh?"

"Yep, like brothers. It was the same with the whole team— me, Blade, Cole." His jaw tightened. "Joe, Chris, and Rick didn't make it back from our last op."

"I'm sorry."

He'd lost a lot of people in his life, she realized. She supposed it was common in his line of work. Still, it couldn't be easy.

And then losing his wife. How tragic.

"Was that when you got ambushed?" she asked, remembering the story.

He nodded, the SUV continuing to eat up the miles.

"I'm sorry," she whispered. "You don't have to talk about it if you don't want to."

"It's fine." He glanced at the clock on the dashboard.

"We've got fourteen hours to go. Might as well talk about something."

She smiled.

He took a deep breath. "We were on a routine mission in Afghanistan, hiking through a mountain pass, when rebel militia ambushed us. One minute, we were marching along the path, the next, we were in a full-on firefight." His grip on the steering wheel tightened.

She wanted to reach out, put a hand on his thigh to comfort him, but it felt too intimate, so she didn't move.

"There was no cover," he said, his voice hollow, like he was still in that moment. "Rick went down first, mowed down by machine gun fire. Then Joe... he got hit too."

"He was Pat's son?"

"Yeah, took a bullet to the leg. Blade and I tried to help him, but they got him in the gut and chest. He died in Blade's arms."

She could picture it now—a serene mountain pass ripped apart by gunfire, her heart aching as she imagined Stitch in the middle of it. "What did you do?" she whispered.

He exhaled slowly. "We had to leave them behind. There was nothing we could do. Blade, Chris, and I split up, hoping we'd be less of a target if we scattered." His expression darkened. "Chris didn't make it either. Only Blade and I got out."

"I'm sorry," she whispered.

"Blade took it hard," Stitch said, glancing briefly in the rearview mirror at his sleeping friend. "He was leading the op."

She followed his gaze. "It wasn't his fault though, was it?"

"No." His jaw clenched. "Our translator betrayed us. The Taliban got to him. Threatened his family. He gave up our location, and Blade felt like he should've seen it coming. Like he could've prevented it."

"How could he? There's no way he could've known," she said, shaking her head.

Stitch shrugged, a haunted look crossing his face. "Doesn't change the fact that good men died. After that, I just... couldn't go back. It was like something died inside me too."

She swallowed hard. Seeing your brothers gunned down, barely making it out alive—it wasn't something you could just move past.

"Didn't they look for you?" she asked softly. She knew how serious it was to vanish from a unit, especially in a war zone.

He hesitated, then nodded. "I made it to the RV point. The chopper was waiting. I saw it, but I couldn't get on. I hid and watched while Blade boarded. They waited as long as they could, then flew back without me. They thought I was dead."

""You were in shock," she said gently. "It wasn't your fault."

"I was messed up, yeah," he admitted, eyes still on the road. "Wandered the mountains for days until I found a village. We'd done a goodwill mission there the year before. Soraya's family took me in."

"She blinked. "Blade found you though, right?"

He nodded. "Yeah, eventually. But he kept quiet. He knew if anyone found out I was alive, I'd be in deep shit. So, he let everyone believe I was gone. I didn't exactly argue."

"Why not? You could've gone back."

His lips pressed into a thin line. "At the time, I couldn't face it. I wasn't ready. By the time I came to my senses, it was too late. Easier to stay 'dead.'"

Sloane's heart ached for the man beside her.

"My biggest regret is leaving Blade to face the fallout alone," he said after a pause, his voice thick with guilt. "There was an investigation, and he took the heat. Ended up retiring early."

Her chest tightened. "That's awful."

"Yeah," he said, his voice rough. "It is."

The silence between them hung heavy for a moment. She could see it now—Stitch hadn't run because he was a coward. He'd been shattered, lost, and too broken to face the aftermath. And now, all these years later, the pain of it still clung to him.

She blinked back the sting of tears. "I'm so sorry for what you went through," she said, her voice soft. "I didn't know."

He cleared his throat, brushing it off, but she could see it still weighed on him. "It was a long time ago," he said. "Everyone's moved on."

Except you, she thought.

"What will you do when this is over?" she asked, tentatively.

He sighed. "I don't know. If I go back to the States, I'll probably get arrested."

Her head snapped around to face him. "What? Why? You didn't do anything wrong."

His lips curved into a grim smile. "Walking away without an official discharge... the Navy doesn't care why. It's still desertion."

"But there has to be a way to fix it, right?"

He shrugged, his eyes wary. "Maybe. We'll see."

"What happens tomorrow at the docks?" she asked, a short while later. The landscape hadn't changed much in the last few hours, and she was growing bored with the view.

"When the *Arabian Princess* sails, we'll pass the information on to Pat, who'll loop in his CIA contact. They'll coordinate with the DEA and the Coast Guard to intercept the ship when it enters U.S. waters. At least, that's the plan."

She didn't know much about how these things worked, but it sounded familiar enough. She'd seen enough news footage back home of Coast Guard raids and DEA drug busts at sea. It always looked so slick, almost effortless.

"You think the crew has any idea they're transporting heroin?"

He shook his head. "Doubt it. The cargo will be buried in containers, probably hidden in legal goods—textiles, electronics, food shipments, whatever won't raise suspicion. It's the dock workers you need to worry about. They're the ones who get paid off to make sure certain containers slip through customs unnoticed."

"You make it sound so easy," she mused.

He shrugged. "If you know the right palms to grease, anything's possible. The cartels have it down to a science."

She let out a low whistle, shaking her head. "Until I came here, I was living in this safe, little bubble. Now that it's burst, the world is suddenly a very scary place."

"It can be," he agreed. "But don't worry. I'm not going to let anything happen to you."

Those words.

That's what he'd said that night, right before they'd kissed, even though he'd been talking about Soraya. Now he was saying them about her.

A warm flush mixed with something deeper flowed through her. It was heady, intoxicating. A glimpse of what it would be like to be loved by someone like him.

She gulped. Like that would ever happen.

As soon as this was over, she'd be going back to her old life, and Stitch would soon be a distant, but very fond, memory.

"What about you?" he asked, breaking the silence that had

stretched out for nearly twenty miles. "You got anyone to go back to? Parents? Siblings?"

She glanced at him, surprised by the question but shrugged. "Not really. My mom died when I was young, and my dad... well, he wasn't exactly father of the year."

Stitch raised an eyebrow, glancing over briefly. "What happened?"

She hadn't planned on talking about it, but once she started, the words just spilled out. She told him about her mom's death and her dad's downward spiral—how the drinking had taken over and eventually, how it all ended.

"I got there too late," she said quietly. "He'd already jumped."

"Shit," he muttered. "That's rough. How old were you?"

"Almost seventeen. Two days before my birthday."

"Damn," he murmured, nodding slightly. "I get that. Birthdays are... hard."

She knew he was thinking about Soraya. There was a silence, heavy but not uncomfortable, just the two of them processing their own grief.

"So, what happened after?" he asked.

"I went to live with my grandmother. She's the one who taught me Urdu."

"Is she from the Middle East?" he asked, glancing at her again, curious.

"No, but her mom was. She married an American engineer and moved to the States. Grandma was born in Seattle. I'm the only one who's ever been back to her birthplace."

He gave a low whistle. "That's why Matthew was so keen on you, huh? Not just the language, but the whole package."

She sighed, the mention of Matthew still a sore spot. "Yeah. Makes sense now. I thought he cared about me, but I was just... useful. Pretty naive, right?"

"Hey, don't beat yourself up," he said, a slight edge to his voice. "Love makes fools of us all."

"Oh, I don't know if it was love," she admitted quickly. "Maybe just... infatuation. Definitely not love."

Stitch shot her a look, a small grin tugging at his lips. "Never been in love before?"

The engine's steady hum filled the pause before she answered. "No. Not really. My dad kind of ruined the whole idea of marriage for me. He was awful to my mom. I don't ever want that."

"Not all men are like that, you know," he said, his voice low.

She knew he wasn't like that. Not after everything. Not after the way he'd held her the other night, how gentle he'd been despite the rough edges.

Stitch wasn't some out-of-control drunk who hit his wife—no, he was something else. A fighter, sure, but not in the way her dad had been. He fought for real. He killed people when he had to.

Like Jeremy. That had been hours ago, and she had almost forgotten. But how many others had there been? How many lives had he taken?

But then she thought about Fatima, how tender he'd been patching her up, making sure she was safe.

"I'm not going to let anything happen to you."

He was such a contradiction. Tough, deadly, a force to be reckoned with—yet he could be so gentle.

A delicious, mind-bending, pulse-racing contradiction.

And somewhere along the line, she'd fallen for him. Hard.

But of course, he wasn't hers to have. He belonged to someone else, someone he'd lost but would never forget.

Soraya.

How could she ever compete with a memory?

Her heart ached, and she leaned back, closing her eyes, letting the silence of the car wrap around her.

CHAPTER 33

Stitch glanced over at Sloane's pale, exhausted face. He loved that she'd tried to stay awake with him but had eventually passed out herself. He felt oddly lighter after all that talking. Maybe the shrinks were right—opening up did help.

What she'd said about her dad had surprised him. He'd always pictured her having a comfortable, middle-class upbringing. She just had that vibe. Well-spoken, elegant, classy.

But she'd been through some stuff too. Like him, she'd lost someone close—her mom. Then her dad had killed himself right in front of her.

Jesus, and she was only seventeen.

Everybody had tragedy in their life. Everyone had to deal with pain.

He wasn't alone in that.

Even if it still hurt like hell.

He drove for a few more hours, then pulled into a gas station to fill up and stretch his legs. They'd been on the road for six hours.

Sloane stirred and opened her eyes. "I must've dozed off," she said, looking a little embarrassed. "I was trying to stay awake to keep you company."

He smiled. "Don't sweat it. You obviously needed the rest."

He was used to going days without sleep. Six hours was nothing.

A loud yawn came from the backseat. "Are we there yet?"

He grinned. "Only about ten more hours."

"Fuck." Blade stretched. "You want me to take over?"

"Yeah, why not. I could use a break."

"You take the back," Sloane said. "I'm good up front."

"You sure?"

"Yeah, you need it more than I do."

After they used the restroom and filled up, they hit the road again. Stitch heard Sloane chatting with Blade, and despite what he'd thought, and he fell asleep.

The next thing he knew, the sun was up, and Sloane was driving.

What the—?

He glanced out the window. They were in a built-up area, surrounded by industrial warehouses and container yards.

Karachi.

"Good morning." Sloane caught his eye in the rearview mirror.

He sat up, glaring at the city. "I can't believe I slept that long."

"Nothing short of mortar fire would've woken you up, man," Blade teased from the front seat. Stitch couldn't help but grin. The banter between them felt like the old days, back in the team. He'd missed that.

"What time is it?"

"Eight," Blade said. "I called the harbor master. The

Arabian Princess leaves at six tonight, so we've got plenty of time to get down there and do a recce."

"Perfect," Stitch said.

Blade turned around. "But first, we gotta make a stop. I need a gun."

The Clifton was a four-star hotel just a stone's throw from the port. Definitely a step up from what they were used to, but no one was complaining.

After a quick breakfast of eggs and naan, they checked into two adjoining rooms. Stitch left the box of supplies he'd picked up from his contact in the trunk.

"Wow, this is nice," Sloane said, grinning as she flopped down on the king-size bed.

Pat called to give them an update. Stitch put the phone on speaker.

"The Pakistani police haven't ID'd Jeremy Vale yet. They're looking for the Pakistani guy who reserved the room, but he used a fake name. You're in the clear."

Blade chuckled. "Smart taxi driver."

"Matthew Sullivan is under 24-hour surveillance, according to my contact. CIA Inspector General Robert McCarthy has been fully briefed on the upcoming shipment and is launching an investigation into Ghost Company, both during the war and after."

"That's good news," Sloane said after they hung up. "If they're watching him, he can't come after me."

Stitch wasn't so sure it was good news. Matthew Sullivan had risen to the top of his list, and he wanted the mastermind for himself. An investigation, a deal, and a few years in minimum-security prison wouldn't be enough for the man who'd ordered the attack on his village and ruined his life.

But there'd be time to settle that later.
First things first: Omari.

CHAPTER 34

The 1,150-foot *Arabian Princess* sat low in the water. Bright yellow cranes loomed above her, their job complete. She was fully loaded and ready to set sail.

"I don't see Omari," Stitch muttered, scanning the loading dock and surrounding area. "He should be here by now. The ship leaves in less than one hour."

"Maybe he's not coming," Blade suggested.

Stitch frowned. "I was sure he'd want to see it off."

Blade grunted in agreement.

A few minutes later, three black SUVs rolled onto the loading dock. Stitch heaved a sigh of relief. "They're here."

Blade eyed out the entourage. "That's some heavy security detail."

Stitch nodded. "He's paranoid. Can't blame him—he's on the CIA watchlist."

"While in cahoots with the CIA," Blake murmured, under his breath.

The convoy rolled to a stop, and a bunch of big, heavy hitters piled out. They didn't bother hiding their weapons—

AKs and M16s gripped tight, ready to fire. The message was clear: *Don't even think about it.*

"You sure about this?" Blade asked, voice low.

Stitch nodded grimly. "Omari's not getting away this time."

"Then, we're going to need a distraction." Blade glanced around.

"Only after they set sail," Stitch reminded him. The shipment had to get underway first, then they could go after Omari.

"What about the exit road?" Blade suggested. "If we blow that, they'll have to stop."

Stitch thought about it. "We don't have enough ammo for a full-on firefight." Two against nine armed mercenaries weren't the best odds.

"We won't need it if things go to plan. We'll blow the first car, the rest will scatter, and we'll pick them off one by one. Easy."

Stitch knew Blade was working the problem. They had to divide and conquer. It was their only hope. In reality, it could go sideways fast, but he didn't have a better plan.

"Alright, you wanna set the charges, or should I?"

"I'll do it." Blade didn't hesitate. "You keep watch on Omari. If he makes a move, let me know."

"Copy that."

Stitch turned back to the convoy as Blade ducked behind a container and vanished.

He could always count on his Navy brothers. That was the great thing about their team. They had each other's backs. Not just in combat, but for life.

Last year, when Blade and Lilly had been stuck in Afghanistan and on the run from the Taliban, Stitch had helped them escape. Together, they'd managed to get Lilly out of the country, but only because Blade had sacrificed himself at a roadblock. It was the bravest—and most reckless—thing Stitch had ever seen.

Now, Blade was helping him track down the man responsible for Soraya's murder and the destruction of their village. That's how it was between them—and always would be.

As Blade crept away to plant the charges they'd gotten from the same arms dealer who'd supplied their weapons, Stitch kept his eyes on Omari. The Afghan warlord was talking to someone on the dock—a port official, by the looks of things. Someone paid to let the heroin containers through. Stitch snapped a quick photo with his phone.

The two men shook hands, and the official walked off. Omari hung back, overseeing the final checks as the massive container ship prepped for departure. His entourage stayed near the SUVs, on edge, scanning their surroundings.

Fifteen minutes later, Blade returned. "All set." He patted his pocket, where the detonator was tucked away. "Just say the word."

"Soon."

They watched as the ship's engines roared to life, churning the dark water beneath it into a foaming frenzy. The steel hull groaned and creaked as it pulled away from the dock.

"There she goes," Stitch murmured.

"And there goes Omari." Blade nodded toward the Afghan leader as he climbed into the middle vehicle in the convoy. Once Omari and his men were safely inside the SUVs, they began to drive away.

Stitch raised his hand. When Blade hit the detonator, the C4 would go off, stopping the convoy dead in its tracks.

"Ready... now!"

Blade pressed the button, and a split second later, the first SUV was blown off the ground, engulfed in flames.

"Nice shot." Stitch watched the wreckage burn. There were no survivors.

The remaining two vehicles screeched to a halt.

"Let's do this," Blade said, springing into action.

"Ready."

They opened fire, unleashing a hail of bullets on the SUVs. The mercenaries scrambled out of the cars, trying to take cover. Stitch and Blade managed to take down six of them before the last three, including Omari, found shelter behind some crates.

But they weren't together—while the mercs huddled behind the crates, Omari bolted into the maze of shipping containers.

"Damn it," Stitch growled. "I'm going after him."

"I'll deal with the others," Blade said. "Watch your back."

"You too."

They split up.

Stitch tracked Omari through the narrow gaps between the containers. The Afghan was armed and dangerous, a seasoned fighter with years of experience as a rebel soldier and Taliban officer. He wasn't going to be an easy target.

Crouching low, Stitch moved quietly, his rifle at the ready. Where had the bastard gone?

He had a couple of rounds left in his AK and ten shots in his Glock. Enough to take down one man.

The alleyways between the containers were dark and narrow, the sun barely touching the gaps. Stitch's pulse was steady, his senses sharp.

I'm coming for you, you son of a bitch.

A sudden burst of gunfire forced him to duck behind a container. He peeked around the corner—nothing. He fired a few shots to cover his advance, then ran to the next intersection.

No sign of Omari.

He paused, listening. Footsteps echoed to his right. He followed, hearing gunfire in the distance—Blade taking care of the other mercenaries. A short, controlled burst. One down, two to go.

Stitch kept moving. Another round of bullets tore through the container ahead, forcing him to dive for cover. He returned fire, spraying bullets down the alley.

Eventually, the shooting stopped. Must be low on ammo.

Stitch continued his pursuit.

When he reached the end of the row of containers, he spotted a robed figure darting toward a warehouse.

Omari.

He ran after him, only to hear a voice behind him bark, "Drop the gun!"

Stitch stopped in his tracks.

Fuck.

Then who the hell had he been chasing? Slowly, he set his rifle on the ground and raised his hands in the air.

"And the pistol."

Grimacing, Stitch took out his Glock and tossed it away.

"Turn around," the Afghan warlord barked.

Stitch pivoted, keeping his hands up. He glared at his adversary, feeling the rage firing hot molten lava through his veins. Instead of losing it, it gave him total clarity.

Omari's eyes narrowed. "Who are you?"

"I'm the man who's been hunting you down."

The dark eyes narrowed. "Why?"

"You burned down my village, killed my people, and murdered my wife."

Omari frowned. "I don't know what you're talking about."

"Don't play dumb. You ordered my village destroyed because the elders wouldn't support your drug operation."

Omari sneered. "You're insane. I don't deal in drugs."

Stitch laughed bitterly. "You can say that with a straight face as your heroin sails out of this port?"

Omari's expression hardened. "I don't have time for this."

"May 25, 2023. Ring any bells?"

A flicker of recognition flashed across Omari's face.

"I saw you there," Stitch hissed. "And now, you're gonna pay."

Omari smirked. "You forget—I'm the one holding the gun."

Stitch shrugged. He could kill Omari with his bare hands if he had to. He just needed a distraction.

He stared over Omari's shoulder. "Took you long enough," he said, dropping his arms. As expected, Omari glanced back.

That was all Stitch needed. He surged forward, tackling the warlord to the ground. The rifle fired harmlessly into the air as they hit the tarmac hard.

Omari fought back. He was stronger than he looked, but Stitch was fueled by hatred and vengeance. The warlord was no match for his brute strength. Getting the upper hand, Stitch reached for the weapon.

Suddenly, a shout rang out, and a second figure appeared, gun drawn. The man Stitch had been following. He fired at Stitch, who rolled over, taking Omari with him, using him as a human shield. The bullets tore through the Afghan's body as he screamed in pain.

Realizing his mistake, the guard froze, horrified. Before he could react, Stitch grabbed Omari's rifle and fired back. It only took one shot, center mass, for him to go down.

With a growl, Stitch shoved Omari's lifeless body off of him. The Afghan's once sharp eyes were now glazed over, unseeing. Death had claimed him.

"Serves you right, you bastard," Stitch muttered.

. . .

It wasn't over yet. Sporadic gunfire resonated from between the containers. Picking up his weapons, along with Omari's, Stitch headed in that direction. He rounded a corner only to find Blade standing over the dead body of one of the mercs.

"That was the last one," he said, wiping his forehead with the back of his hand.

Stitch grinned. "Great work."

Blade looked at him. "Omari?"

Stitch gave a quick nod. "He's dead."

Blade patted him on the back. "Job done, then. Let's get the fuck out of here."

Already sirens could be heard screaming up the road towards the dock.

Together, Stitch and Blade melted into the shadows.

CHAPTER 35

Sloane paced up and down the hotel room. Where the hell were they? They'd been gone for hours.

A short time ago she'd heard police sirens race past on their way to the harbor. Something had gone down, and she had a terrible feeling she knew just what it was.

Please let them be okay.

Nausea rose in her stomach.

What if Stitch was dead? What if he wasn't coming back? Her heart twisted painfully in her chest.

She shook her head. No, she mustn't think like that.

Of course, he was coming back. It would take more than a few armed mercenaries to put him down—and he had Blade for backup. She didn't know the former SEAL team leader that well, but she could tell he was a force to be reckoned with. He wouldn't go down without a fight. And he'd protect his friend until the end.

She just prayed this wasn't the end.

Sloane was close to wearing a path in the carpet when she finally heard the keycard in the door and the two disheveled sailors walked in.

"Oh, thank God!" She flung herself at Stitch. "I was so worried. I heard the sirens and thought something terrible had happened."

"Something terrible did." Blake's eyes twinkled. "But not to us."

Sloane realized she was still hanging onto Stitch and let go. Glancing at his face, she was relived he didn't seem uncomfortable with the attention. If anything, he looked pleased.

"Omari?" she asked.

"He's dead."

Two short words. No emotion.

Stitch walked further into the room, his back to her.

"Are you okay?"

"Yeah, why wouldn't I be?" He kicked off his shoes.

"Er, because you just killed a man."

The man that murdered your wife.

"We just killed a lot of men." His voice was stark and matter-of-fact, like he was telling her he'd just weeded the garden.

Blade cleared his throat. "I'm going to take a shower, and then call Lilly. Catch you later." And he left through the interleading door, leaving them alone.

"I need a shower too," Stitch said, heading for the bathroom.

She let him go, sensing his need to be alone. To process what had happened. How could they be so blasé about death? Then again, when they were operators they'd lived with it on a daily basis. The SEALs were an elite assault force. Death was what they did. It was their constant reality—maybe they'd become immune to it.

"Are you hungry?" she called after him, as he disappeared into the bathroom. "I can order room service."

No reply. Only the sound of the door locking behind him. Seconds later, she heard the sound of running water.

Stitch took a long time in the shower. When he emerged, it was in a billow of steam, towel wrapped around his waist. For once, his mouthwatering body didn't distract her—she was too worried about him. He seemed so detached like his head was in the clouds. She wanted to reach out and pull him back to earth. "You know, if you want to talk—" she began.

"I'm fine," he interjected.

"Okay." She gave a little sigh. If he didn't want to talk, she wasn't going to make him, but all her senses were telling her he wasn't right. Maybe he just needed some time. After all, it had just happened.

"Look, Sloane, you don't need to worry about me. This was just another op, at the end of the day."

"No, it wasn't," she said softly. "You got the man responsible for attacking your village and murdering your wife. You've waited over a year for this moment. I'd say that was a little more than just another op."

He shrugged and sat down on the edge of the bed. "I thought it was too. I thought it would feel different, but it doesn't. After all that, it just feels like another mission. We've taken out a bad guy who deserved to die, along with a bunch of armed mercenaries. It doesn't make anything better. It doesn't bring them back. It doesn't bring *her* back."

"No," she whispered. "It was never going to do that."

The massive shoulders slumped. He looked up and she realized his eyes were moist. He wasn't crying, but the emotion was spilling over.

"Oh, Stitch," she whispered.

Without a word, he reached for her, pulling her into his warmth. Still standing, she wrapped her arms around him, feeling the solid strength of his body as he laid his head against her stomach. Her fingers instinctively moved to his hair, still damp from the shower, her touch gentle as she stroked it. She could feel the wetness soak through the shirt she was wearing, but she didn't care. If she could offer any comfort to this brave, broken man, she would.

He held onto her for a long moment, and she could feel the tension in his muscles, as if he was drawing strength from her. A flash of vulnerability, a side of him she hadn't seen before, like he needed her as much as she needed him.

Eventually, he looked up, and her breath caught in her throat. His eyes burned with an intensity that sent heat rushing through her, igniting every nerve in her body. His gaze was filled with longing—no, desire—and it was aimed at her.

That look made her feel powerful, cherished, and wanted in a way she hadn't known was possible.

He lay back on the bed, pulling her down with him, and she followed without hesitation, her lips meeting his as if it were the most natural thing in the world. There was no hesitation, no awkwardness. Just the rightness of being together, like this was exactly where they both belonged.

His kiss was gentle at first, as though he was savoring the moment, learning her taste. It was different from the kiss they'd shared that night in the apartment when he'd mistaken her for Soraya. Now, there was no confusion. He knew exactly who she was.

And he wanted her.

Not Soraya.

Her.

That realization made her shiver as she tangled her fingers in his hair, feeling him groan softly against her mouth. He deepened the kiss, more demanding now, as if he liked what he'd discovered and wanted more—needed more.

His hands roamed over her back, sending ripples of pleasure down her spine. She had wanted this man from the moment he'd walked into her life, fierce and protective, with a heart as scarred as his body. And now, she had him. All of him.

Her world shrunk to the two of them, everything else fading away. It didn't matter what happened tomorrow, or that the world outside was full of danger. Right now, it was just them.

His hands slipped beneath her shirt, fingers grazing her bare skin, and before she knew it, he was lifting the fabric over her head. She broke away from his kiss just long enough to let him pull it off, and then it was gone, discarded on the floor.

When her gaze met his, the intensity in his eyes made her heart race. He didn't smile, but the way he looked at her—with such raw hunger—made her knees weak. Slowly, almost reverently, she traced her fingers over his abs, down to the faint line of hair that led beneath the towel. His skin was warm, the muscles beneath hard and unyielding.

He never took his eyes off her.

When her exploration stopped, he reached up, cupping her breasts in his hands. She moaned softly at the sensation, as the heat between them grew even more intense. He caressed her, savoring every second, and her body responded, a pulse of desire radiating from her core.

She lowered herself onto him again, their mouths meeting with a sense of urgency this time. His kiss was fiercer now, hungrier, and her body tingled in response. He wrapped his arms around her, pulling her tightly against him, her breasts crushed against his chest.

She could feel his hardness through the thin fabric of her pants, and as their kiss deepened, the desire between them became a palpable force, impossible to ignore.

He growled softly, tugging at the waistband of her pants, and she kicked them off easily. His towel loosened and fell away, leaving nothing between them but the charged air.

When their bodies met—skin on skin—she sucked in a breath, her heart pounding. He was so hot, or maybe it was her. Her skin felt like it was on fire, every nerve alive with need for this man.

In one swift move, he flipped them, pinning her beneath him, and there was no mistaking his desire now. It was in his dominant kiss, in the way his body moved against hers, in the rigid heat pressing against her thigh.

Her breath hitched as his body rubbed against her in all the right ways. She opened her legs, granting him entry, her entire body aching for him.

With a low growl, he slid inside her, filling her completely. Her head spun, stars bursting behind her eyelids. She gripped his shoulders, holding on as he slowly pushed deeper into her, their bodies melding together perfectly.

"Oh, God, Stitch," she whispered, overwhelmed by the intensity of the moment. Tears threatened to spill over, but she blinked them back. He had ruined her for anyone else.

She gasped as he began to move, each thrust sending waves of pleasure through her. His eyes were locked on her, filled with something deeper than desire. As he moved inside her, he brushed a tear from her cheek, then smiled softly and kissed her again.

That smile—it melted her. In that moment, he told her everything she needed to know. She could trust him. She could give herself to him completely.

So she did.

Their bodies moved together, finding a rhythm that was both urgent yet unhurried, as if they had all the time in the world. She clung to him, savoring every touch, every kiss.

No one had ever made her feel like this.

His sculpted back rippled under her fingers, each thrust

making his muscles tense beneath her hands. She kissed his neck, her lips brushing over the pulse that throbbed against his skin.

"Fuck, Sloane," he groaned, his voice ragged. "I don't know how much longer I can take this."

She wrapped her legs around his waist, pulling him closer, needing him deeper. His pace quickened, and she gasped as pleasure built to an almost unbearable intensity. Her body trembled beneath him, every nerve alight with sensation, every inch of her filled with need.

Her breath came in ragged gasps, and as his weight pressed her into the mattress, she let out a cry, the sound a mix of longing, need, and pure, unrestrained pleasure.

CHAPTER 36

Stitch had stopped fighting it. Whatever this thing was between him and Sloane, he was done pretending it didn't exist. He wanted her—had wanted her from the moment he'd broken into her apartment and seen her standing there, naked and vulnerable. She'd slipped into his mind and heart from that day forward. And now, finally, he had her in his arms.

Her body was perfect, every curve made for him. The feel of her skin beneath his hands, soft and warm, made him ache with need. She tasted like everything he'd been craving for months. He kissed her like he was drowning, desperate for the air only she could give him.

This time was different. He knew exactly who he was holding, and she wasn't a ghost from his past. This was real, and she was real. Sloane. Her kisses, her touch, everything about her grounded him in the present, pulling him out of the darkness he'd been living in for so long.

When he felt her lips on his skin, all the tension and bitterness he'd carried after killing Omari melted away. He'd expected to feel something, some rush of vengeance fulfilled, but instead, he'd been left with nothing. No satisfaction, just emptiness. But with Sloane, there was no emptiness. She filled him, chased away the grief, the guilt, and the regret.

She was his now, and he wanted to claim her in every way. He knew she felt it too—the way she responded to him, her body moving in perfect sync with his, like they'd always been meant to be together.

He didn't have to hide anything from her. She accepted him, all his scars, all his darkness. She wanted him anyway, and that was a gift he hadn't expected. He buried his face in her hair, breathing her in, grounding himself in her scent. Vanilla and something sweet, something uniquely her.

She was so responsive, so alive under his touch. He loved the way her skin flushed beneath his fingertips, the way her breath caught when he kissed her neck. It made him feel powerful, like he could give her everything she needed, everything she deserved.

He kissed her again, more fiercely this time, pulling her tighter against him. He couldn't get enough of her—her taste, her warmth, her quiet strength. The way she kissed him back, eager and just as desperate, made him feel like he'd found something he didn't even know he'd been missing.

He groaned when her hands tangled in his hair, pulling him closer, holding on as if she couldn't bear to let go. And he didn't want her to. Ever.

She was everything.

He'd been so focused on revenge, so wrapped up in the past, that he hadn't realized what was right in front of him. Sloane. She was the light he hadn't known he needed, and now that he had her, he wasn't letting go.

As she moved beneath him, her breath coming in short gasps, he felt himself losing control. The way she wrapped around him, the way her body clamped down on his—it was too much, and he was too far gone to stop. He didn't want to.

He thrust deeper, feeling her nails dig into his back as she cried out his name. That sound—God, it did something to him. Made him feel like he'd won some kind of battle, like he'd conquered something much more important than the enemies he'd hunted down.

His name on her lips was everything.

He groaned, feeling the surge in his body, knowing he was about to explode. His fingers tightened on her hips, and then he was gone, lost in the sensation of her. The world narrowed to this moment, to the way her body moved with his, the way they fit together so perfectly.

He buried himself deep inside her, giving her everything he had, his breath coming in ragged gasps. "Sloane," he groaned, his voice hoarse and filled with something he couldn't quite name.

She was with him, her body shaking beneath him, her soft cries mingling with his as they both found their release. It was primal, overwhelming, but so goddamn perfect.

When it was over, he collapsed beside her, pulling her close. Her head rested on his chest, her hair brushing against his skin, and he let out a long breath, feeling more at peace than he had in years.

He hadn't felt like this in so long—content, grounded, whole. Like all the anger, the grief, and the chaos had melted away, leaving only her. Sloane. The woman who had managed to slip past all his defenses and make him feel again.

He stroked her hair, running his fingers through the dark strands. "Where'd you learn to kiss like that?" he murmured, still catching his breath. "You're lethal."

She laughed softly, the sound like music to his ears. "You must bring out the best in me. I've never kissed anyone else like that, ever."

Her confession sent a warm rush through his chest. He

liked that. Liked knowing he was the one who made her feel this way.

"I'm glad to hear it," he said, pressing a kiss to the top of her head.

Her hand slid over his chest, fingers teasing the sparse hair there, and she kissed his neck again, nuzzling against him. "This is nice."

"It is." He couldn't help himself, he traced his fingers over her nipple, watching it pucker under his touch. She was so damn responsive, it made him want to do things to her, just to see how she'd react, to hear those gasps of pleasure or soft moans that drove him wild.

They were just starting to get lost in each other again when there was a knock on the door.

"Housekeeping," came a voice from the hall.

"We're okay," Stitch growled, not wanting to be interrupted.

She slid toward the edge of the bed, laughing softly. "Should I get that? They probably want to turn down the beds."

"Too late for that." He looped his arm around her waist, pulling her back against him.

Her laughter filled the room, and he smiled as he nuzzled her neck, kissing her skin. "I'm not done with you yet," he growled, his voice of promise.

She gasped as he lowered his mouth to her breast, sucking gently, her body arching beneath him. "Oh, that feels so good," she moaned.

"Hmm…" he murmured, flicking her nipple with his tongue, loving the way she writhed beneath him, completely open and unguarded.

He couldn't get enough of her. After weeks of wanting her but holding back, now there was no stopping him. She was his, and he planned to show her just how much he wanted her, over and over again.

He could feel the heat building between them again, a fire that wouldn't be extinguished. He glanced up into her eyes, already hazy with desire, and gave her a look that said everything he was feeling.

"Ready?" he asked, his voice rough with need.

In response, she pushed him onto his back, straddling him. God, she was a sight—beautiful, confident in her womanhood, and so damn sexy it made his cock shudder.

They kissed again, deeply, until his whole body ached for her. She teased him, sliding over his skin, driving him wild.

"You're driving me crazy, woman," he growled, gripping her hips.

With a wicked smile, she positioned herself above him and sank down. He groaned, his body consumed by her fire.

Her movements were slow at first, deliberate, but he could see the desire building in her eyes. As she rode him, her breath coming in soft moans, Stitch knew he'd never felt this way before. Not with anyone.

She was everything he didn't know he needed. And he was never letting her go.

CHAPTER 37

Sloane clutched Stitch's hand, her fingers trembling against his as the chaos of Jinnah International Airport swirled around them. It felt like she was standing in the eye of a storm, the relentless noise and movement a stark contrast to the silence stretching between them. Her heart hammered against her ribcage, nerves coiled tight enough to snap. Every second felt like a countdown to disaster—any moment, she expected the crack of a gunshot to echo off the walls, or the sudden sting of a blade slipping between her ribs. It wasn't paranoia. There was a price on her head.

Jeremy was gone, but Matthew wasn't—and he was the one calling the shots, according to Pat.

Patrick Burke.

It was clear both Stitch and Blade looked up to the former SEAL commander. They spoke about him in almost reverent tones. Sloane had never met the man, but she trusted him, if only because they did. Pat had promised he'd pull every string he could to get Stitch home. But it wasn't fast enough, not for this moment.

"Matthew's gone dark," Pat had told them. No surprise

there. He'd know the heat was on after Jeremy's death. He wasn't stupid. He was dangerous, calculating. Airports and ports were on lockdown, and an APB was out, but somehow Sloane doubted that would stop a man like him.

Still, for now, she could go home.

Home. The word hit her with a strange mix of emotions. Elation—because it meant she was safe, she could breathe again. Relief—because this nightmare might finally be over. But underneath all that was a heavy ache, a bitter disappointment that gnawed at her. This wasn't how she wanted it to end. Not like this. Not with a hurried goodbye, not with Stitch left behind.

"I can't go back to the States," Stitch had said, his voice gruff but tight with frustration. "Not until they clear things up. Besides, I've got unfinished business."

She gulped. Rahul Ghani. She knew he was going after him. Alone.

"You sure you don't want me to stay?" Blade asked, for the hundredth time.

"No. It's more important you get Sloane back safely." He grinned. "And I know how much you love Afghanistan." There was an undercurrent there, something between the two men.

Blade gave a nod. "Watch your six, brother."

"Always."

Sloane couldn't believe he was sacrificing his safety for hers. Tears welled in her eyes, but she blinked them away.

Blade would be flying back with her, not Stitch. The thought made her heart twist painfully in her chest. She liked Blade—respected him even—but it wasn't him she wanted by her side.

She wanted Stitch.

What if she never saw him again? The thought lodged in her throat, making it hard to breathe. Was this how it ended, after everything they'd fought through, after all the bullets and blood and sleepless nights? A rushed, awkward farewell in a crowded airport, the last kiss stolen between security lines?

More tears threatened, but she gritted her teeth and stopped them falling. She couldn't let him see her break. Not now. Not like this. Stitch squeezed her hand, but it wasn't enough. It wasn't nearly enough.

Blade clapped a hand on Stitch's shoulder, a silent promise passing between them. "Pat's talking to Commander Mattison as we speak. He'll get things sorted. It won't be long before you're stateside, man. You can trust him."

Stitch shrugged, trying to play it cool, but the look in his eyes betrayed him. He was desperate to go home, to finally walk free without the weight of the past few years hanging over him. But the system wasn't that simple. Sloane knew that hunger, saw it in the way his jaw clenched, and his gaze flickered to the doors leading to the terminal. The place where he should be walking through with her.

They hugged, the kind of tight, bone-crushing embrace only brothers-in-arms understood. Stitch's voice was low, rough. "Take care of her, Blade."

Blade gave a sharp nod. "You know I will."

It was time. The words echoed in Sloane's head as she took a deep, shuddering breath, forcing herself to let go of his hand. The warmth of his touch slipped away, leaving her cold and empty. She tried to smile, but it trembled at the edges. "I'll miss you," she whispered, her voice barely audible over the crowd. "Thank you for... everything."

His eyes locked on hers, piercing through the noise and chaos like a lifeline. "Stay safe, Sloane. I mean it. Matthew's still out there, and he's dangerous."

"I know." Her throat burned with the words she couldn't say. *I love you. Don't let this be the end.*

"Damn, I wish I could be there to hunt him down," he muttered, the frustration spilling over now, raw and unfiltered.

"Give it a few days." Blade's voice was steady, slinging his backpack over his shoulder. "You'll be back in the fight soon enough. We'll get him."

Stitch gave a reluctant nod, but his gaze never left hers.

Her heart screamed at her to stay, to fight against the inevitable, but there was no choice. Not now. She gave him one last, lingering look, hoping somehow he could see everything she wasn't brave enough to say.

Then she turned, her stomach twisting with every step she took, Blade at her side as they moved through security. Every beep, every scan felt like she was walking away from something she wasn't ready to let go of. And even as the crowd swallowed them up, she knew she'd left a part of her heart back there, standing with Stitch in the middle of a busy airport in Karachi.

CHAPTER 38

"It's time to come home," Pat said over the phone. "I've explained the situation, and you will be taken into custody when you get here, but I think we can argue your case."

Stitch leaned against the wall, glancing out the grimy airport window as planes came and went on the tarmac. Islamabad felt too small, too suffocating, now that home was almost within reach.

He'd just got back from seventy-two hours in Afghanistan. It hadn't been hard to track down Rahul Ghani, the Afghan drug lord who'd helped destroy his village. His life.

Stitch had snuck into his house in Lashkar Gah in the dead of night, moving like a ghost through the heavily guarded estate. Ghani had only been awake long enough to see Stitch's face and hear him utter one word before ending his life.

Soraya.

The terror in Ghani's eyes had been brief but satisfying. Justice had been served—or vengeance, in this case. Now, with Ghani dead, there was only one target left. Matthew Sullivan.

Which was why he needed to get on that plane.

"They're really going to buy that I was *undercover* for over a year?" He'd seen how the system worked, how unforgiving it could be.

Pat let out a long breath on the other end. "I know it sounds like a stretch, but we've got an angle. Classified operations, black ops missions, it all gets murky, especially when they don't have the full picture. That's where we come in. You disappeared because you went deep undercover. We make them believe that. They'll listen because they have to—especially when it comes to someone with your record."

Stitch let the silence stretch, mulling over the words. A year. He'd been off the grid for over a year. It wasn't just about him not going back—it was everything that had happened during that time. Things he couldn't even put into words, things that wouldn't fit neatly into a report. The government wouldn't care about the trauma, the sanctuary he'd found with Soraya, the heartache or the vengeance. They only look at the details, the black and white—and his situation was all kinds of gray.

"And what if they don't buy it?" Stitch finally said, the question hanging heavy between them. "What if I get back, they slap cuffs on me, and throw me into a black hole somewhere?"

"They won't," Pat said firmly, but even through the phone, Stitch could hear the undercurrent of uncertainty in his former commander's voice. "Listen, man. I've been talking to some people in the DoD. High-level people. They're intrigued, Stitch. They want to know what you know. What you saw. You took down Omari, you rooted out a mole in the CIA. That stands for something. They see you as an asset."

Stitch snorted. "An asset? I've been out of the loop so long

I barely remember the last time I was in a clean fight." He paused, lowering his voice. "You're telling me they're not pissed off that I just disappeared?"

Pat's response was quick. "They're pissed, but they're more interested in why you disappeared. That's where we've got leverage. I've framed it like this—classified black ops. I told them you went dark as part of an assignment that got compromised. It's believable enough, after the ambush. You disappeared to track down the people responsible. With me and your former commander backing the story, they'll accept it."

"Then what?" He knew his Navy career was over. He'd never be an operator again.

"You'll debrief, you'll cooperate, and they'll keep you under watch, sure, but it won't be a prison cell. They won't throw you to the wolves."

"Debrief," Stitch repeated. How many of those had he sat through in his life. After every mission, every deployment. "And what happens if they want to pick apart every detail? If they want answers I can't give?"

"We play it smart." Pat's voice was low, serious. "Look, they don't know everything you've been involved in. They don't know Vale is dead, or that you guys took out Omari—and they don't need to know. Talk about the CIA agent you rescued, and how you bust open the heroine scam. That'll satisfy them."

"Sloane will have to be briefed. She knows what really happened. She could blow it for me." Even though she wouldn't on purpose, he knew that. He trusted her, but he also knew these people had a way of getting information out of you, and she wasn't experienced enough to know when it was happening.

"I'll get Blade to have a word with her before they clear customs. Don't worry, she'll cooperate."

Stitch pinched the bridge of his nose, feeling the weight of it all crashing down on him. "You're putting a lot of faith in them playing nice, Pat. You sure about this?"

Pat's tone softened, but didn't lose its edge. "I've been in this game long enough to know how the pieces move. It's not about playing nice, Stitch—it's about playing smart. They want you alive, talking, and cooperative. And with Commander Mattison backing us, we've got enough political clout to push this through. But you gotta come in willing, ready to cooperate. Play your part and we'll make sure you walk out free."

It was a gamble, but he was willing to take a chance. He deserved this. Even trauma didn't excuse what he'd done. He'd deserted the rest of his team, even if it was only Blade who'd gone home. He should have been there, should have taken his brother's back. It was something he'd have to live with for the rest of his life. Thanks to Pat, he might have a fighting chance.

"Okay," Stitch growled. "I'll do it. I'll get on the next flight out."

But only because he wanted to be there to protect Sloane. Matthew would be gunning for her, and he couldn't let anything happen to her. Not now, not after everything they'd been through.

She was his to protect, and he wasn't going to let anyone else have that honor.

He didn't know when he'd started thinking about her as his. Maybe after they'd made love in Karachi, after he'd taken out Omari. She'd cleaned the blood off his hands, figuratively speaking, healed the hole in his heart, and made him whole again.

He missed her, and she'd been gone less than twenty-four hours.

"It's the only way," Pat said, resolutely.

For a long moment, Stitch didn't speak. He stared out at the distant runway, the hum of the airport fading into background noise. The idea of setting foot back on U.S. soil, after all this time, felt surreal. Part of him had stopped believing he'd ever make it back.

"Thanks, Pat," he finally said. "I owe you."

"I might have a way you can return the favor," Pat said, and Stitch could almost hear him smirk down the line.

"Oh yeah?"

"More about that when you get back. First things first. Let's make sure you're in the clear, and then we'll talk."

Stitch frowned, wondering what Pat wanted from him. "Sure, no problem." Whatever it was, he owed the guy big time, and he'd do whatever it took to repay his debt.

"See you on the other side," Pat said, and ended the call.

Stitch slipped the phone into his pocket, feeling the tightness in his chest finally ease. It was time. Time to step out of the shadows and face whatever waited for him on the other side of that flight.

CHAPTER 39

Sloane stared through the dirty windows of the fleabag motel, wishing she was anywhere but here. Blade didn't trust the CIA, since they couldn't be sure who was working with Matthew, and so he'd booked them into a dingy motel outside of town. "Just until we know the lay of the land," he'd explained.

She knew it was because they were still trying to find Matthew. So far, he'd evaded capture, staying off the radar. He hadn't used any of his credit cards, hadn't gone home, hadn't visited his ex-wife or his children.

"He knows what he's doing," Blade told her. "He was trained for this. Special ops, remember?"

"That was a long time ago," she'd countered.

"It's not something you ever forget."

"How's Stitch?" she asked. The good news was that he'd landed earlier that morning, but the bad news was he'd been taken into custody, and nobody had heard from him since.

"Pat met him at the airport and is arguing his case," Blade said, reassuringly. "He's a powerful man, with a lot of clout. If anyone can get Stitch out of this mess, he can."

"I hope what I said helped," she said. They'd been debriefed at the airport. Two men from the Agency had taken her into an interrogation room and questioned her for hours about her assignment, about Matthew, and about the shooting in Peshawar. They'd asked her about Stitch, or Vance, to use his real name, and wanted to know what part he'd played in exposing the former Ghost Company unit who were transporting heroine out of Afghanistan and into the United States.

"It will have. It back's up what Pat will argue. He's been undercover all this time, hunting down those responsible for the ambush in the valley where he lost half his unit. He infiltrated a local tribe, earning their trust, and when their village was destroyed, in an attempt to find him, he tracked Omari to Peshawar, where he met you."

"But Omari wasn't responsible for the ambush."

"Doesn't matter. Nobody knows what really happened out there." His eyes were cold, and Sloane recalled he'd been team leader on that mission. "It was Taliban led, so it could have been."

She knew it wasn't, but the whole thing did kind of make sense. A covert op, and a classified, undercover mission sanctioned by his commanding officer at the time. She hoped it would work.

God, she longed to see him again, to hold him in her arms. The ache in her chest grew heavier with each passing minute. It was like her heart had been carved out, and the only thing that could fill the empty space was him. She hated feeling this way—vulnerable, desperate, unsure of what the future held. But after everything they'd been through, she couldn't lie to herself anymore. She *needed* him.

That last night together had been more than just comfort. It had been raw, real, a promise of something more. She could still feel the way his lips had brushed against hers, slow at first, like he was afraid to cross that line, and then with all the pent-up emotion he'd been holding back. It had felt like a release, a breaking of all the tension that had built between them since the moment they met. His hands on her skin, the way he'd whispered her name like it was the only thing that mattered in the world. God, she'd felt *alive* in his arms, like she could breathe for the first time in weeks.

But now... now she was suffocating without him. The uncertainty was killing her.

She wondered if he felt the same way. He hadn't said much, even then. But she saw it in his eyes. The way he'd looked at her, like he was memorizing every detail, like he didn't want to forget her face. It had been more than just physical. She *knew* that. She'd felt it, deep down in her bones.

But there was so much she didn't know—so much he hadn't told her. His wife's death still weighed heavily on him, she could see it in the way he sometimes closed off, retreating into his own mind.

Stitch was a man who carried his pain quietly, like a burden he didn't think he deserved to let go of. But that night, for the first time, she'd seen him let a little of it go. He'd been there with her, fully, not as the haunted man who kept himself at arm's length, but as someone who wanted to let her in. It hadn't been perfect—it had been messy, intense, even a little awkward at first—but it was real. *Real.* And that's what she clung to now.

She'd never been the type to believe in fairy tales or happily ever afters. Her life had taught her better. But this— what they had—felt like the beginning of something. Something that might just be worth fighting for.

If only they'd let him go.

The thought of him locked up, alone, waiting for bureaucrats to decide his fate—it made her stomach turn. Pat was doing everything he could, and she believed that. But what if it wasn't enough? What if the government decided Stitch was too much of a liability? What if they buried him under red tape, locked him away, and she never saw him again? The idea of it was unbearable.

She squeezed her eyes shut, pressing her forehead against the cold window. *Please, let him come home.* She didn't care if it took weeks, or months—she just needed to know he'd be safe. That he'd be able to walk out of this mess and into her arms again. That they'd have a shot at a future.

Because she wanted that. She wanted a future with him. And it terrified her to admit it. After everything they'd been through, all the near-death experiences, the danger, the violence—it was this, the not knowing, that scared her the most. The idea that they might not get the chance to see what could have been.

She couldn't lose him. Not now. Not after what they'd shared.

Sloane turned away from the window, pacing the small, dingy room. Her body hummed with nervous energy, and her heart raced with the fear of what could go wrong.

She'd never felt this way before—not about anyone. Not even Matthew had awakened her soul like Stitch had. It made her feel sick to her stomach thinking about how naïve she'd been. How Matthew had played her, seducing her, recruiting her for a damned mission then sending her out there on her own. Her only job to report back.

Dispensable.

She thought about her last conversation with Stitch, the way he'd looked at her right before she boarded the plane. He hadn't said the words, but they were there, unspoken between them. She'd felt them in his touch, in the way his lips lingered on hers for just a moment longer than necessary.

Stay safe, Sloane. I mean it. Matthew's dangerous.

He hadn't been talking about the danger she was in, though. She knew that now. He was talking about his own fear—his fear of losing her, of never seeing her again. She could see it in his eyes, even if he couldn't bring himself to say it. He was still too wrapped up in his own pain, in the loss of his wife, to admit what was growing between them.

But she wasn't going to let that stop her.

She loved him. And if she had to fight the entire damn government to get him back, she would. She wasn't giving up. Not now. Not ever.

Blade had said Pat was powerful, that he had connections. But even those connections could only go so far. It was all up to the people in Washington now, to whether they saw Stitch as an asset or a liability.

Sloane wrapped her arms around herself, feeling the cold seeping through the room, and closed her eyes. All she could do now was wait.

Even if it was killing her.

CHAPTER 40

The door slammed behind him, the heavy thud echoing like a final punctuation to days that had felt like a never-ending interrogation. Stitch inhaled deeply, the cold, sharp October air of D.C. filling his lungs, reminding him that he was *free*.

He still couldn't believe it. After all those days of being dragged through one sterile government office after another, the grilling, the endless hours of trying to keep his story straight—it had finally worked. He was out. Walking across the parking lot, he tugged his worn jacket tighter around him, trying to shake off the disbelief. The Department of Defense had bought it. Hell, he wasn't even sure *he* bought it. But with Pat and his former commander arguing in his corner, they'd convinced the brass that his disappearance was part of a covert op—off the books, a black mission so sensitive that no one had clearance to know about it.

Pat had done most of the talking, but the story stuck. His supposed undercover work had "led" to the exposure of a heroin smuggling ring operating out of Afghanistan. Apparently, that was enough to sway the decision-makers. In their eyes, he wasn't a liability anymore—he was a goddamn hero, a "valuable asset to the U.S. government." He huffed out a laugh. *What a crock of shit.*

The truth was, it was all a lucky coincidence. Yes, he'd survived after the ambush in the valley. Yes, he'd been working with a local tribe to track down the people responsible, but he hadn't been some covert hero on a mission. He'd been surviving, trying to make sense of his life, trying to forget... her.

But none of that mattered now. He was free, and he had Pat to thank for it.

A black SUV pulled up, the familiar silhouette of Patrick Burke behind the wheel. Pat had been waiting for him, as always. Stitch slid into the passenger seat, feeling the weariness of the past few days catch up with him.

"You look like hell," Pat said, glancing over at him as they pulled out of the parking lot.

Stitch grunted. "Feels like it."

Pat smirked, but his voice held a note of sympathy. "You did good back there. Kept your cool. Most guys would've folded under the pressure. They really had you under the microscope."

"Yeah, well, it's not like I had a choice." He leaned his head back against the seat, staring out the window at the city lights. "You think they really bought it?"

Pat's hands gripped the steering wheel tighter. "They didn't have a choice. Between your intel and the heroin ring takedown, we gave them just enough to make it worth their while to keep you out of a cell. Plus, Mattison owed me a favor, so that didn't hurt."

Stitch shook his head. "I still can't believe it worked. I was prepared to be locked up for a long time."

Pat let out a low chuckle. "You and me both. But they see you as an asset now, and that's all that matters. You're out."

Stitch looked over at him. "So what now? You really think I can just walk away from this?"

Pat gave him a sidelong glance. "Depends on what you want. You're a free man, Stitch. You've got options. But... if you're looking for a way to stay in the game, I've got a place for you at Blackthorn. We could use someone like you."

Stitch didn't answer right away, the offer hanging in the air between them. Pat had always been straight with him, always had his back. If there was one person he could trust, it was him. But the thought of going back into the field, of putting his life on the line again... he wasn't sure he was ready for that. Not after everything that had happened. Not after Sloane.

"I'll think about it," Stitch finally said, his voice low. "But right now, all I want is to see her."

Pat smiled. "That's why we're heading there now. Sloane's holed up at a motel just outside the city with Phoenix. Blade had to head back to D.C. for some work, but Phoenix is keeping an eye on things."

Stitch's heart raced at the mention of her name. Sloane. The thought of her waiting for him, not knowing if he'd even make it out of this mess... it tore at him. He hadn't told her he'd been released. He wanted to see the look on her face when he walked through the door.

"Thanks for doing this," Stitch said, glancing over at Pat as they sped down the highway.

"You don't need to thank me. You earned this. And hey, just think about my offer. We're building something special with Blackthorn, and I know you'd be a perfect fit."

Stitch nodded, but his mind was already elsewhere—on Sloane, on what it would feel like to hold her again. He wasn't the same man he'd been before, not after everything they'd been through, but maybe, just maybe, they could start fresh. If she still wanted him.

The motel came into view, a dingy, low-rise building with a faded sign that flickered in the night. Pat pulled into the parking lot and parked the car. The place was just as grim as Blade had described—no one would look for them here. Stitch's stomach clenched with anticipation as he climbed out of the SUV.

Pat clapped him on the shoulder. "Go get her, man. You deserve this."

Stitch took a deep breath and nodded. "Thanks, Pat."

He walked across the cracked pavement toward the room number Pat had given him, his pulse pounding in his ears. His hand trembled slightly as he knocked on the door. For a moment, there was silence. Then he heard movement on the other side, the sound of footsteps approaching.

The door swung open, and there stood Phoenix, holding a hand to his head. Blood seeped between his fingers, his eyes unfocused, his usually steady stance wavering like he was trying to find solid ground beneath him.

Stitch's heart lurched. "What the hell happened?"

Phoenix blinked slowly, his face pale. "I—" He stumbled, gripping the doorframe to keep from collapsing. "I went outside... heard something." His voice slurred, eyes darting past Stitch's shoulder like he was still trying to make sense of it all. "Someone hit me."

Stitch's blood ran cold, adrenaline surging through his veins. "Where's Sloane?"

Phoenix's head dipped, his body swaying, and the silence that followed felt like a knife twisting in Stitch's gut.

"Where the *hell* is Sloane?" Stitch barked, grabbing Phoenix by the shoulders, giving him a sharp shake.

Phoenix winced, pulling his hand away from his blood-matted hair, his gaze finally locking on Stitch's. "She's gone. Matthew... it was Matthew. He took her."

The world tilted.

Stitch felt his grip tighten on Phoenix's jacket, white-knuckling the fabric. His mind raced, the pulse pounding in his ears nearly drowning out the words coming from Phoenix's mouth.

"I looked up and saw him," Phoenix muttered, his voice hoarse, slurred from the blow. "Just before he took off with her."

Matthew. The name was like acid burning through Stitch's brain, his fists clenching, every muscle in his body coiling like a spring ready to snap. He'd *had* her—right here, where she was supposed to be safe—and now she was gone.

"How long?" The words were more of a growl, raw and guttural. His mind was already racing with calculations—how long it would take Matthew to get out of D.C., how far he could've gone by now.

Phoenix swayed again, grabbing the doorframe tighter. "Maybe... half an hour. I don't know, Stitch. Everything's... hazy."

"Half an hour..." Stitch released him, mind reeling. He turned sharply, heading back toward the SUV, his heart thudding like a drumbeat. Matthew had a head start, but it wasn't enough to disappear—not yet.

"Pat!" he yelled as he stormed back toward the car, where Pat had stayed behind, watching from the vehicle. He slammed a fist on the hood to get his attention.

Pat opened the door, eyes narrowing as he saw Phoenix leaning weakly against the doorway. "What the hell's going on?"

"Matthew's got her," Stitch ground out, his breath coming in short, harsh bursts. "He hit Phoenix, took Sloane. He's on the run."

Pat's expression hardened instantly. "Goddamn it."

"We don't have time to wait for backup," Stitch snapped, already yanking open the passenger door, his mind racing through every possible escape route Matthew could have taken. He could feel the rage bubbling under his skin, the desperation. "He's not getting away this time. I swear to God, Pat—"

"I know," Pat said, sliding into the driver's seat with grim determination. "We'll find him."

They had to. There was no other option. Sloane was out there, with a man who would stop at nothing to destroy them both. But this time, Stitch wasn't going to let him get away.

Not again. Not with her.

Pat started the engine, and with a screech of tires, they tore out of the motel parking lot, heading into the dark, toward whatever hell awaited them next.

CHAPTER 41

The blow came out of nowhere, a sharp, searing pain exploding across the side of Sloane's head. Her vision blurred instantly, stars dancing in front of her eyes as she stumbled backward, clutching the side of her face. Matthew stood over her, his expression cold and calculating. The friendly charm she once knew was gone—replaced with something ruthless, terrifying.

"Matthew?" Her voice was shrill, a mix of shock and fear. He was supposed to be in hiding—half the police force in D.C. was hunting him down, and yet here he was. In the flesh. Her pulse thudded so hard in her ears she could barely hear herself.

"Yes, it's me, darling." His smile twisted as he towered over her. "Now, don't make this harder than it needs to be."

He reached for her, but she stumbled back, adrenaline flooding her body. *Run*, her brain screamed, but her legs felt like lead, her head still spinning from the hit. She tried to make a break for the motel door, her hand reaching for the handle, but Matthew's fingers closed around her arm like a vice.

"Let go of me!" she screamed, trying to twist free, but he yanked her back with brutal strength, his grip digging into her skin.

"You're only going to make this worse for yourself," he growled, pulling her out of the room and toward the parking lot. She fought against him, kicking and thrashing, trying to break free, but Matthew was too strong. He grabbed her by the waist, dragging her across the tarmac, his arm clamped around her like a steel band.

Her heart pounded with terror. Where was Blade? Pat?

The sharp sting of cold metal dug into Sloane's back as Matthew shoved her into the backseat of the car, her body slamming against the door. Her pulse was racing so fast she could barely hear anything but the pounding in her ears. How had this happened? How had Matthew found her here? She struggled to keep her thoughts straight, but everything was slipping into chaos. Phoenix had gone outside to check out that noise, and the next thing she knew, he was down, and Matthew was dragging her out of the room.

She was trapped.

Her heart twisted in her chest as the full weight of her predicament pressed down on her. The man she once thought she knew—the man who'd shared his bed with her—had turned into a stranger, a monster. She didn't know who he was any more. How could he be capable of such violence? *Of wanting her dead.*

She tried to move, push herself up, but her arms were shaky and the dizziness from the blow to her face made it impossible to sit up straight. Everything around her seemed to blur and spin.

Phoenix.

The last thing she'd seen was him hitting the ground outside the motel, blood running from his head.

Was he okay? Would someone find him? Would Pat find him?

The car jerked forward as Matthew hit the gas, the sudden motion slamming her back into the seat, knocking the air from her lungs. She gasped, her heart racing.

"Where are you taking me?"

Matthew didn't answer. From her position, she could see his jaw clenched, the reflection of the city lights flashing across his cold, hardened face. That same face she used to touch. That face she once thought she loved.

Her thoughts drifted back to those early days when he'd recruited her. The dinners, the charm, the way he made her feel like she was part of something bigger than herself. She'd been drawn in by his confidence, by the excitement of the missions. They'd shared more than just professional moments—there had been real intimacy once. Or so she thought. Now, all of it felt twisted, like a nightmare she couldn't wake up from.

How did I ever trust him?

Now she'd gone from being his asset to being his target.

Matthew's voice cut through the dark haze in her head. "You had one job, Sloane." He glanced at her in the rearview mirror, his tone dripping with disappointment. "Just one. Watch Omari. Report back. But no, you had to go digging, didn't you?"

She swallowed hard, fear prickling her skin. "I was just doing my job. I thought—"

"Too damn well. You saw too much," he interrupted, his voice a low growl now. "And you couldn't let it go. Jeremy warned me about you, said you were getting too close to the truth, but I thought we could control you. Keep you on a leash."

Sloane felt her stomach turn. "You sent Jeremy to kill me."

Matthew didn't deny it. He laughed bitterly instead, eyes

fixed on the road ahead. "I didn't want it to come to that, but you forced my hand, sweetheart. You got too close. When you saw him with Omari, you sealed your own fate. I wasn't gonna let you destroy everything I've built."

Tears stung her eyes, but she fought them back. She wouldn't give him the satisfaction of seeing her break. But the reality of it—the man she'd once trusted, even *cared* about, wanted her dead—was suffocating.

"I thought we had something," she said, her voice trembling. "I thought you cared about me."

Matthew's gaze flickered to the rearview mirror, and for a moment, something like regret flashed across his face. But it was gone as quickly as it had appeared. "I was fond of you, Sloane. I won't lie about that. But I can't afford sentimentality. Not in this game."

The coldness in his words pierced her, and a shudder ran down her spine. The man she'd known was gone, replaced by someone ruthless, heartless. She had no more illusions. He wasn't sparing her. He wasn't going to let her live.

And Stitch... Stitch had no idea what was happening. He didn't even know she was gone.

Maybe Blade would find her. As soon as they realized she'd been taken, they'd be on the lookout. But how were they going to find her. She glanced out the window, her vision still hazy from the earlier blow. The city lights faded as they sped down the highway, moving further away from the city. She tried to push herself up again, but her head spun, making her collapse back onto the seat.

"What... what are you going to do?" she managed to ask, though deep down, she already knew the answer.

Matthew's lips curled into a twisted smile. "You know exactly what I'm going to do. There can't be any witnesses, Sloane. No one can know what's really going on. That means you."

The terror surged through her, turning her limbs to ice. She had to find a way out, but her body was weak, her head swimming. Her pulse roared in her ears as panic clawed at her throat. She had to keep him talking, had to buy time.

"The CIA's onto you," she blurted, her voice shaking. "You'll be caught. It's just a matter of time."

Matthew laughed darkly. "You're delusional if you think the Agency can stop me. By the time they figure out you're missing, I'll be long gone."

She couldn't think, couldn't strategize. Her mind was slipping, the darkness closing in faster than she could fight it. She shifted, feeling the cold leather seat beneath her as the road blurred outside the window.

Blade. Pat. Phoenix. *Someone* would come for her, wouldn't they? She had to believe that. She had to.

But the effort of staying conscious, of keeping herself together, was too much. She tried to lift her head again, tried to focus, but her vision swam and her body felt too heavy, too far away from her control.

Please, she thought one last time, her eyelids fluttering shut as the world around her dissolved into black. *Don't let me die.*

With a soft sigh, Sloane gave in to the encroaching darkness.

.

CHAPTER 42

One way or another, Stitch was going to find her—and Matthew Sullivan was going down.

Pat hauled out his phone and dialed 911. Stitch stood beside him, fists clenched, his heart thudding with the violent rhythm of helpless rage. Every second that passed without Sloane felt like a knife twisting deeper into his gut.

Twenty minutes later, the cavalry arrived.

A local sheriff named McCloskey took charge, asking them rapid-fire questions. They explained the situation: a wanted felon and rogue CIA agent had abducted a key witness, and they feared for her life. It was imperative they get her back.

Pat was on his phone again, calling his CIA contact, Stuart Rider. It wasn't long before a cavalcade of blacked-out SUVs swarmed the motel parking lot, drawing stares from every guest still lingering near their rooms.

"We'll have the press here soon," McCloskey groaned, adjusting his hat.

Stitch didn't care. Whatever it took to get Sloane back.

For the first time in his life, he felt utterly useless. This wasn't his neck of the woods. He had no contacts here, no strings to pull, no networks to exploit. He had to trust the authorities to do their job. But trusting others had never been his strong suit—it felt like everything was moving in slow motion, and meanwhile, God only knew what was happening to Sloane.

Back at the CIA field office, they reviewed CCTV footage from outside the motel.

"Sullivan's driving a gray Chevrolet," Pat pointed out, his finger tapping the screen. "We got the plates."

They immediately put out an APB on the vehicle, but an hour later, the news came in—the car had been found abandoned in an industrial area, miles away.

"He must've had a second vehicle waiting, or someone helping him," Stitch muttered. "We need to look at his known associates. There has to be a lead."

An agent at a nearby desk typed furiously on his keyboard, eyes scanning data as he worked. "Sullivan's got a long list of contacts. He knows almost everyone in the local CIA field office and probably has half a dozen unofficial informants and associates."

Stitch swore under his breath. Sullivan had been operating under the radar for so long, hiding his true self behind his cover as a respected agent. Now they were up against a man who knew the system better than anyone.

Fuck. They had to find a lead.

"What about properties?" said Stitch. "Does he own any properties, cabins, warehouses, anything like that?"

"He owns two houses in D.C.," the agent responded. "One his wife and kid live in, the other is his official residence. But nothing else that we know of."

Stitch racked his brain. What did they know about Matthew? "If he's moving drugs, he needs a place to store them. A container yard, a warehouse—something. They've been moving shipments for years, so there's gotta be a system in place."

"We've got the names of his cohorts from Ghost Company, but most of them are off the grid. We're tracking down leads now."

Stitch nodded. It wasn't much, but it was something. His gut told him that Sullivan wouldn't disappear without tying up his loose ends. "Maybe one of them hired a warehouse or storage space somewhere?"

"Looking into it," said a petite female agent. "I'm running their names now."

Stitch was impressed by how efficient the department was. He had no idea which branch of the CIA this was or what they were called, but Rider was a solid leader, and his team seemed loyal, smart, and capable.

Which made it all the more surprising that a rotten apple like Matthew had operated unnoticed for so long.

"We had no idea he was dirty," Rider said, almost as if he'd read Stitch's mind. "The first we heard was when Pat walked into my office last week. I thought he was talking bullshit, but once we started digging into Matthew's affairs, we found a lot of suspicious activity."

"What kind of activity?" Stitch asked.

"Various dummy corporations, shell companies, investments. All the red flags, though nothing can be traced directly back to him. All his assets in the States are legit, paid for through his salary and some smart investments. On paper, he's an exemplary citizen."

Not anymore. The game was up.

A call from one of the agents made Stitch look up.

"Sir, I've found an old lease taken out by Ryan Osbourne almost four years ago. It's for a warehouse near the Anacostia River."

"Who's Ryan Osbourne?" Rider asked.

"He was part of Matthew's unit that was deployed to Afghanistan, sir. Part of the original Ghost Company."

"Address?" Stitch barked.

The agent scribbled it down and handed it to him on a Post-it note.

Stitch glanced at Rider and Pat. "Let's go!"

"THAT'S THE PLACE," Stitch said, his voice grim as Rider pulled up in front of a two-story, prefab structure. It had a flat roof and a metallic sliding garage door. By warehouse standards, it wasn't large, but it was big enough to hide several shipping containers.

Situated several blocks back from the docks, the building blended into its surroundings—just another warehouse in a forgotten part of the city. If you didn't have a reason to be here, you'd drive past without giving it a second thought.

The team jumped out of the agency vehicle, weapons drawn, as they approached the front. Stitch's pulse quickened. Sloane could be inside. He wanted to charge in, guns blazing, but years of training held him in check.

"There's a side door," he called, circling the building.

"I'll go around the back," Pat said, breaking away.

Stitch moved fast, checking the side entrance. Locked, as expected. He glanced up, and his heart stuttered. Smoke—thin wisps curling from one of the upstairs windows.

"Fire!" he yelled, his voice breaking the stillness.

He threw his shoulder against the door, but it didn't budge. "I need help here!"

Rider came running, and after three hard heaves, the door broke open, flinging inward as smoke billowed out. They were instantly engulfed in the stifling cloud. Stitch pulled his T-shirt up over his nose and mouth.

"I'm going in," he said, determination hardening his voice.

"Not advisable," Rider warned, already pulling out his phone. "I'm calling the fire department. This whole place could go up."

Ignoring him, Stitch ducked inside, staying low. The dense smoke made his eyes sting and water. Every instinct screamed to stop, to get out, but the fear of what might happen to Sloane overpowered his sense of caution. He pushed forward.

In the main area downstairs, visibility was better—the smoke hovered near the ceiling, probably coming from the second floor. The garage door mechanism caught his eye, and Stitch ran over, flicking the switch. It groaned, lifting halfway before jamming.

"Sloane!" he shouted.

His eyes darted up to the offices on the second floor, where the smoke was thickest. That's where the fire had started. He heard something—a faint cry.

"Sloane!"

Sure as hell, the hazy outline of two men could be seen through the smoke, their muzzles flashing. They didn't know where the intruders were, so they were firing randomly in all directions. Stitch slid forward on his stomach and took aim. He pulled the trigger and heard one man cry out. The figure fell to the ground.

Pat took down the second with precision, the man collapsing as the room echoed with gunfire.

"I'm going up!" Stitch yelled. "Sloane's trapped!"

He sprinted for the stairs, but more gunfire rained down, forcing him to retreat behind a plywood wall.

"More shooters!" he shouted.

Pat darted across the room, taking cover beside Stitch. "I'll cover you," he said.

From across the floor, Rider opened fire, sending bullets toward the stairwell.

Stitch bolted, sprinting up the stairs before the shooters could react. He was almost at the top when a hand appeared around the corner, gun ready to fire. Instinct kicked in—Stitch grabbed the man's wrist, twisting it hard before hurling him down the stairs. Pat finished him off at the bottom.

His breath came in ragged gasps as he rushed toward the office. Smoke thickened around him, making it almost impossible to see. But he didn't care. All that mattered was getting to Sloane.

He kicked in the door, and there she was—slumped over a table, coughing uncontrollably, tears streaming down her face.

"Matthew's getting away," she gasped, pointing weakly down the corridor.

"Where?" Stitch shouted, pulling her to her feet.

"The roof..."

She could barely stand. He considered going after Matthew, but Sloane wouldn't make it out alone. His jaw clenched with frustration.

The glass partition between the office and the next room shattered, flames licking across the floor. Within seconds, the fire was everywhere.

Sloane collapsed against him, her body wracked by another fit of coughing. "I can't breathe..." she wheezed.

Stitch didn't hesitate. He hoisted her over his shoulder in a fireman's lift, his lungs burning with every breath he took. "Hang on," he rasped, forcing his way back toward the stairs.

"Pat!" he croaked, but it came out as more of a squawk. His throat burned. He couldn't risk going after Sullivan now—he had to get Sloane out.

He found the exit, pushing Sloane's limp body through the half-open garage door and dragging her to safety. His chest heaved with each breath as he collapsed beside her on the pavement, the warehouse behind them consumed by flames.

Sirens blared, fire trucks arriving too late to stop the inferno. Stitch coughed violently, his lungs protesting against the smoke that still lingered in his chest.

He turned to Sloane. Her pulse was strong, but she was out cold.

Rolling onto his back, he looked up at the roof just in time to see a helicopter rising from the smoke, its rotors slicing through the air.

Matthew was getting away.

Stitch watched helplessly as the chopper banked right, disappearing into the night sky.

CHAPTER 43

They took off from the CIA helipad in a Mi-17 just before five.

Time wasn't on their side. If they wanted to reach the cabin before dark, they had to move fast.

Stitch prayed Sullivan hadn't already headed for the border.

"Who do you think he's meeting?" Stitch asked Pat as they soared across the sky, the sun dipping lower.

"Could be a money man," Pat guessed. "He'll want to clean out his accounts before fleeing the country. You need cash to hide effectively."

"Maybe he's meeting a coconspirator," Stitch suggested. "A member of Ghost Company."

"I think that's who those guys were back at the warehouse," Pat said dryly. "I had to stop that last merc with my bare hands. He kept coming at me. Those guys knew how to fight. Not even the smoke slowed them down."

"How's the leg?" Stitch asked.

Pat shrugged. "I'll walk it off."

Stitch nodded. His boss wouldn't let something as small

as a twisted knee slow him down. Pat was tough—pushing forty-five but still fit, muscular, and stronger than most men half his age. Apart from Blade, there was no one Stitch trusted more in a firefight.

The four-hour flight took them to San Antonio, where a vehicle was waiting to transport them to the cabin.

One of the young analysts had tracked down an isolated cabin near Medina Lake, owned by Sullivan's ex-wife's mother. The local sheriff said it had been vacant for years.

"Why can't we fly there?" Stitch growled. Every moment wasted gave Sullivan more time to escape.

"Nowhere to land," Pat explained. "Even Sullivan would've had to drive there."

"At least that buys us some time," Stitch muttered.

They sped down the freeway, sirens blazing, racing through Medina County toward the lake.

By the time they arrived, it was dark. The driver from the Texas office killed the lights and parked behind a clump of trees, out of sight.

Stitch, Pat, and another agent approached the cabin, guns drawn.

Pat, who was leading, suddenly stopped and raised a hand. Stitch peered over his shoulder.

Lights.

There was someone inside.

Maybe Sullivan had decided to stay the night and make his run for the border tomorrow. It was dark, after all, and he probably thought he was safe.

The cabin was well hidden. Not even Sullivan's ex-wife knew it existed.

A sharp CIA analyst had dug through a property purchase from thirty-two years ago. When the analyst contacted Sullivan's ex-wife, she said the cabin had been sold after her mother passed away five years ago. That much was true, but the buyer was one of Sullivan's dummy corporations.

A tangled web of deceit that led right back to Matthew Sullivan.

"Let's check it out," Stitch said.

They split up and circled the cabin. When they regrouped, the agent said, "I see two people inside. You?"

"Same," confirmed Pat.

Stitch nodded.

Parked outside was a powerful, black SUV. Stitch felt the hood. It was cold. "They've been here a while," he whispered.

"So, what now?" the CIA agent asked the two former SEALs.

"They're probably armed," Stitch said.

Pat nodded. "I'm not looking for another shoot-out."

"We could wait until they come out, then arrest them as they get into the car," the agent suggested.

It wasn't a bad idea.

But Stitch had something different in mind. "How about we lure them out?"

Pat narrowed his eyes. "What are you thinking?"

"A little diversion, maybe?" He nodded toward the getaway vehicle.

The agent pursed his lips. "I'll see what we've got in the trunk."

He returned with a can of fuel, some old newspapers, and a lighter. "Will this do?"

"Perfect," Stitch said.

Once Sullivan was out in the open, he was bound to fight back. Stitch was counting on it. He needed a reason to take the bastard down.

Pat doused the SUV while Stitch stuffed paper up the exhaust and under the carriage. It wouldn't do much damage, but it would burn harder.

The agent lit the fire, and they stepped back as the flames started to lick at the car.

Stitch kept his eyes on the cabin. He'd seen enough flames to last a lifetime.

He wondered how Sloane was doing. His chest warmed at the thought. He hadn't wanted to leave her, but he had to finish this, or she'd never be safe.

As long as Sullivan was alive, there'd be a target on her back.

He didn't know when her safety became more important than his need for revenge, but it had. All he could think about was killing Sullivan and getting back to her.

A shout came from inside the cabin, and the door swung open. A man Stitch didn't recognize stood there, rifle in hand.

"What the—?" the man growled.

Sullivan appeared behind him.

"Shit!" Sullivan hissed, darting back inside.

At first, Stitch thought he was going for his gun, but then Pat yelled, "He's going out the back!"

"He's mine," Stitch shouted, taking off after Sullivan before Pat could react. "You get the other guy!"

STITCH TORE through the dark woods. He could barely see a few feet ahead of him. The moonlight didn't stand a chance against the thick tree coverage, so he used the light on his phone to guide him.

He strained to listen, but there wasn't much to hear. Stitch was impressed. Even in this dense forest, Sullivan moved quietly—a testament to his training.

A crack echoed as a twig snapped underfoot. Stitch followed the sound. Then there was a rustle, the brush of a tree branch, and the crunch of leaves.

He followed the trail, heading northeast. He knew there was a lake nearby—he'd seen it on the map.

Is that where Sullivan's heading? Does he have a boat waiting for a getaway?

A well-trained agent always had a contingency plan. If Sullivan was anything like Stitch, he'd already thought through every scenario and counter-scenario.

The rustling stopped.

Stitch paused, listening hard. Just the chirps and chatter of the night creatures.

Nothing human.

He moved cautiously, half-expecting Sullivan to double back. It was a tactic Stitch had used on several jungle ops—let your pursuer think they're still on your trail, then ambush them from behind.

Through a break in the trees, Stitch spotted the shimmering, dark blue surface of the lake. A shadowy figure bolted down the beach toward a wooden jetty.

"Sullivan!" Stitch exploded into a run, adrenaline fueling his muscles. As he hit the sand, he saw the motorboat moored at the end of the pier.

Fuck.

He pushed harder, ignoring the burn in his calves. If Sullivan got away now, they'd never find him again.

Stitch sprinted down the jetty as Sullivan untied the moorings and pushed the boat into deeper water. The motor sputtered to life.

Sullivan's boat was packed with a holdall and a cooler box of supplies.

This wasn't Plan B. This was always Plan A.

They weren't going to risk driving away from the cabin. Smart. There was only one access road, and it'd be easy to block and check. The plan was to motor across the lake, then take a chopper or some other transport to Mexico. Unchecked. Undetected.

Then it hit him. There was only one holdall in the boat. One cooler of supplies.

Sullivan had never planned to take his sidekick. A cabin fire would have covered up the bullet wounds, leaving Sullivan free to escape with the money—if that's what was in the bag he was carrying.

Moonlight glistened off the water. It would have been a peaceful scene if Stitch wasn't chasing the man who'd almost killed Sloane and destroyed his life.

"Sullivan!" he bellowed.

But the rogue agent didn't respond. The boat was nearly a meter out, its engine kicking up frothy water.

Stitch didn't slow down.

He put everything he had into his last few strides and launched himself off the end of the pier. He wasn't letting the bastard get away this time.

It was only midair that Stitch saw the gun in Sullivan's hand.

Then Sullivan pulled the trigger.

CHAPTER 44

 NE MONTH LATER

LIFE WASN'T FAIR.

Sloane threw her clothes on the floor and climbed into the shower. She'd finally found the man of her dreams, and he'd disappeared off the face of the earth. After Stitch had left her in the ambulance, she'd told him she'd wait. That she'd be here for him. Surely, he'd understood what she meant.

Hadn't she been clear enough?

She tilted her head back and let the water pound her face. Why was she second-guessing herself? Of course she'd been clear. He knew. He'd felt it too. She hadn't imagined it.

Yet, a month had passed, and there was still no sign of him.

Or Pat.

She'd tried reaching out through official channels, but no one knew anything. It was like the whole thing had never happened. She was beginning to wonder herself. The last contact she'd had with anyone in authority was when a young agent came to see her in the hospital a few days after the fire, handing her a letter terminating her contract.

Her job was over.

It hadn't even been a real assignment. Nothing about the entire operation was legitimate. Matthew. The mission. It had all been a farce.

She'd been played—completely.

Her cheeks burned, remembering how easily she'd fallen for it all. She had been flattered by Matthew's attention, eager to impress, and so quick to trust.

She squeezed her eyes shut. What a fool.

After her shower, she stepped out onto the bathmat and wrapped herself in a big, fluffy towel.

Never again.

Never again would she be deceived by a man.

Had they even arrested Matthew? She'd asked the young agent, but he'd given her the standard response. He couldn't share any details about an ongoing investigation. But she shouldn't worry—there was no longer any threat to her.

"So, that's a yes, then?" she'd asked, but he'd only repeated the same line.

Which left her wondering. Was Matthew in prison? Or had Stitch taken him out, just like Jeremy and Omari? Was that why no one was talking?

Was that why Stitch hadn't come back? Had he been arrested for killing Matthew?

Nobody was giving her any information!

She'd tried calling Stitch's burner phone, but it went straight to voicemail. It had probably been destroyed or deactivated. There was nothing she could do but get back to her life.

What life?

She rubbed herself dry, gripping the towel. What was she supposed to do now? Maybe she'd go back to teaching. She had always loved that, but something was holding her back.

It was because she wasn't ready. The past few months had been insane, and she needed time to process everything, not least her feelings for Stitch, and how to move forward without him. A hot tear rolled down her cheek, something that happened more and more frequently these days.

What did you expect? she scolded herself. That he'd stick around? Move in? Live happily ever after? Yeah, right.

They'd had a passionate affair, but it was over now. He'd obviously moved on. His line of work meant he couldn't stay in touch. He probably wasn't even in the country anymore.

A familiar ache settled in her chest as she pulled on a black nightgown she'd once bought to impress Matthew, back when they were dating.

Funny enough, she'd never had the guts to wear it for him. Now it seemed like a fitting end to her love life—funereal.

Stitch was irreplaceable. No man could compare.

"I prefer you naked."

She gasped and spun around. "Stitch!"

She hadn't noticed him sitting quietly on the bed, his broad shoulders taking up half of it. He hadn't changed—still rugged, still brawny, totally gorgeous.

He grinned. "Did I catch you at a bad time?"

She stood frozen, her heart thudding in her chest. Part of her wanted to throw herself into his arms and never let go, but another part of her hesitated. It had been a month. A lot could change in a month.

Did he still feel the same way?

Maybe he was here to say goodbye.

"Why are you here?" she choked out.

"I said I'd come back, didn't I?"

"Yes," she said cautiously. "But it's been a while."

"Sorry. I got held up. Had to go back to the SEAL teams and finalize my discharge paperwork. It wasn't handled right the first time. Pat insisted."

She bit her lip. "So, you're not going back? You're not here to say goodbye?"

"Not yet." He got to his feet, eyes gleaming.

Her heart pounded. Was this really happening?

When he reached her, he buried his face in her hair, murmuring, "I've been dreaming about this moment."

"Really?" She shivered as he nuzzled her neck. Could this be real? Could he truly be here?

"Really."

Without thinking, she launched herself at him, wrapping her arms around his neck.

He laughed, catching her easily, holding her against his strong chest. She felt his heartbeat, strong and steady. Hers was firing like a machine gun.

"I missed you so much." She buried her face in his neck. "I thought you weren't coming back. That you'd forgotten about me."

"How could I forget the woman I love?" he whispered into her ear.

"What?" She pulled back, her eyes wide. Had she just hallucinated, or had he just said he loved her?

"You heard me." He kissed the side of her neck, his breath warm against her skin. "Don't make me say it again."

Stunned, she shook her head.

He snorted. "It's not often I can render you speechless. I can see I'm going to have to prove it to you. Right now."

She giggled, happiness bubbling up inside her, an emotion she hadn't allowed herself to feel in weeks. "I'd like that."

In one swift move, he carried her to the bed and laid her

down, his eyes dark with desire. But as he leaned over her, she noticed the thick white bandage wrapped around his side, just above his waist.

"Stitch... what happened?" Her fingers brushed against it gently.

"Matthew shot me," he said, his voice casual, though his face tightened with a flash of pain as she touched him.

"You were shot?!"

"Hey, I'm fine." He gave her a reassuring smile. "They patched me up good as new, but... that's why it took me so long to get to you. Discharge and a bullet wound, not the best combination." He winced when she touched the bandage again. "But don't worry, it's healing. All the important things still work."

He was making light of it, but her heart clenched. "I wish you'd told me."

"I didn't want to worry you until it was all over," he murmured, pulling her hand away and kissing her knuckles. "Now that I'm here, I'm not going anywhere."

She wanted to argue, to demand more details, but when he kissed her again, all her protests melted away.

In that moment, it didn't matter.

Their lips met, and with every touch, he unleashed a yearning in her so deep it nearly overwhelmed her. She clawed at his T-shirt, and he helped her pull it over his head, wincing slightly as the movement tugged on his wound.

"I don't want to hurt you," she whispered, worry flitting through her gaze.

"You won't." He smirked down at her, eyes filled with heat. "I'll take it easy. Maybe."

She grinned, her hands sliding over his bandaged side, careful but determined.

God, how she'd missed him.

Her hands fumbled at his belt, desperate to feel him close.

She needed to believe this was real, that he was here, that this moment was actually happening.

His jeans hit the floor, and he lowered himself onto her, careful but sure, claiming her mouth with his. Her breath hitched as their bodies pressed together.

Everything about him was strong, intense, and right where she needed him.

He groaned as she tugged him closer, pulling him down, opening herself up to him, making room for him in every sense of the word.

"Stitch," she whispered, her voice trembling as she gazed into his eyes, "I love you too."

His kiss was his answer, and the way he moved, slow and sure, was a promise of everything she had been waiting for.

CHAPTER 45

Stitch smiled as he looked down at her flushed face. "Believe me now?"

Sloane laughed, her chestnut hair splayed over the pillow, her eyes bright with love. She was the most beautiful thing he'd ever seen.

"I'm starting to."

He kissed her again, unable to stop. Now that he had her back, he wanted to hold on to her forever.

"I'm sorry I didn't call sooner," he murmured. "I thought about it, but if I'd been arrested during the process, I didn't want to get your hopes up. Until my discharge was sorted, I wasn't free to come see you."

"I understand," she said softly. "Is everything okay now?"

"Yeah. I was medically discharged, citing trauma from our last op. Pat pulled some strings, and helping bust the heroin trafficking ring worked in my favor. I've agreed to some therapy, but the main thing is—I'm not a wanted man anymore."

She smiled, but her gaze was curious. "What happened to Matthew? Did you get him?"

He nodded. "Yeah. We tracked him to that cabin he used to hide out in."

"And?"

"There was another guy with him, a finance guy. He'd cleaned out their accounts, brought Matthew a bag of cash. The plan was to split it and head to Mexico."

"But you stopped them."

"We got the money guy, but Matthew made a run for it. He took off toward the lake, jumped into a boat he had ready."

"And?" she asked, eyes wide.

"I caught him. He tried to shoot me, but I kicked the gun out of his hand. He fell into the water, hit his head, and never resurfaced. They pulled his body out of the water a couple of hours later."

Her gaze softened. "So, it's over. He's really gone."

Stitch wrapped his arms around her, pulling her close. "Yes, he's gone. You're safe now."

She snuggled into him, resting her head on his chest. "You got your revenge."

There was a pause as he processed her words. "I thought that's what I was after... but it wasn't."

She tilted her head to look up at him. "What do you mean?"

He sighed softly. "When I got to the cabin, I realized I wasn't chasing him for revenge anymore. I wanted him dead because I couldn't let him hurt you. It wasn't about the past anymore. It was about protecting you."

She placed a hand on his cheek. "You did it for me?"

"I didn't realize it until that moment, but yeah. You're what mattered most to me. More than vengeance."

His heart swelled as she gazed up at him. He hadn't just saved her life, she'd saved his too.

"I love you," she whispered, pulling him down for a kiss.

He smiled against her lips. "I love you too."

After a moment, he pulled back and took her hand. "There's something I've been meaning to ask you."

"Should I be worried?"

"Only if you don't want me around."

She scoffed, her hands tracing the muscles in his shoulder. "Like that would ever happen."

He grinned. "Pat offered me a job with Blackthorn Security. As a private contractor."

She stared at him. "You'll be operating again?"

"Yeah. I just wanted to make sure that was okay with you."

"You don't need my permission," she said.

"I know I've been given a second chance, and I don't want to waste it. I don't want to lose you again, Sloane. I want you by my side. Always."

Tears welled up in her eyes. It made him want to kiss them away. "I want you to do what's right for you. If working with Blade and Pat is what you want, I'm okay with it."

In that moment, he didn't think he could love anybody more.

"Even though it'll take me away from time to time?"

She forced a smile. "As long as you always come back to me."

"Copy that."

They kissed again, and Stitch held her close, breathing in the moment. He was so goddamn lucky to have found her. After everything—after all the loss and pain—he had found love again. With Sloane by his side, there would be no more nightmares. Only love, laughter, and a lifetime of happiness.

He thought about the ring in his jeans pocket. He'd been carrying it for weeks, waiting for this moment. He wanted to give it to her now, but he had to be sure first. Sure that she wanted him too. That she loved him as much as he loved her.

Now he was.

Sloane leaned her head on his chest, her fingers tracing lazy circles over his skin. He kissed the top of her head, his heart pounding in his chest. This was the moment.

He shifted, reaching into his pocket, feeling the small box between his fingers. "Sloane," he began, his voice low but steady.

She looked up at him, her eyes curious. "Yeah?"

His heart hammered as he reached over, pulled out the ring box and opened it, holding it between them. The diamond sparkled in the soft light, but it was her expression —her wide eyes, the way her breath caught—that made his chest tighten.

"I've been carrying this around for a while," he said, his voice a little rough. "I was waiting for the perfect moment, but the truth is... every moment with you is the right one."

Her eyes welled up, her lips parting in a soft gasp, but she didn't say anything.

He continued, keeping his voice steady. "I don't want to waste any more time. I've almost lost you more than once, and I'm done with that. I don't care where life takes me, or how many ops I have to run—I want to come home to you. I want you by my side, every damn day, for the rest of my life."

Her hand trembled as it rose to her mouth, her eyes locked on his.

He swallowed, his heart racing. "Sloane, will you marry me?"

For a moment, time seemed to stand still.

"I can't," she said, her eyes filling with tears. She turned her head away, refusing to look at him.

Her words cut through him like a blade."What? Why?" His chest constricted painfully.

She turned away, wrapping her arms around herself as though shielding against the blow she'd just delivered.

"Because of Soraya," she whispered, her voice breaking. "I know how much you loved her. I can't compete with that.

He reached for her, but she stiffened. "Sloane, I'm not asking you to compete with her. I'll never forget Soraya—how could I? But she's gone, and you're here. You're my future now." His voice cracked, vulnerable, but steady. "I know she'd want this for me—for us. She'd want me to be happy."

Sloane's shoulders trembled. When she finally turned to face him, her eyes were red, raw, and full of doubt. "I don't know if I can live my life wondering if I'm just... second best. The consolation prize." Her voice wavered, as if the words themselves pained her.

He took her hands gently, pulling her closer. "You're not second best, Sloane. You're everything." His grip tightened as if he were afraid she'd slip away. "Out there, all I could think about was you. Getting back to you. Making sure you were safe. You healed me when I didn't think I could be healed."

She blinked, her lips trembling as her walls started to crack. "Really?"

His gaze softened, filled with something deeper than she could have imagined. "This isn't settling. This is me realizing that lightning can strike twice, that I'm the luckiest bastard alive because I found someone I never thought I'd deserve. You made me whole again, Sloane. I wasn't sure I'd ever feel that way again... but you did it. You're the one I want. I'm not letting that go."

Her breath caught, and the flicker of a smile ghosted her lips. "You really mean that?"

"More than anything." His voice was rough but sure, like he was offering her every piece of himself.

A tear slipped down her cheek, and her heart—so carefully guarded for so long—finally gave way. "Then... yes," she whispered, her voice trembling but full of conviction. "Yes, I'll marry you."

Relief and joy surged through him. He slipped the ring onto her finger, his hands shaking just a little.

She threw her arms around his neck, laughing as the tears fell, and he pulled her close, his own eyes stinging. This was it. This was everything.

"I love you," he murmured into her ear, holding her tight.

"I love you too," she whispered back, her voice thick with emotion. "Always."

They kissed again, slow and sweet, sealing the promise they'd just made. It was perfect.

It was forever.

WHAT'S NEXT?

Want more Blackthorn Security? Take a look at the next book in the addictive romantic suspense series.

HEAT FORCE

GEMMA FORD

HEAT FORCE

Runaway bride, untamed jungle, and a brooding ex-soldier billionaire collide in this sizzling romantic suspense.

Lexi ditched her glitzy New York life *and* her high-profile wedding to follow her heart to a gorilla sanctuary deep in the African jungle. Life's simpler here—until *Hawk* shows up. A former soldier turned billionaire CEO, he's on a mission to fix his company's eco-friendly image, and the last thing Lexi needs is another rich guy who doesn't care. But why does his brooding intensity have her questioning *everything* she thought she wanted?

Hawk's mission? Boost his company's reputation. But one encounter with Lexi, the fiery sanctuary worker, and suddenly, it's more than just business at stake. She's wild, passionate, and impossible to resist—and he's not the type to back down from a challenge.

When danger strikes and Lexi goes missing, Hawk will stop at nothing to save her. The jungle may be unforgiving, but he's not leaving without the woman who's captured his heart.

Adventure, steamy chemistry, and heart-stopping action collide in this unforgettable romance set in the wild heart of Africa.

Paperbacks available from Amazon and Gemma's website store at www.authorgemmaford.com.

ABOUT THE AUTHOR

Gemma Ford is a romantic suspense novelist who enjoys writing about feisty, independent women and their brave, warm-hearted men. *Steel Vengeance* is the sixth book in Gemma's bestselling Blackthorn Security romantic suspense series.

You can browse the rest of the series or sign up to Gemma's mailing list for discounts, promos and the occasional freebie at her website: www.authorgemmaford.com.

www.ingramcontent.com/pod-product-compliance
Lightning Source LLC
LaVergne TN
LVHW021653060526
838200LV00050B/2340